An Owl Too Many

Also available in Large Print
by Charlotte MacLeod:

Vane Pursuit
Mistletoe Mysteries
Recycled Citizen
Plain Old Man

An Owl Too Many

CHARLOTTE
MACLEOD

G.K.HALL &CO.
Boston, Massachusetts
1991

Also available in Large Print by
Mysterious Press/Warner Books, Inc.
A Time Warner Company.

G.K. Hall Large Print Book Series.

Set in 18 pt. Plantin.

Library of Congress Cataloging-in-Publication Data

Macleod, Charlotte.
An owl too many / Charlotte Macleod.
p. cm.—(G.K. Hall large print book series)
ISBN 0-8161-5235-7 (lg. print)
1. Large type books. I. Title.
[PS3563.A31865088 1991b]
813′.54—dc20 91-14541

For Elizabeth Walter
with deep respect, sincere gratitude,
and much affection.

1

Professor Peter Shandy spied it first, to nobody's surprise. Shandy, hot-shot horticulturist at Balaclava Agricultural College, wasn't the man to miss much. "Saw-whet," he whispered.

"Screech." Dr. Thorkjeld Svenson's gentlest whisper still brought to mind the roaring of maddened trolls in caverns measureless to man.

"Too small. No ear tufts." Associate Professor Winifred Binks, newly appointed to the chair of Local Flora, was not to be intimidated even by the college president. This was her first time out with Balaclava's traditional Annual Owl Count; she clearly saw it as a chance to burnish the name of Binks, which had acquired an ugly greenish patina through no fault of hers.

"Maybe it's a young screech owl that hasn't grown its ear tufts yet." Emory Emmerick wasn't even a member of the faculty, nobody quite knew how he'd managed to muscle his way into this august company. "Or a Richardson's owl?"

His suggestion was greeted with the silence it deserved. The small avian settled the matter itself by emitting a weak, two-toned rasping cry instead of a mournful whinny (screech) or a song like the dropping of water (Richardson's). Svenson conceded.

"All right, Binks, saw-whet. Write it down, Shandy. Yesus, look at that!"

October's bright blue weather had given way to crisp autumn night. Here in the woods behind the campus, dead oak and maple leaves lay ankle-deep. Low in the sky rode a harvest moon just past the full, veiled off and on by fast-scudding rags of gray cloud. At the moment, the huge orange disk showed clear. Across its face was flitting, huge and silent, a feathery form of ghostly white.

"*Nyctea scandiaca,*" gasped Professor Stott, head of animal husbandry and the greatest owl-watcher of them all. "President, this cannot be! The snowy owl is an arctic day-flier, habituated to marshes and meadows. One might find a snowy owl in Maine or Minnesota during the winter months, but rarely this far south unless driven to forage abroad by a shortage of lemmings in its customary haunts. I have it on excellent authority that there is an abundance of lemmings in Canada this year."

"Then might what we saw have been merely the white underbelly of an extra-large barn owl?" suggested Professor Binks.

Stott shook his head, deliberately and ponderously, for he was not a man given to haste. "That was not a barn owl. I would know a barn owl. Barns, after all, are my own native habitat." Stott could wax jocose upon occasion.

"How about a short-eared owl?"

That was Emmerick putting his foot in it again. Nobody paid any attention to him, the bird had been far too large and much too white.

"Loki, maybe."

Dr. Svenson was a student of Norse mythology, so his jokes tended to be on the obscure side. Emmerick, who'd just become acquainted with the college's magnificent draft horses, all named for Norse gods and goddesses, naturally missed the point.

"I thought Loki was one of your Balaclava blacks."

As usual, the rest ignored him. "An interesting suggestion, President," murmured Winifred Binks. "Loki was a shape-changer, was he not? Didn't he once turn himself into a woman?"

"Into a mare. Got knocked up by a horse named Svadilfari while he was trying to con a rock giant into rebuilding the wall of Asgard for nothing. Served him right. Bore an eight-legged colt and gave it to Odin. There it goes again! Come on."

They stepped up their pace, still in single file according to owl watch protocol. President Svenson led, of course. Daniel Stott, Balaclava's most dedicated owl watcher, was second; the knowledgeable Winifred Binks third. Emory Emmerick, the novice, made an annoyingly erratic fourth; Peter Shandy came last as whipper-in.

Each was anxious for a clear sighting. Rules demanded that each bird be positively identified by at least two members of the team. What judge was going to believe a snowy owl in Massachusetts in October without an oath sealed in blood by the entire group, or at least a reasonable facsimile thereof?

"There's something almost eerie about that bird." Winifred Binks excelled any of the men in woodcraft. She was sharp as a fox, quick to catch each teasing glimpse as it flitted along between the trees. "It's flying so slowly, one might almost think it was leading us on. Dear me, how fanciful!"

"The owl may be wounded, or simply confused," said Professor Stott. "That would explain its being so far out of its customary habitat."

Professor Stott had on the same owl-counting garb he'd worn every year for two decades: ankle-high boots, green porkpie hat with a speckled guinea-hen feather stuck in the band, vast brown tweed knickerbockers, and matching Norfolk jacket. Completing the ensemble were a dark-green flannel shirt and Argyle plaid stockings in tones of brown and green, knitted years ago by his late wife, Elizabeth, and kept in repair by the second Mrs. Stott. Iduna, née Bjorklund, had been named after the Norse goddess who kept the golden apples of youth, and might have been feeding them to her husband. Though a man of mature years and considerable size, Stott was gliding along behind the leader without even panting.

Winifred Binks had recently inherited her grandfather's fortune and was still trying to count her ever-multiplying millions. Still, she hadn't put on any show of affluence. Her customary working clothes were plain gray or brown slacks and knitted pullovers in neutral shades or gentle pastels suitable for a woman of indeterminate years. Tonight, though, she'd surprised the men by appearing in the well-worn tunic, pants, and moccasins she'd cobbled together out of home-tanned deerskins during her leaner days.

The head and tail of the line were less exotically garbed. Thorkjeld Svenson, even taller than Stott and a good deal brawnier, could have passed for a rock giant himself in his gray flannel shirt and work pants if he hadn't also been wearing a red wool cap with a huge white bobble like an overgrown rabbit's scut. Peter Shandy, bringing up the rear with field guide, clipboard, first-aid kit, flashlight, and a pint of brandy just in case, was dressed much like the president, except that he wore a shapeless old tweed hat in place of the bobbled cap.

Emory Emmerick, in natty flannels and a Fair Isle pullover that would have suited Miss Binks better than him, looked too much like an ad from a men's mail-order catalog to fit in with this congeries of individualists. Nor did he act like them. Owl-count protocol demanded that members of each team keep in single file; all at once Emmerick put on a burst of speed, snapping a twig under his foot to everyone else's fury, and moved up toward the front of the line. This was practically lèse-majesté; who did the damned fool think he was?

Peter couldn't figure out why in Sam Hill Emmerick had invited himself along tonight. He was an engineer, or called himself one. He obviously didn't know anything about owls, he didn't know how to behave on an owl count, and he didn't have sense enough to keep his big mouth shut at any time. He'd been airing his opinions right and left every time Peter had seen him at the station this past week.

"Station" was a portmanteau word encompassing the college's new field station out on the western border of Balaclava County and the small television station that was about to get built under Emmerick's supervision. The thirty-acre tract had been the old Binks estate; both the land and the buildings being erected on it were gifts of the heiress. Professor Binks and her longtime idol, Professor Emeritus of Local Fauna John Enderble (author of *How to Live with the Burrowing Mammals*, *Never Dam a Beaver*, *Our Friends the Reptiles*, et al.), had set up a museum of local flora and fauna in a prefabricated building where they were already conducting nature-study classes. Winifred had built herself a house from a kit. Television stations, they were learning, were a great deal more complicated to set up, even though this one would be producing and airing nothing but environmentally oriented programs.

Peter was a member of the steering committee; he'd already lined up his old friend Professor Timothy Ames to star in a rip-snorting, soul-stirring epic on soil conditioning. Emmerick had aired his opinion that they ought to get some sex and violence into the program, so Tim had offered to cut an earthworm in half with a switchblade knife. He would thus have created not one dead worm but two perfectly viable live ones, without all the fuss and bother to which the mammalia, including *Homo*-allegedly-*sapiens*, are subjected. However, Emmerick had said that wasn't quite what he'd had in mind. Peter had a hunch that once he really got to know Emmerick, he was going to have him kicked the hell off the station and replace him with somebody whose brains weren't wired to a cathode-ray tube.

But all things in their own time. At the moment, that improbable great bird was still allowing them to catch quick glimpses of it through the trees. If anybody was going to get a sight of the snowy owl, or ghost, or whatever it was, P. Shandy was determined to be among those counting.

Of course Svenson's group was not the only one working on the owl count. Several other faculty members, the more avian-minded among the students, and a number of Balaclava Junction's townsfolk were out owling, too; they'd all be prowling the fields and woodlands for as much of the night as they could stick. Territories had been divided off and assigned to groups, usually of eight spotters. Svenson had claimed for himself the trickiest plot and the fewest spotters but had snaffled the cream: namely Stott, Binks, and Shandy, in that order. Emmerick could have been added to the group by way of penance, Peter supposed; the president never felt comfortable making things too easy.

What the flaming perdition was that confounded blob of feathers up to now? Peter had never before seen an owl behave like this one; it was beginning to give him the heebie-jeebies. Miss Binks—she'd asked him to call her Winifred but so far he hadn't been able to work himself up to it because she reminded him so much of his fourth-grade teacher—could be right about the creature leading them on. This was probably not a bird but a bogle, he decided. When they got to wherever it was taking them, it would emit a hideous squawk and vanish in a puff of sulfur. Maybe he ought to begin a second list for specter-spotting. Thus musing, he tripped over a root or something and went down on his knees.

The leaf mold was deep and spongy. Peter wasn't a big man. He fell so lightly that those in front of him didn't even notice. No matter, he wasn't hurt and hadn't dropped his tally-board or spilled the brandy. He was clambering to his feet and dusting off his pant legs when all hell broke loose.

"Get down!" Svenson was roaring. Peter felt a mighty thud as he saw the president hit the ground, carrying Winifred Binks down with him. Even Dan Stott moved fast, a fusillade of shots was a powerful motivator. Peter rolled over to flatten himself behind a boulder. Who the flaming perdition was trying to slaughter them all? It sounded like a squad of machine gunners.

Or did it? He heard the rapid-fire explosions, he saw the quick, sharp flicks of light, and the sudden puffs of smoke; he smelled the gunpowder. But where was the whine of bullets? Now came a new noise, a strange fizzing overhead. Peter glanced up at the sky, just in time to see three skyrockets explode together in a cascade of red, white, and blue fire.

He leapt to his feet. "Emmerick! You crazy son of a bitch, you've scared off every owl in Balaclava County."

Now Thorkjeld Svenson was on his feet, too, shaking the tree like a maddened gorilla. "Come down here, you yackal! I want to tear your arm off."

"That seems a splendid idea, President." Dan Stott, normally the mildest of men, was nodding enthusiastically. "I shall be happy to assist you."

Winifred Binks's was the sole voice of reason. "Peter, is your flashlight working?"

"Er—" He pressed the switch, and it was. That was when he learned it was not a boulder he'd taken shelter behind.

"Good God! Emmerick, how'd you get into that net?"

Emmerick didn't say anything, nor did he make any movement.

"He made a sudden rush to the front of the line," said Winifred, "and tried to pull me with him. Then all at once he was being flung up into the tree. I think he started to call out, but the banging started and he thumped down again. He must have had the wind knocked out of him. I couldn't see what happened next because President Svenson—whose gallantry and courage under fire I cannot sufficiently—"

"Urrgh!"

"Oh yes, of course. First things first." She leapt for a limb and swarmed up the tree.

"Binks!" If there was by chance an owl still left in the area, Svenson's roar would surely have discouraged it from lingering. "Come back here!"

"I'm just looking."

Her voice fluted down from far overhead. This tree, Peter noted, was an oak, still clinging to the leaves it would continue to hold long after the maples and birches were bare. It was at the top of another giant oak that he'd first met Miss Binks; he wasn't at all surprised she'd made such excellent time climbing this one. The really astonishing development was that net.

He shone his flashlight again on Emmerick, trussed up like a supermarket turkey. The engineer had had time enough by now to get his wind back; why wasn't he breathing? Then Peter realized he wasn't going to breathe, not ever again. And Miss Binks was up there alone. Or not. Peter grabbed for that same branch, pulled himself up, and scrambled to meet her.

The moon kindly obliged by coming out from behind its veil of clouds, the pair of them were able to search the oak fairly well. They found the makeshift contrivance that had been used to launch the rockets, they found signs of burning and a few scraps of paper from the fireworks, but that was all.

So the spooky whiteness had been no snowy owl, merely a ruse to lure them here. Emmerick's unseemly behavior along the way had been due to his anticipation of the stupendous practical joke that was going to be played on this bunch of stuffed shirts from the college. He might well have engineered the fireworks display himself.

But if he was in on the joke, how had he got caught in the net? It would seem he must have had an accomplice up in the tree to fire off that opening salvo. Had his partner decided to turn the joke on Emmerick? There'd been something pretty damned selective about the way that net had managed to snare only one of four people who were still bunched up close together. Had it been dropped from above, or laid on the ground?

Had Emmerick fallen from the tree because the ropes gave way, or had he been deliberately dropped? And was it really supposed to have been a joke?

There must be marks up here that would give them information, if only they had enough light to see by. This flashlight was about as much help as a lightning bug. Peter snapped it off and stuck it in his pocket.

"We may as well go down, Miss Binks, before the president bursts a blood vessel. We're wasting our time, we'll have to get the state police out here with searchlights. If this was meant to be a joke, it's backfired very badly. I'm quite sure Emmerick's dead."

2

"Oh dear," said Winifred, "how very distressing. Mr. Emmerick was a tiresome man, in my opinion, but one would not have wished him so bizarre and untimely an end. I wonder what on earth that explosive retiarius thought he was going to catch. The net must have been rigged with some kind of automatic tripping device, wouldn't you think?"

"It's possible," said Peter. "I hope I wasn't it."

He didn't pause to elaborate. Dr. Svenson was still bellowing for them to come down; perhaps he was irked because they hadn't tossed him a culprit to mangle. For a college president, he did have a rather wide streak of the berserker in him. Anyway, there really was nothing more to be done until they had lights; the police must be called without further delay.

Winifred was the fleetest of foot among them, but Peter wasn't about to let her go alone with a retiarius loose in the woods. He himself was second fastest but was damned if he'd be pried away from the scene of the crime. Dan Stott would be no earthly use, he'd get to ruminating somewhere along the way and forget what he was going for. Svenson himself would have to act as Miss Binks's bodyguard, and who better? Peter slid down the last ten feet of trunk and got straight to business.

"President, you gallop on back and get hold of the state police. Miss Binks, you'd better go with him as guide, you know all the shortcuts. Tell them to bring some portable searchlights and a stretcher, and to keep their confounded sirens turned off.

We've had all the noise we need for one night."

"Ottermole?" barked Svenson.

Peter shook his head. "We'd never find him, he's already out owling. Anyway, he hasn't the equipment we need."

Fred Ottermole, Balaclava Junction's own chief of police, comprised fifty percent of the force's strength, not counting part-time help and unpaid deputies, of whom Peter was one. Peter couldn't recall which territory the chief had been assigned to and didn't care. Ottermole was a good man in a scrap, but when it came to detecting, owls and litterers were his forte. He might as well stay with the hunt.

"This way, Dr. Svenson."

Winifred Binks darted off between the trees in what would seem to be the wrong direction but assuredly was not. The president followed without question, knowing she couldn't get lost in the woods if she tried. Professor Stott remained where he'd been standing ever since he'd seen Emory Emmerick snatched up into the oak. After due deliberation, he uttered.

"Peter, I believe we may now say with confidence that the apparition of a snowy owl was a mere ruse to gain our, or probably Mr.

Emmerick's, attention. Though the outcome of the adventure has been far more deplorable than I anticipated, I cannot say that I was ever wholly sanguine about the probability of a satisfactory sighting. Shortages of *Nyctea scandiaca*'s accustomed prey occur cyclically, as a rule in a span of five to seven years. To the best of my recollection, only three and a half years have elapsed since a snowy owl was observed by one Mr. Wendell White of Durham, Maine, attacking a raven on a byroad connecting Route 9 to Route 136. Mr. White got out of his pickup truck and rescued the raven from the owl on the ground that the raven was a local bird and he didn't hold with foreigners coming in and trying to take over. One sees the force of Mr. White's argument."

"Many in Balaclava County would feel the same way," Peter agreed. "I suspect our so-called owl may in fact have been nothing more than a bunch of white feathers tied to a fishing pole. Some wisenheimer was running along beside us, sticking it up in the air every so often to keep us moving toward the net."

"Your brain is more agile than mine, old friend, I would not have thought of a fishing pole. Indeed, the runner himself must have been inordinately agile to have traversed so irregular a terrain without alerting any of us to his or her presence. Your own ears are exceptionally keen, Peter, and your perceptions acute. Those of our esteemed colleague Winifred Binks are even keener, as I believe you will concede."

"I certainly will, Dan, and you've raised an interesting point. I suppose the lure could have been slung on something like a trolley wire and was being pulled along just fast enough to keep it ahead of our party. Or else the runner was keeping his distance, casting the lure like a trout fly and reeling it back."

"That would not have been easy to do in these woods," Daniel Stott objected. "Would there not have been great risk of the line's being fouled on a branch or the lure's getting caught in the undergrowth?"

"Maybe there were crooks stationed all along the way with separate casting rods. Drat! I wish they'd get here with those searchlights."

Peter knew he was being unreasonably impatient. The president and Miss Binks couldn't even be out of the woods yet, much less have got to a phone and alerted the state police. He and Stott would be here alone for at least an hour, probably longer. They might as well make what use they could of the time.

"Dan," he said, "hold the flashlight for me, will you? I want to take a closer look at Emmerick."

"By all means," his friend agreed. "Poor fellow, to have met an untimely demise through a mistimed and ill-judged Halloween prank."

"Think so?" Peter was down on his knees beside the grotesque bundle of netting, trying to get a better look without disturbing the body. "Shine the beam down this way, will you? M'yes, I can see well enough now. This would have had to be one hell of a Halloween prank, Dan. I can see blood on the sweater. It looks to me as if somebody's shoved the point of a damned great big hunting knife into the back of Emmerick's neck."

"Right at the base of the skull, thus effecting his instant demise," Stott agreed after careful scrutiny of the ugly wound. "We must be thankful that the poor fellow did not suffer. You speak of a hunting knife, Peter. That would have required a sharp blow by a powerful hand. Might we not also consider the possibility of a hunting arrow, a javelin, or a bolt from the sort of harpoon gun used by scuba divers?"

"We might," Peter conceded, "though it would have taken some fancy shooting to hit a vital spot by moonlight with the target up a tree, bundled into a net. Unless the hit was plain fool luck."

"The element of luck cannot be discounted, Peter. Moreover, a harpoon bolt would have a line attached by which it could be retrieved even from a distance. The same might conceivably be true of an arrow or a spear, might it not?"

"I suppose so." Peter wasn't too sold on the arrow, javelin, or harpoon concept, and Dan Stott noticed.

"In any event, we are agreed on the element of premeditation and the likelihood of a human agent, are we not? Unless some kind of infernal device was set up in the tree which was triggered by Emmerick's sudden rise. Do you think that possible?"

Peter shrugged. "Miss Binks and I didn't find one, but we could easily enough have missed it. I'd far rather believe in an infernal device than in the possibility that somebody's over there in the bushes right now, aiming a harpoon gun at us."

"Surely you do not seriously entertain such a possibility?" Daniel Stott asked the question only after due consideration. "It would seem to me that should further mayhem have been intended, this would have had to be effected while our party was still all together, since the would-be perpetrator would not have known in advance which of us would go for help and which would stay behind. Had the plan been to wipe us all out, I venture to suggest that live bullets would have been used instead of firecrackers."

"Good thinking, Dan."

"Thank you, Peter. I am, however, still nonplussed as to why Mr. Emmerick was stabbed after he had already been trapped in the net. Though," Dan added after further pondering, "I also fail to see whether there would have been any point to his having been stabbed first."

"I can't see that, either. Besides, it doesn't fit with what Miss Binks told me. She claims Emmerick dashed to the front of the line just before the fireworks went off, and tried to take her with him. You must have noticed him, Dan, you were next in line to the president."

"I was indeed, but I cannot truthfully say that I observed the occurrence. I was wholly preoccupied with the aberrant behavior of the snowy owl, as I then still supposed it might be. I believe I was weighing the alternative possibility of an albino *Tyto alba pratincola*, although I had no substantial grounds on which to do so. But for a member of the group to have advanced himself ahead of our leader was a serious breach of owl-count etiquette. Had Mr. Emmerick not been made aware of our accustomed protocol?"

"Certainly he had; I explained the rules to him very carefully, in words of one syllable insofar as possible, before we started out. I couldn't imagine why he wanted to come in the first place. Now, of course, I realize it was because he thought the net and the fireworks were a practical joke and wanted to be in on the fun."

"Peter, you say Miss Binks told you of Emmerick's movement. Did you yourself not see it happening? You were directly behind him, were you not?"

"I didn't see him pass the president. I was flat on my face at the time. I'd tripped over a root. Or thought I had. In retrospect, I wonder if it mightn't have been Emmerick's foot that tripped me."

"A viable hypothesis, in my opinion. I must say I myself found Mr. Emmerick's behavior quite incomprehensible in one who was neither a member of the faculty nor even a fellow townsman. His absurd pronouncements betrayed his abysmal ignorance of the Strigiformes, his forwardness amounted at times almost to rudeness. Can you account for his having forced himself upon us as he did, Peter?"

"Dan, I cannot account for one damned thing that's happened tonight. So where do we go from here?"

"Since we cannot in point of fact go anywhere at all until our reinforcements arrive, I see only one course open to us." Stott began fishing in the capacious pockets of his Norfolk jacket, bringing out squarish, thickish bundles carefully wrapped in foil. "Here, old friend, have a sandwich."

Iduna Stott's sandwiches were always expertly engineered and nutritionally balanced. The one Peter opened first had been started with slices of home-baked rye bread and honey-cured ham, progressing thence to smoked turkey, sage cheese, fresh tomato, cucumber, lettuce, and alfalfa sprouts, all subtly enhanced by a mustard dressing whose secret recipe Iduna had promised to will to the college's home arts department should she ever get around to shuffling off her mortal coil.

Dan's trove also included a thermos of hot tea. With this and the sandwiches, plus a few fig squares, apples, and chocolate cookies along with a swig apiece from Peter's brandy flask by way of *bonne bouche*, the two old friends whiled away the time pleasantly enough, although Emmerick's by now stiffening corpse was not the companion they would have chosen for an al fresco picnic. They even managed to add a pair of barred owls and a more exciting long-eared *Asio otus wilsonianus* to their checklist before Miss Binks and Dr. Svenson showed up with a fairly long arm of the law in tow.

"Did you bring the floodlights?" was Peter's greeting.

"Battery lanterns." The officer in charge held up the one he'd been using to light the path. It was a fairly impressive affair with a bulb half the size of an automobile headlight. "We understand you've had an unfortunate incident here."

"M'yes, you could say that. My name is Shandy, by the way, and this is Professor Stott. I assume Professor Binks and Dr. Svenson have explained how we watched one of our group get caught up in a net, hauled up into this tree here, then dumped back on the ground. He's also been stabbed in the neck."

"Well, that's an interesting development. I'm Sergeant Haverford. Is this your man? You haven't moved him?"

"Oh no, that's exactly how he landed. We just—er peeked under the net with our flashlight."

"I see. Let's have a couple more lanterns over here."

Two of Haverford's men stepped forward. The battery lanterns made a big difference, it was easy enough to see the dried blood and the gaping slit.

"Commando tactics," Haverford remarked. "Neat job. We understand from Dr. Svenson that his name was Emory Emmerick and he was an engineer helping to set up a television station for the college. Had you known Mr. Emmerick long, Professor Shandy?"

"No, not at all until he showed up last week and introduced himself to the steering committee as the site engineer. We were surprised to see him, as a matter of fact, because there was still nothing for him to do and won't be, I gather, until the subcontractors are ready to pour the foundations. However, Emmerick seemed to feel it was important for him to get the lie of the land, as it were. We assumed he knew what he was doing."

"'We' meaning this steering committee you mentioned? Who's on the committee?"

"Of the present company, Professor Binks and myself. Plus some other members of the faculty, of course."

"Including Dr. Svenson?"

"Certainly. As president of the college, Dr. Svenson is an ex-officio member of all committees."

"I see. How well have you people been getting along with Mr. Emmerick?"

"Well enough, I suppose."

"You don't sound very enthusiastic."

"It's just that, since he couldn't get on with his own job, he tended to be a bit too ready to get involved in other people's," Peter replied.

"Such as how?"

"Such as inviting himself along tonight, for one thing," Winifred Binks put in. "Mr. Emmerick seemed to think owl counting was some sort of campus frolic instead of serious ornithological research. Even before that quite terrifying grand finale with the fireworks, he'd been talking too much and too loudly and offering stupid observations that showed he knew virtually nothing about owls. Am I not right, Professor Stott?"

"One is loath to speak ill of the dead, but there remains the fact that he confused *Aegolius acadica acadica* with *Aegolius funerea richardsoni*," Stott confirmed in a tone from which he had not succeeded in eliminating a note of rebuke. "Not being myself a member of the field-station steering committee, I had held small converse with Mr. Emmerick before this evening. My initial impression was that his acquaintance would not be one I should care to cultivate further."

"So what you're saying is that Mr. Emmerick had already started making enemies at the college. Can you give me any names, Professor Shandy?"

"Of course I can't." Peter was beginning to fray around the edges. "Emmerick hadn't made enemies. We thought of him as a pest, not a menace. We knew he wasn't going to be around long, and we also knew that if he got to be too much of a nuisance, it was quite within our power to ship him back to his bosses and get them to send somebody who'd mind his own business and leave us to manage ours as we saw fit; which we'd certainly have done if he'd survived tonight's caper. Er—speaking of business, I expect Professor

Binks told you that she and I searched the tree."

"She did mention it. I assume what she meant was that you shone a flashlight up through the branches."

"Oh no. We climbed the tree and shone the light—er—laterally."

"You climbed the tree?" Haverford looked to be about thirty-five years old, and a few inches over six feet. He smiled tolerantly down on their two graying heads. "How did you manage that?"

"Easily enough." Winifred Binks reached up to the same branch she'd used the first time, swung herself over it in a neat flip, and was forty feet in the air before Haverford could wipe the grin off his face. "If you're coming up, Peter," she called from the top, "bring one of those lanterns so we can take a better look this time."

Peter held out his hand. "May I, Sergeant?"

"You're going up there with her? Like that?"

"It's how we generally go. I might point out that Miss—er—Professor Binks and I are not only experienced climbers but also trained naturalists. We'd both have recognized unusual damage to the tree and would have been careful not to make it any worse. We couldn't see too much because our light wasn't strong enough, but we did find the place where the net crashed down through the branches, for whatever good that might do. If you'd like to go up yourself or send one of your men, we'll be happy to serve as guides."

"Thanks, Professor." Haverford didn't grin this time. "I think the best thing for us to do now is leave a guard around the tree and come back with ladders and search dogs in the morning. Can you get your friend down out of there all right?"

"Certainly." Peter raised his voice a little. "Come on down, Miss Binks. The sergeant's decided to wait for daylight."

Less than a minute later, Winifred Binks was on the ground. "I daresay you've made the right decision, Sergeant Haverford, though I'm sure Professor Shandy and I could have managed well enough with those nice lanterns of yours. I did notice a wisp of transparent fishline tied to a branch."

Haverford made a strange gurgling noise, Professor Stott nodded.

"Then that supports your conjecture, Peter. Professor Shandy," he explained to the sergeant, "has proffered the hypothesis that what we hoped was a snowy owl may in fact have been merely a bunch of white feathers pulled along on some mechanism analogous to a trolley wire. Do you not find this reasonable, Professor Binks?"

"Oh yes, certainly. An alternative possibility might have been someone running along parallel to the path with the lure on a pole; but it's not easy to move silently through the woods at night unless one is on a well-marked path, as we were. And not even then if you're in a hurry. We were walking briskly, we naturally didn't want to miss the chance of a definitive spotting. A snowy owl would have been a real coup. Pity, but there it is. You weren't planning to leave poor Mr. Emmerick here till morning too, I trust?"

"Oh no," the inspector reassured her. "We'll take him with us when we go. Let me just try to get straight about this net. Which of you was nearest to Mr. Emmerick when he got caught in it?"

Thorkjeld Svenson, who'd been chewing a handful of trail mix, gulped and growled, "I was."

"Do the rest of you corroborate that?"

"Of course we do." Winifred Binks sounded as though she found Sergeant Haverford a trifle slow in the intellect. "Dr. Svenson is our group leader, his place is always in front. Mr. Emmerick had had that explained to him before we started, but he either forgot the rule or chose to disregard it. If he hadn't suddenly taken that notion to dart ahead—dear me!"

Haverford pounced like a hawk owl on a mouse. "Wait a minute, Professor Binks. You're saying Dr. Svenson should have been in front; do you mean he should have been the one to get caught in the net?"

Peter stifled a snort. If they'd meant to catch Svenson, they should have dug a tiger pit.

Winifred Binks must have been thinking much the same thing, she shook her head violently. "I'm not offering any conjectures, Sergeant, I'm merely attempting to sort out the facts. The net was only big enough for one person. The question is whether they—I say 'they,' though of course it may have been only a single he or she—intended to snare a particular member of our group, or just the first one who happened along. You'll note that a fair number of dead leaves are caught up in the net along with Mr. Emmerick's body. This indicates to me, though of course I may be wrong, that the net had been spread across the path and camouflaged so that it wouldn't be spotted before somebody stepped into it. How anybody could have mistaken Mr. Emmerick for Dr. Svenson is a question I'm not prepared to answer."

"Maybe they didn't know Dr. Svenson by sight, but just that he'd be the first in line," one of the other officers ventured.

"That would mean we're dealing with a set of paid assassins," said Peter. "Can you think offhand who'd want to put out a contract on you, President?"

"Anybody."

Svenson was being overmodest. Fearsome though he might appear, and indeed often was, Thorkjeld Svenson was admired by many, revered by some, and loved by a surprising number, of whom Peter Shandy and Daniel Stott were two, although either would have been hideously embarrassed to say so. Through weal, through woe, through sun and storm and general cussedness, each to each had held the steadfast fraternal devotion of a Damon to a Pythias, a Roland to an Oliver, a Mason to a Mason, an Elk to an Elk. Peter was more shaken than he ever wanted to be again at the thought that it might have been Svenson bundled up inside this depressing tangle of cords. He wished he hadn't been so flip about the putative contract.

The hell of it was, that stab in the neck would have made some sense if the trappers had been under the impression that they'd snared the president. Thorkjeld Svenson's reputation as a warrior in the old berserker tradition was too well known for even a squad of hired retiarii not to have had some inkling of what they'd be running up against. But why then the fireworks? Why the net at all? Why the stabbing? Why not an elephant gun from a safe distance?

Through an often bizarre concatenation of circumstances, Peter had come to be regarded as Balaclava County's apology for Renfrew of the Mounted. Sooner or later, a small voice from some other dimension was murmuring, he was going to get stuck with this mess.

The hitch was, the state police would be perfectly willing to go on with the case, but only to the extent that Chief Ottermole asked them to. Ottermole was not one to let outsiders hog any glory that might be hoggable. As soon as he found out what had happened, he'd insist on taking charge, relying mainly on local talent for whatever help he needed.

And when Fred Ottermole thought of local talent, he thought first of P. Shandy.

That was a bridge to be crossed when they got to it. Right now Haverford was saying, "I know you folks want to get home, but I'd like to get statements from all of you while everything's fresh in your mind."

"That's quite all right, Sergeant," replied Winifred Binks, at whom Haverford's semi-apology had been mainly directed. "We were planning to stay out all night, anyway. President, will you go first?"

"You, Binks. Emmerick was your man."

The outdoor life, while good for the soul, tends to be rough on the complexion. Haverford stared from the youngish, dapperly clad male body, which had by now been extricated from the net and laid out on the stretcher, to the spare, gray-haired woman whose wrinkled face was almost as thoroughly tanned as her ill-made deerskin suit. "You and he were—er—ah—?"

Winifred Binks took his flounderings calmly. "What President Svenson means, Sergeant, is that I'm the one responsible for having brought Mr. Emmerick to Balaclava. It was my idea to build the television station."

"Binks's money, too," Svenson barked.

"Binks's? You're—you're not the missing heiress to the Binks estate?"

Winifred shook her head. "I was never missing, Sergeant; I was merely too uninteresting to be kept track of until the media discovered that Grandfather was dead and I'd inherited his money. Nor am I all that interesting now, I'm afraid. There's not much I can tell you that hasn't already been said, except that when Mr. Emmerick rushed to the head of the line, he tried to take me with him."

"How was that?"

"He'd been walking behind me. As he came up to my side, he took hold of my arm and started urging me forward."

"Did he say anything?"

"I believe he whispered something like 'Let's move up.' I assumed he'd got the childish notion of being first to spot the snowy owl and wanted me along as co-witness. The evidence of a single spotter is not accepted in the owl count, you see, there must be at least two. Since Mr. Emmerick knew I was also doing my first owl count, he apparently thought I'd be willing to help him confound the experts."

"Did you say anything to him?"

"No. I did take a few steps forward,

mainly to regain my balance. He'd practically knocked me off my feet trying to hustle me along. Needless to say, I wanted no part of his nonsense, so I pulled away and got back into line behind Professor Stott. This all happened very quickly, you know. I'm not sure Mr. Emmerick realized immediately that I wasn't still with him. Once he'd bolted past Dr. Svenson, I saw him turn his head as if he might be looking around to see where I was. Then all at once he was up in the air and into the tree."

"Just like that, eh?"

"Oh yes. For a moment I was quite nonplussed. Then I realized that Mr. Emmerick must have been caught in a snare because nothing else made sense. I heard him cry out—we all did—"

"What did he say, Professor Binks?" By now Haverford's address was almost reverential. "Can you remember?"

"No. One couldn't have heard what anybody said, that was when the firecrackers started banging. They made a horrendous noise, we thought they must be guns, so we threw ourselves down to dodge the bullets. After a bit—it seemed forever but probably wasn't more than a few seconds—Peter—Professor Shandy—caught on that there weren't any. By that time, the skyrockets were starting, so we knew it was a trick. We blamed Mr. Emmerick for setting them off, he'd been acting the clown all along, as I believe I mentioned a while back."

"Yes, you did say he'd been disruptive."

"He'd been a pest. We were furious, not so much at having been made fools of, though of course one never likes being scared out of one's wits for someone else's amusement, but because the noise would have frightened off the owls and ruined our count. Really, that was an unconscionable thing to do, no matter who did it."

"I couldn't agree more, Professor Binks. So then what happened?"

"Good question. Peter, what happened next?"

"Well—er—a couple of us began berating Emmerick, assuming he was up in the tree. Then it dawned on me that what I'd thought was a boulder in the path was in fact Emmerick trussed up in a net, as you saw him earlier. That reminded me of a heavy thud I'd heard just as the explosions began and I concluded he'd either fallen or been dropped out of the tree. At first I thought he'd had the wind knocked out of him, then I realized he was dead. So Miss Binks and I went up to see what we could find."

3

"You went up?"

Haverford's voice was going up, too. "This guy gets caught in a net, hauled into the tree, and stabbed to death. And you went up?" His voice ended on a squeak.

"We didn't know he'd been stabbed," said Peter. "That high neck on Emmerick's sweater seems to have absorbed most of the blood. I never noticed the wound in his neck until Miss Binks and the president had gone to get help, leaving Stott and myself to guard the body. As for searching the tree, we may have been a trifle precipitate but I don't see where we were all that foolhardy. Bear in mind that this didn't all happen in rapid succession. When the firecrackers started banging, we reacted quite as the—er—perpetrators no doubt expected, trying to shelter ourselves from the apparent shooting, then focusing our attention on Emmerick's body. Whoever'd been in the tree had plenty of time to get down and away without our noticing."

"On a bicycle," said Winifred Binks.

"A bicycle? Why, Professor Binks? Did you see it?"

"No, I merely hypothesize one. They're fast, silent, easy to hide, and easy to ride on a path like this. I myself would have ridden a bicycle. But then I always do."

"You do?" This was clearly not what Haverford would have expected from a multimillionairess, but he nodded. "That's a good point. Edwards, you and Andrews take a look around. See if you can find any bicycle tracks."

The two officers scouted the area with their lanterns. They didn't find any bicycle tracks, but they did turn up a sizable heap of black plastic not more than twenty feet from the oak tree. It looked brand new.

"This is interesting," said Peter. "It wasn't here this morning."

"How do you know?" Haverford demanded.

"At the president's request, I walked the path to make sure there were no obstacles that might give us trouble. We'd be working in the dark, you understand, so as not to disturb the owls. They don't like light, it interferes with their hunting."

"I see. And you're quite sure the plastic wasn't here?"

"Oh yes. I spent a fair amount of time walking around the tree; big old oaks like this are apt to have holes in them where owls can nest. I also searched the ground for owl pellets, those little balls of fur and bones they regurgitate after they've eaten a mouse or whatever. I couldn't have missed a great wad like that, I'd either have taken the plastic away myself or sent one of the college groundsmen over to pick it up. That's not to say it wasn't around, I probably wouldn't have noticed if it had been still rolled up and hidden under the leaves."

"What do you mean, still rolled up?"

"Just that it looks brand new and is the kind of plastic sheeting that comes in rolls. Gardeners and landscapers use the stuff as a mulch, to keep weeds from growing and to reflect heat up on their plants. It also prevents moisture from soaking into the ground and can turn your garden into a desert if you don't watch out, but I'll spare you the lecture. Could we spread it out and have a look?"

"I guess so, if we're careful."

Handling the plastic through paper napkins left over from Iduna's picnic, pages torn from Sergeant Haverford's notebook, President Svenson's red cap, and anything else they could find to protect the surface from their fingerprints and preserve any others that might be present, the lot of them worked the bundle carefully over the path. Stretched to full length, and paced off by Peter, it measured all of a hundred feet and didn't show them a thing.

"Maybe they just used it to wrap up the bicycle," one of the state policemen suggested.

Haverford gave him a look. "No sense trying to guess. We may as well roll it up and take it to the lab. Careful, try not to pick up any leaves or twigs."

"What about the rope that must have been attached to the net?" Peter asked.

"We haven't found any on the ground, maybe it's still up in the tree. Did you have anything special in mind, Professor?"

"I was just wondering whether the rope had been cut or broken. That could indicate whether Emmerick fell by accident or was deliberately dropped. I forgot to look before the body was taken away."

Haverford clearly hadn't thought to look, either. "We'll know definitely when we get the lab report," he fudged. "Thank you,

Professor Shandy. Now could we get your statement, Dr. Svenson?"

He got it in about seven words, then wasted a good deal of time trying to extract the names of persons who might have had both the inclination and the ready funds to hire somebody to assassinate the president. By the time he got around to Professor Daniel Stott, Haverford was visibly shaken. When Stott said he hadn't noticed Emmerick's getting caught in the net because he'd been ruminating, the sergeant got downright nasty. Peter's efforts to convince him that Professor Stott was only telling the plain truth because Dan always ruminated met with little favor. Since they were also insistent that he'd never once stepped out of line, there wasn't much Haverford could do but table the question.

"All right, I guess we won't be needing you people any longer tonight. You aren't any of you planning to leave town in a hurry?"

"Hadn't better," snarled the president. "Classes."

"Oh, right. Then I expect we can find you at the college if Chief Ottermole requests our further assistance."

Peter said they'd be looking forward to it,

and the two groups parted company. Most of the policemen headed back the way they'd come, two stayed to guard the tree. The owl counters walked on the way they'd been heading for half a mile or so, but none of them spotted so much as a regurgitated pellet of mouse fur, and not a hoot was to be heard. After a while, Dr. Svenson voiced what was by now the consensus of the group.

"Hell with the owls. Let's go home."

They were a silent lot as they followed Winifred Binks's lead back to where Peter had parked his car. He automatically headed back toward the college, since most of his passengers lived within its purlieus, then realized he was being less than courteous to the lone female member, who lived miles out of town. To cover his gaffe, he said, "I'll just drop the others, Miss Binks, then run you back to the station."

"Indeed you will not," Winifred protested. "I'll get a security guard to let me into the gym, and doss down on one of the tumbling mats."

After a certain amount of argy-bargy, she agreed to the pull-out sofa in the Shandys' upstairs den. Truth to tell, Peter was glad not only that he wouldn't have to make the long drive but also that Miss Binks would be safe under his roof instead of out on a thirty-mile tract in the middle of nowhere. He managed to get her settled without waking his wife, then climbed gratefully into the conjugal bed.

Considering how late it was by then, Peter had expected to sleep like one of the logs he'd spent so much of the night clambering over. Instead he lay wide awake, thinking about the many who might still be out there owling. He hoped none of them had got tangled up with a phantom netter.

Or netters. How many hands would have been needed to run that operation? One could have done it, maybe, if the person was strong enough. Hauling Emmerick up into the tree would have been the hardest part. Maybe that was why he'd got dropped so fast; whoever had pulled him up couldn't hold him any longer. Could that mean the netter had been a woman, or a young kid? Or that the netter had tried to hold him with one hand while stabbing him with the other?

It wasn't as though Emmerick had been a big man, he'd been a few inches shorter than Peter himself, and Peter was no giant. Say five feet six or so, about Winifred Binks's height. He'd no doubt weighed twenty or thirty pounds more than she; her mostly vegetarian diet kept her weight down, although the muscles developed by her arboreal habits made her look heftier than she was. Emmerick had not been noticeably muscular, he mightn't have been able to put up much of a fight even if he hadn't been pinioned by the net. Easy to stab, then; maybe hard to hold.

And so what? Peter dozed off at last and had a not particularly amusing dream about Emory Emmerick, dressed in Miss Binks's deerskins, being chased through the woods by an unidentifiable absentminded professor with a minnow net. He woke gummy-eyed and heavy-headed, wondering why the sun was so high and why Helen wasn't here beside him. Then he heard her talking to somebody downstairs, and remembered.

The time was half past eight, at least he hadn't wasted the whole morning. Not that it mattered much, this being Saturday, but he might as well get up. Peter didn't feel obliged to put on the dog for Miss Binks, she'd seen him in far worse shape than this. Four minutes later, unshaven but showered and more or less respectably clad, he was downstairs drinking his first cup of coffee and lending his voice to the postmortem.

Usually Peter got breakfast, but today

Helen was officiating at the stove. "Shall I poach you an egg, dear?" she offered. "Winifred and I are having one. One each, that is. Maybe you'd better have two, you've got to keep up your strength."

"Why?"

"I don't know, but you're bound to have a reason before long. I'm surprised Thorkjeld's not on the phone right now demanding to know why you haven't found out who bagged Mr. Emmerick. What a totally bizarre way to kill somebody! You don't suppose it could have been a joke that went wrong?"

"Some joke! A hunting knife smack in the medulla oblongata."

"You don't know for sure that it was a hunting knife. What if the person who hauled up the net happened to have been holding something sharp in his hand, like a—"

"A sword cane?" Peter offered.

"Exactly. I see you're in one of your moods."

"If you say so, my love. May I trouble you for the jam? And the butter?"

"Of course, my precious. Would you care for a piece of toast to put them on?"

"I was working up to the toast," said Peter

with what little dignity he could muster in his present condition. "Thank you. As to the question of how Emmerick was stabbed, my suggestion is that we wait and see what the police pathologist turns up. Drat! I'd like to take another look around that tree, but I suppose Haverford, or whoever's taken over for him, is out there with a posse already. I wonder if anyone's thought to notify the Meadowsweet Construction Company that they're short one site engineer?"

"It's a bit early for that, isn't it?" said Miss Binks. "Don't business offices generally open at nine o'clock?"

"I believe that depends on the nature of the business. Construction workers start early, so perhaps their inside people do, too. Anyway"—Peter glanced up at the kitchen clock—"it's almost nine now, so we may as well try them. Let's hope they stay open Saturday mornings."

"But it's not your responsibility," Helen protested. "Shouldn't Fred Ottermole be the one to tell them?"

"Why? We're Meadowsweet's customer, aren't we? At least Miss Binks is. Who better than she to break the news?"

"And who better than you to be listening in on the upstairs extension when she calls?

At least eat your eggs first. Do you have any idea who Mr. Emmerick's superior might be, Winifred?"

"I expect Mr. Gyles would be the one we should talk to. He's the man who handled all that business about the bidding with us. I don't mind a bit making the call, and do please listen, Peter, in case I don't explain properly. You know what an ignoramus I am. Now let's see, I'm quite sure I have the office number here in my compendium. One does need to be organized."

Now that she was a woman of property, a member of the college faculty, and the driving force behind Balaclava's new field station, Winifred Binks had equipped herself with a large leather tote bag from which she was seldom parted. Along with a good many other things, it held a thick loose-leaf notebook into which Winifred scrupulously entered every scrap of information that she or anybody else involved with her project might by any chance require. She hauled out the book and thumbed quickly down the bristle of index tabs.

"Here we are. Addresses and phone numbers. E-F-G—Golden Apples. I must remember to—J-K-L—ah yes. M for Meadowsweet. Why don't I run upstairs and straighten the sofa, then put the call through from the den? By the time I've changed the sheets and got hold of Mr. Gyles, you'll have had time to finish your eggs, Peter. Unless, of course, you'd rather I waited till you've had another cup of coffee?"

"No, no, you go right ahead."

Peter was banking on that Old Boston accent of Miss Binks's to overawe any receptionist or secretary who might otherwise have obstructive tendencies, nor did he bank in vain. By three minutes past nine, Miss Binks had Mr. Gyles on the wire and was saying her piece about his late employee. She said it well, she said it succinctly and with exactly the proper note of compassionate concern. What went wrong was Mr. Gyles's reply.

"Just a moment, Miss Binks. You say this man's name was Emory Emmerick and our company sent him out to your job as site engineer?"

"Yes."

"Could you hold on a minute, please?"

"Certainly."

Peter, on the downstairs phone, raised his eyebrows at Helen.

"What's happening?" she murmured.

"God knows. Maybe he's gone to take up

a collection for the funeral wreath. He's being long enough about it."

He was, indeed. It was a long time before Mr. Gyles came back.

"Sorry to keep you waiting, Miss Binks, but we seem to have a major problem here. Our site engineer's name is Patrick Henry O'Gorman and he's not scheduled to go out to your site until a week from Tuesday. We have nobody named Emory Emmerick on our payroll. As far as our personnel department can tell, we never did have."

4

"But then who was he?"

That was what Viola Buddley wanted to know. That was what everybody had been asking everybody else ever since Winifred's startling conversation with the man from Meadowsweet. So far, nobody had come up with an answer. As soon as he'd hung up the phone, Peter had passed on his astounding piece of non-information to Dr. Svenson and state-police headquarters, then driven Winifred Binks and her bicycle back to the field station. At the moment, she was over in her new house changing out of her deerskins while Peter broke the news about Emmerick to the two full-time members of the field staff.

Viola Buddley was receptionist, secretary, and general assistant, which could mean anything from dusting the exhibits to picking the flowers for Winifred's camomile tea. The name Viola suggested somebody willowy and wistful; Peter thought Ms. Buddley's parents would have done better to call her Heliantha. This strapping young woman reminded him of jolly round red Mr. Sun in the Thornton Burgess stories his third-grade teacher used to read to the class when they'd been good, as children had often been in his day.

Since the bulk of her duties were in fact secretarial, Viola had no practical reason that Peter could see to show up for work in hiking boots and khaki shorts. He personally thought a tight green T-shirt with "Have you hugged a tree today?" sprawled across the bosom was carrying Viola's enthusiasm for environmental concerns a step too far, but if Miss Binks didn't mind what she wore around the office, he supposed he shouldn't, either. For the rest, Viola had a great many blotchy tan freckles, strawberry-blond hair frizzed out into a bush, and a radiant smile that had just now been wiped from her face by the news about Emory Emmerick.

"The state police are checking to see whether he had a criminal record," Peter explained. "If they don't come up with an identification, I expect they'll send photographs out to the newspapers and television stations. Just asking around won't help, I don't suppose. We don't know where he came from, and his name might not have been Emmerick."

"Emory told me he came from New Jersey," said Viola.

"When was this?"

"Thursday night. He took me out to the Bursting Bubble. You know it?"

"M'yes, in a manner of speaking." Earlier in the year, Peter had watched Lumpkin Upper Mills's sole apology for a nightclub burn down, along with the historic Lumpkin Soap Works. "I understand the Bubble's reopened in that former bowling alley out on the Clavaton Road."

"Yes, and they've done a really nice job with it. There's a three-piece combo, and they've opened two lanes as a dance floor. It's great fun, as long as you don't mind dancing back and forth in a straight line. Emory and I had a marvelous time. I sort of thought it might be the start of something beautiful, but after what you said, I don't know whether to feel bereft or relieved."

"He wasn't worthy of you!"

This burst of pent-up emotion came from the lips of the station's research fellow, Knapweed Calthrop, who was at Balaclava on a teaching fellowship. Knapweed was doing his fellowship dissertation on the bedstraw or madder family, which he himself always referred to as the Rubiaceae. Like the bedstraws, he could be rough and bristly, but never with Viola.

These two were more or less of an age, Peter thought, although you never could tell with women. Emmerick must have been well into his thirties, perhaps even older; why wouldn't Viola have preferred a younger chap? Knapweed wasn't bad-looking in his unassuming way, and he was fairly sound on the Rubiaceae.

But was that enough? On reflection, Peter could see why the picaresque temperament that must have underlain Emmerick's having the face to present himself here under false colors, and the breezy enthusiasm he'd displayed for jumping in with both feet when he had no idea where he was going might have had more appeal for the flamboyant

Viola than her co-worker's penchant for sitting on rotten stumps brooding over wisps of bedstraw. There was something basically uncharismatic about the Rubiaceae by and large, Peter had to admit, though the bluet offered its shy appeal and the wild madder at least had more pizzazz than the sleepy catchfly.

Well, such was the way of the world. Peter supposed he ought to get back to college, though he couldn't think why. This wasn't a week for tutorials, Svenson hadn't called a faculty meeting. Still, he had a nagging hunch that there was something he'd meant to do and hadn't done. Had he promised to take Helen somewhere today? No, that couldn't be it. Both a librarian and a respected writer, Helen had planned to work on her latest article for Wilson's Library Bulletin while Peter slept off the fatigues of the owl count, then spent whatever might remain of the day grading papers.

The field-station lobby had big picture windows on both sides. Peter could see Winifred Binks emerging from her log cabin, looking much more the professor than the pioneer in neatly pressed gray flannel slacks and a sky-blue jersey. As she entered the station, she asked, "Would you care to join me in a cup of coffee, Peter?"

Coffee was in this case a misnomer; Winifred made her brew from dried chicory and dandelion roots ground by hand between a rock and a hard place. Peter thought he might as well accept, maybe the healthful brew would jog his memory. He was sipping from a slightly wopsical hand-thrown pottery mug and listening to Viola's mournful reminiscence about what a swell dancer Emory had been when a red 1976 Dodge sport coupe with white stripes around the sides and BALACLAVA COUNTY FANE AND PENNON painted on the door whizzed into the parking area.

"Ah," said Winifred. "Our friend Mr. Swope, in his new staff car. I've been wondering why we hadn't heard from him."

"Good Lord, that's whom I meant to call," said Peter. "Swope didn't get in on what happened to us last night because he was covering the owl count up behind Valhalla."

Cronkite Swope, star reporter for the *Balaclava County Fane and Pennon,* had never been one to let a night's sleep stand in the way of a good story. It was a burning shame that he'd elected to go out with a group of students that included two of Dr. Svenson's seven beautiful daughters, instead of sticking with the president's team and getting first-hand coverage of Emmerick's bizarre demise. He must be ready to cut his own throat.

But no, Cronkite was chipper as a bee. "Wow, what a night! I got this terrific shot of Gudrun Svenson in profile, looking up just as this great horned owl flew smack-dab across the face of the full moon with a bunch of wispy little clouds streaking along behind. The chief's going to put her on the front page."

"M'well, perhaps you may want to phone your chief and tell him to hold the presses." Peter felt like a rat for not having alerted Swope sooner, after all they'd been through together. "I gather you haven't heard what happened to Emory Emmerick last night."

"Emmerick? You mean your site engineer?"

"We thought he was, but it seems he wasn't."

"Huh? How come?"

"According to Mr. Gyles of the Meadowsweet Construction Company, Emmerick not only didn't work for them but they'd never even heard of him. The reason I'm speaking of Emmerick in the past tense is that he got netted last night."

"Netted?"

"Exactly. Have you something to write with?"

Peter need not have asked, Cronkite Swope was a summa cum laude graduate of the Great Journalists' Correspondence School. "Shoot, Professor!"

Peter shot. He'd barely dropped Emmerick out of the tree before Swope was on the phone to his paper, howling for a rewrite man.

"Here, Professor." He thrust the telephone into Peter's hand. "You tell'em. I've got to whiz over to the state-police barracks and see if I can con them out of a photograph. Darn it to heck, why didn't I go with you instead of Gudrun?"

"You couldn't be everywhere, Cronkite," Winifred Binks consoled him. "Here." She fished in her tote bag and brought out a small camera. "As it happens, I took a few snaps myself, some of Mr. Emmerick in the net and some of the police working around his body. There should be one or two of them carrying him away on a stretcher, too. The police had battery lanterns and I was using extra-sensitive film because I'd hoped to get some photos of owls by moonlight, so the chances are that at least some of my exposures will be usable."

"Miss Binks, I love you!" Swope grabbed the roll of film she'd taken out of her camera, gave her a kiss that all but shattered the windows, and galloped back to his car.

"Wow!" Viola Buddley had watched the embrace with unconcealed envy. "How come you got kissed instead of me, Prof?"

Miss Binks bridled a bit and fluffed her short gray hair. "Some women just can't keep them off, my dear, though goodness knows I make every effort. More coffee, Peter?"

"Thanks, but I'd better get moving. I feel like a skunk for not having alerted Swope earlier, now I'm having qualms about Fred Ottermole."

"Oh gracious, yes, Chief Ottermole should certainly know. But perhaps the state police have already got in touch with him."

"His wife may not have let them."

Edna Mae Ottermole had a tendency to be over-protective of her husband, whom she appeared to regard as a cross between Sir Launcelot and Eliot Ness. If Fred had stuck with his owling until after daybreak, as he most likely had unless he'd somehow got wind of what was happening on the president's territory, he'd still be asleep and Edna Mae would be guarding his slumbers. Peter decided he'd better call before going. He did and she was.

"I hate to wake Fred unless it's desperately urgent, Professor."

"It's desperate but not urgent. I'll be along in a while; let him sleep till I get there."

"I gather Ottermole hasn't yet heard about Emmerick," Peter remarked to Miss Binks as he put down the receiver.

"Lucky man. I suppose you do have to wake him."

"According to protocol, he should have been the one to call in the state police."

"But we couldn't wait to find him," Winifred protested.

"I know that. What we did was the right thing. Anyway, he wouldn't have had the facilities to cope. But he's got to be told. The only way we'll get any information about Emmerick from the state police is to approach them through Ottermole. At least he looks like a cop."

"Indeed he does, with his uniform always so beautifully pressed, and that black leather jacket with all the zippers. Though it might be a trifle warm for his jacket today. There's that gentle feeling in the air and that soft haze over the sky which means the Great Spirit is smoking his peace pipe. I do hope it's the Great Spirit, and not the power plant at Clavaton acting up again. Now who's this man driving in? Oh dear, and there's that wretched squirrel caught inside the bird feeder again. Come, Viola. Talk to him, Peter. The man, I mean."

Winifred rushed out, with Viola and Knapweed at her heels. Peter went to the door. "Yes, sir," he said, "what can I do for you?" Here was somebody who thought he was somebody; tanned and groomed like a three-year-old on Derby Day, although he was assuredly no colt. Nearer fifty than forty and on his way to play golf at some country club, was Peter's guess.

The visitor returned Peter's appraising glance with a Dale Carnegie smile. "I'm looking for my site engineer. Is Emory Emmerick around?"

He glanced over to the windows that made up the entire back of the reception area, and caught sight of the squirrel-rescue party, rushing toward the back of the clearing with Winifred well in the lead. "Oh, I see him. What's he running away for? Would you mind stepping out and telling him Mr. Fanshaw is here?"

Peter was mildly interested to note that Mr. Fanshaw had been taken in by Winifred's superficial back-view resemblance to the late Emmerick. "They're after a squirrel," he said noncommittally, picking up a length of rope that was going to be used for something or other when somebody got around to it, and idly rigging a noose in one end. "Mr. Fanshaw from where?"

"From Meadowsweet Construction, of course. You do work here, don't you?"

"Oh yes." Peter tested his noose and found it good.

"Look, I have some things to check out with Emmerick and I'm rather short of time. Can't you just open the window and give him a yell?"

"Sorry, Mr. Fanshaw. It wouldn't work."

"Why not? Has he gone deaf all of a sudden?"

"M'yes, in a manner of speaking. You're under arrest, Mr. Fanshaw."

"I'm what?"

Taken wholly off-guard, Fanshaw stood there goggling an instant too long. Peter had time to flip the noose over his head, pinion his arms to his body, and trip his feet out from under him.

Fanshaw kicked, he butted, he even tried to bite Peter on the nose. That was a sad mistake; whatever dental adhesive he might have been wearing failed to hold. Peter was a man of the turnip fields; by the time Miss Binks returned saying she'd left the others to cope, he had Fanshaw neatly trussed and hobbled. He'd even retrieved the dentures and restored them to Fanshaw's denuded gums, but got only a curse for his efforts.

A lady of the old school is never surprised by anything. Winifred Binks didn't even raise an eye-brow when she discovered a trussed-up prisoner on the station floor.

"Oh dear, Cronkite appears to have missed out on another scoop. Just a moment, Peter, I know I have another roll of film. Ah yes, here we are. If you'll prop the outer door open and switch on the overhead light, I believe we can get the proper exposure. Do you suppose a light tap behind the ear would quiet the gentleman down enough to keep him in focus?"

Fanshaw started to yell, "You can't do this!" However, an appraising look from Peter, and the fact that Miss Binks was handing her colleague a fancy brass-bound gavel that some kind soul had donated to the field station, for no reason that any of its members had yet fathomed, had a marvelously quieting effect. He did keep trying to turn his face away while Miss Binks was snapping his picture, but she was using fast film again and refused to be disconcerted.

"There," she said at last, "these should make Cronkite happy. Now what do you propose to do with your bird, Peter?"

"I thought I might as well take him along to Ottermole, since I'm going there anyway. Too bad you missed the fun, he breezed in here and introduced himself as Mr. Fanshaw from the Meadowsweet Construction Company. He wanted to check some things out with Emory Emmerick."

"How very interesting," Winifred replied. "And what was it you wanted to check, Mr. Fanshaw?"

"Can't you just go and get Emmerick?" The man was pleading now, all the fight gone out of him.

"No, I'm afraid we can't. I'm sorry to tell you that Mr. Emmerick is dead. Furthermore, he does not appear to have been connected with the Meadowsweet Construction Company. So our logical assumption is that you're not, either, which I presume is why

Professor Shandy has tied you up. Am I not right, Peter?"

"In every particular, Miss Binks."

Fanshaw had been lying perfectly still, keeping his eye on the gavel. Now he reacted as though he'd been given a dose of strychnine: his face turned purple, his back arched till only his head and heels were touching the floor. Then he went limp and didn't say a word.

Peter and Winifred observed the phenomenon without comment. After a moment, the latter asked, "Shall you need help getting him into your car?"

Peter shook his head. "I think you and I can manage him. His feet are tied so that he can't run, but he should be able to walk after a fashion and perhaps with a modicum of persuasion. Fortunately I'm—er—packing my rod. Would you care to get up, Mr. Fanshaw, or shall I start persuading?"

Without waiting for an answer, Peter jerked the prisoner to his feet, turned him around, and set him hobbling toward the door. "You're coming, aren't you, Miss Binks?"

"Oh yes, I wouldn't miss it. Mr. Fanshaw and I will do nicely in the back seat. Once we've got him fastened into his seat belt, I'll just nip back and leave a note for Viola and Knapweed. I may as well fetch the gavel while I'm about it, don't you think? You wouldn't care to mess up your nice upholstery with a lot of bullet holes. Sorry, I should have thought of the gavel before we came out."

"That's quite all right, Miss Binks, I'm sure Ottermole would rather have Mr. Fanshaw rapped than riddled."

Peter was relieved that his mere allusion to a firearm had been enough to cow Fanshaw into cooperating. In fact he didn't own one and was carrying nothing more potentially lethal than the horn-handled jackknife his father had given him on his tenth birthday. He drove as fast as he dared to Balaclava Junction and pulled up in front of the trim white frame house with the blue trimmings and the star cutouts in the shutters, where Edna Mae and Fred ran their tight little ship. Half a second later, Cronkite Swope pulled in behind them.

"Hi, Professor! I phoned here and Mrs. Ottermole said you were on your way, so I thought I'd buzz over and see what's cooking. Our darkroom guy says your film is coming out great, Miss Binks. Hey, what's that you got in your car?"

"A present for Ottermole," said Peter. "Mr. Fanshaw's not talking to us, perhaps he'll open up for you. Slide in and be ready to bop him with this gavel if he tries anything funny while I go to the door. Would you care to join me, Miss Binks?"

"With pleasure. I have a recipe for sassafras jelly that Edna Mae wants to try." Winifred picked up her tote bag and preceded Peter into the house, leaving Swope happily taking angle shots of the man in the back seat.

Fred Ottermole was out of bed and into a fancy bathrobe, being plied with coffee and jelly doughnuts by his solicitously hovering spouse as he sat in an armchair reading the comics to his four young sons: one in his lap, two perched on the arms of the chair, and one doing handstands on the back. Peter hated to disturb so charming a tableau of family life, but duty called.

"Sorry to interrupt you, Ottermole, but there's a delivery for you out in my car. Is your lockup available for use?"

"Far as I know. How'd you make out last night, Professor?"

Peter could see that Fred was all wound up to brag about his own owl count, but now was not the time. "That's what I came to talk to you about. I gather you haven't heard about Emory Emmerick?"

"Emmerick who? Hey, you don't mean that new guy over at the field station? What happened to him?"

"He's been—er—netted. You'd better get dressed and shaved, Ottermole. I expect Swope will be wanting to take your picture."

5

"What do you suppose he'll do now?" asked Miss Binks.

She and Peter had helped Ottermole get the alleged Fanshaw tucked away in the village lockup. Now they were on their way to tear Helen away from her literary pursuits and treat her to lunch at the Plucked Chicken, a fairly soigné new eatery that Bathsheba Monk and her sister-in-law Gert had opened in what had formerly been Bouncing Bet's Beauty Barn.

"Fanshaw?" said Peter. "He'll yell for his lawyer."

"Oh dear!" Miss Binks's long face grew longer. "That reminds me, I was supposed to meet Mr. Debenham—my own lawyer, you know—and some of those people from

Grandfather's trust in my office at half past eleven. It completely slipped my mind. Understandably enough, I suppose, but they must be there now, wondering where I am."

"Maybe they forgot, too," Peter consoled her.

"Not a chance. Lawyers don't break appointments with clients as rich as I am. If that sounds a trifle cynical, I assure you it's meant to. May we stop at your house and give them a buzz to say I'll be along shortly? That is, if you'll be kind enough to take me. Perhaps Helen would like to ride out with us, then you and she can go along to lunch together. I shan't ask you to wait, you know what lawyers are like."

That Winifred Binks could break the appointment herself would never have crossed her mind, Peter realized. Mr. Debenham and the people from the trust had, after all, given up their Saturday to her when they might have been out playing croquet or at home polishing their writs of attainder. Himself trained to put duty before pleasure, Peter agreed without demur and drove on to the old rosy brick house on the Crescent where his wife, as it turned out, was entertaining another man.

"President, I'm glad you're here," he lied.

"We've had some interesting developments. You'd better go make your phone call, Miss Binks. Tell them we'll be along as soon as we can. Helen, would you care to drive out to the field station with us? We'd intended to take you to lunch, but Miss Binks remembered she's supposed to meet with her lawyers. Maybe you and I could—"

"Shandy!" roared Svenson. "Developments."

"M'er, yes. Putting it in a nutshell, Emmerick was an impostor. Nobody at the Meadowsweet Construction Company ever heard of him. When I took Miss Binks back to the field station this morning, another one showed up calling himself Fanshaw and pretending to be Emmerick's superior. He clammed up when he heard Emmerick was dead, so we arrested him and delivered him to Ottermole."

"But couldn't you get anything at all out of him?" Helen demanded.

"Nary a yip. Fanshaw was genuinely surprised to find out about Emmerick, I'd bet my Sunday boots on that. Cronkite Swope's been taking his picture, we'll get one over to the state police and maybe they can get an identification. Fred Ottermole's handling that end of the business. Maybe you ought to stroll down to the station and see how he's making out, President."

Peter had already inquired of Officer Dorkin, who'd been holding the desk while his chief slumbered, whether there'd been any report from the barracks. Dorkin could only tell him that the alleged Emmerick had in fact been stabbed through the back of the neck, which didn't get them anywhere that he could see. Peter had made the suggestion mainly in the hope of getting Svenson off their backs, he might have known it wouldn't work.

"I'll go with you," the big man grunted. "Might snare another impostor."

"I should hardly think so," Peter demurred, but of course it didn't do any good.

The upshot was that Helen decided to stay home and work on her article because her editor was growing snappish. Miss Binks mentioned a trifle fretfully that she hoped they might get started soon because those lawyers had already been cooling their heels at the station for the past half hour. While she didn't much care about Mr. Sopwith and his minion, she was solicitous for Mr. Debenham, who'd been kind to her even when she hadn't had two cents to rub together.

Thorkjeld Svenson offered to drive, but

Peter had fortitude enough left not to let him. "No, you don't, President. My hair's falling out fast enough already. Sit in back and rest your brain."

By the time they got to the field station, Peter was beginning to understand how a long-distance bus driver must feel at the end of an imperfect day, even though this day was just hitting its stride. At least, as Miss Binks had prophesied, her visitors were still waiting. She entered the lobby briskly but without undue haste and didn't strain herself on the apologies. She then turned to young Calthrop, who sat at the long table picking at an alien Tyrol knapweed with a pair of needle-pointed tweezers.

"Where has Viola gone?"

"She said she felt like a walk. She's coming back to check the rain gauges and fill the bird feeders."

"Good, they need it. Oh dear, that wretched red squirrel's caught inside the big feeding station again. You'd better go find her and help her cope before he tears it apart trying to get out. Now, gentlemen, what is it you want to talk to me about? I mustn't waste too much of your time."

"Ah, could we go into your office?"

Mr. Sopwith, the speaker, had recently

inherited from a retired senior officer managership of the immense estate which the late Jeremiah Binks had left in trust for his granddaughter. He looked to Peter like the sort of banker who ought to have a heavy gold watch chain strung across his paunch and his thumbs stuck into the armholes of his waistcoat. It was disappointing to find him in flannels and a sports jacket with a discreet but perceptible windowpane check. The garb, Peter supposed, had been selected to remind Miss Binks that Mr. Sopwith was giving up his Saturday in her interests. Debenham, on the other hand, wore a dark business suit much like the suits Peter himself generally wore on occasions when work pants and a flannel shirt wouldn't be quite the thing.

Sopwith had brought along a small, slim, silent individual in unbecoming brown with a self-effacing tie. This was Mr. Tangent, accountant for the trust. Mr. Tangent was carrying a ledger, a couple of file folders, and one of those colored booklets with plastic pages in which presentations to important clients are apt to be arranged. Miss Binks's was green, perhaps in deference to her ecological interests, or to celebrate the magnitude of her inheritance, or possibly even in tribute to her late grandfather. Or else, Peter mused, since he liked to examine all sides of a question, because green was the color of the one they happened to have kicking around the office.

Getting back to the subject of offices, Sopwith's suggestion that they adjourn to Miss Binks's was plainly an attempt to exclude Dr. Shandy and President Svenson from the discussion. Winifred was having none of that. She seated herself at the table near the big windows that was used for such things as examining architects' plans, mounting specimens for the museum, drinking dandelion-root coffee, eating daylily-pollen muffins, and sundry other activities, and motioned for the men to join her.

"Let's stay right here, why lug chairs around if we don't have to? Dr. Svenson, you'd better sit beside me and lend a few extra fingers to count on. I'm hopeless at arithmetic. All right, Mr. Sopwith, what's so pressing?"

"It's a question of your portfolio."

"But I thought my investments were doing quite nicely."

"On the whole, they are," Sopwith conceded. "Tangent, show Miss Binks the figures."

Silently the accountant handed over the green folder, open to a pageful of figures. Winifred scanned it, then nodded to Dr. Svenson. "Satisfactory, on the whole, wouldn't you say, President?" she said. "But there's one I want to get rid of right away."

"Ah yes," Sopwith replied. "You're referring, of course, to Golden Apples. You doubtless recall my mentioning to you a while back that the company, while holding steady and continuing to pay a small dividend, hasn't increased its profits for the past several years. This is a very shaky situation, Miss Binks. I strongly suggest we dump Golden Apples before it takes a nosedive and reinvest the proceeds in a company that offers a more satisfactory return."

"Indeed?" said Winifred. "And what would you recommend?"

"Well, I've given that question a good deal of thought. Considering that Golden Apples is a packer and distributor of what are currently known as—ah—natural foods, and considering the current popular interest in healthful nutrition, I should say we ought to reinvest your proceeds with a similar company in which you already have a relatively small holding. Lackovites is a younger, more aggressive firm which has leaped far ahead of Golden Apples in sales during the past few years. Show Miss Binks the figures on Lackovites, Tangent."

Wordlessly the accountant opened one of his file folders and handed the heiress a balance sheet on Lackovites. She took a cursory glance and handed it over to Svenson.

"Very impressive, but they fail to show one factor which you also don't appear to have taken into account, Mr. Sopwith. You mentioned Golden Apples once before. Since then, I've done a bit of looking into the matter myself. I find that Golden Apples products are highly regarded by nutritionists as being of exceptional quality and flavor. The company's packaging, distribution, and advertising leave much to be desired. This seems to be because their rigidly maintained quality standards require them to buy top-quality ingredients that raise their overhead and eat into their profit margin, leaving them without the capital to compete aggressively. The consequence is that while they hold on to their customers, they don't attract enough new ones."

"That's why I—"

"Let me finish, Mr. Sopwith. Lackovites, on the other hand, has superb packaging, extensive advertising, and an extremely aggressive sales force. They've been taking advantage of that growing interest in natural foods you mentioned to attract a great many new customers, and they've been succeeding so far because people are often too ready to accept ballyhoo as fact. However, the word's begun to get around that their so-called secret magic ingredients are mainly cornstarch and sawdust. Inferior-grade sawdust, at that."

"But Miss Binks—"

"In short, Mr. Sopwith, that Lackovites bunch are nothing but a pack of opportunists out to make a killing. They can still attract customers but they can't keep them because their goods are deplorably bad, and I'm mortally ashamed to have any connection with them. What I want you to do the very first thing Monday morning, Mr. Sopwith, is to dump every share of Lackovites I own before the market starts to fall, and reinvest every penny in Golden Apples."

"But you can't do that!"

Winifred drew herself up and looked down her nose like a grand duchess laying out a miscreant footman. "I'd like to know why not."

"It's impossible!"

"I think what Mr. Sopwith means, Miss

Binks," Lawyer Debenham interrupted, "is that you pretty much own Golden Apples already. You see, the company has never gone public, which is why you've never seen their stock listed anywhere in the reports. What happened was that about twenty years ago—I'd have to look up the exact date—a penniless young couple named Compote approached your grandfather with an idea. They wanted to start a food-packaging enterprise that would produce and market only naturally grown, nutritionally sound, highest-quality products. At that time, as I probably don't have to tell you, the general public was much less aware of such things than people are today, and so-called nature foods were often dismissed as being only for crackpots and faddists."

Winifred smiled. "But Grandfather was himself a crackpot and faddist, so of course he jumped in with both feet, as they'd been wise enough to expect he would. I'm sure he'd have thought theirs a splendid idea even if they'd been as nutty as he, only it just so happened they weren't."

Mr. Debenham smiled back. "I might remind you, Miss Binks, that while your grandfather was of an—um—adventurous nature, he was also a very shrewd businessman. He agreed to finance the new company on condition that he was to hold seventy percent of the stock. The remaining thirty shares were to be held by the Compotes, who would have the option of buying back twenty-one percent of his shares should they desire to obtain controlling interest in Golden Apples. As of this date, they have not seen fit to do so."

"Couldn't if they wanted to," Sopwith grunted. "They don't have the money."

"I have no information on that point," said Debenham. "However, it does bring up another angle of which you should be aware, Miss Binks. You and the Compotes each have first option on all the other party's shares, which means that if you should decide to sell, you'll have to give them first chance to buy. And vice versa, of course. This may pose a dilemma."

"I don't see that it does," said Winifred. "All we have to do is pump in some fresh capital to beef up the Golden Apples's sales force, redesign its packaging, and do some aggressive advertising ourselves. We'll have a major advantage over Lackovites there, because we'll be telling the truth. Since I'm really the senior partner in the enterprise, the Compotes can't object to my taking a hand, can they? Please make an appointment with them for early next week, Mr. Debenham, and explain that I want to discuss our new sales program. Will you be available to accompany me?"

"Of course, Miss Binks. You know you always come first with me."

Peter hadn't thought Lawyer Debenham much for looks, till he smiled at Winifred Binks. The old coot was in love with her, by gum! And Winifred was blushing, though she tried to pretend she wasn't.

"How kind. I'll expect your call, then. And you, Mr. Sopwith, must let me know the minute it's sold how much you get for the Lackovites stock, so that I'll have an idea what else we should sell in order to make up the balance of our advertising budget. Now is there anything else anyone wants to talk about? Mr. Sopwith? Mr. Tangent?"

Neither answered.

"Mr. Debenham? Peter? Dr. Svenson?"

"Fake figures."

While the others talked, Thorkjeld Svenson had been poring over the Lackovites report, jotting down calculations in the margin in his surprisingly small, precise handwriting. Now he was showing Mr. Debenham what he'd written.

"Why, bless my soul!" the lawyer exclaimed. "Mr. Tangent, how could you have overlooked such glaring discrepancies?"

"I—I didn't have time to check the figures," stammered the accountant. "Mr. Sopwith—that is, I was handed the folder just as we were leaving the office. I wouldn't have—I can't imagine why they—" Catching his superior's wrathful eye, he faltered into silence.

"Please don't distress yourself, Mr. Tangent," said Winifred. "Those figures don't matter a bit, since we shan't have anything more to do with Lackovites anyway. I trust this convinces you, Mr. Sopwith, that I did in fact know what I was talking about when I called them a pack of opportunists. A pack of rogues would have been an apter epithet."

"I—ah—"

"Yes, Mr. Sopwith, I quite understand. You've been in charge of the trust only since your predecessor's retirement, and I'm sure you had a dreadful mass of paperwork to cope with in the process of transferring Grandfather's holdings to me. One could hardly expect you to be thoroughly familiar with all the details. So what we must do next is have you and Mr. Tangent sit down with Mr. Debenham and Mrs. Chilicothe, who's our own accountant, and make a thorough check of every single item that pertains to the trust."

"But that would take weeks," Sopwith protested. "Or even more. Maybe months. Even years!"

"Time is what I pay you for, Mr. Sopwith," Winifred replied serenely. "I'm sure you wouldn't want me to get off on the wrong foot with the Internal Revenue Service over somebody's faulty arithmetic. Dr. Svenson, I know you have many demands on your time, but since you're so expert at managing the college finances and since the success of our field station depends at present on my personal solvency, perhaps you'd consent to oversee the checking committee?"

"Pleasure."

Even at his most benign, Thorkjeld Svenson was an awesome figure. Sopwith looked more than a bit taken aback, Tangent was openly terrified.

This one slipup didn't necessarily mean the pair had been cooking the books, Peter told himself. Maybe Sopwith suspected his predecessor had been up to shenanigans and was afraid of making waves lest he lose the account for his bank. Maybe he was just a lazy bastard who'd been loafing on his job, assuming that a woman unused to handling large sums of money would let herself be hornswoggled into believing whatever he told her. He knew better by now, by George. Peter wondered how much overtime Sopwith and Tangent would be putting into the Binks account over this weekend.

6

"I'm afraid Mr. Sopwith may be rather put out with me." Winifred Binks was trying to act repentant. "I wasn't awfully tactful, was I?"

"Can't be tactful to a yackass," growled Svenson.

"You handled him just fine," Peter added. "Of course Sopwith's upset at being made to look like a fool, but it's not your fault that he happens to be one. I expect what really got to him is your starting to whittle away at your stock portfolio. The Binks Trust is no doubt his bank's biggest account and he's going to catch some flak if he doesn't keep it that way. You've already committed yourself to a major expense with no chance of return by underwriting the field station. Once you start bankrolling Golden Apples, you'll be putting another big dent in the pile, at least for the time being."

"And what if I do? My own wants are minimal. I have no dependents to think of, so I'm quite at liberty to have some fun with my money. That's how Grandfather always operated, and it worked for him. Until that last venture, but I'm not quite far enough around the bend for anything like that. At least I don't think I am."

"But you're sure Golden Apples is a sound proposition?" Peter asked somewhat nervously.

"As sure as one can be. I went into their whole situation most carefully with Mr. Debenham and Mrs. Chilicothe. We figure to invest roughly three million dollars in seed money. Counting tax breaks and so forth, we should be able to recoup the entire sum over a period of five to six years. It's not going to be difficult to get Golden Apples rolling because they have so much going for them already. And we don't intend to squander the money recklessly. For instance, I'm planning to give the company lots of free time on our television station once we get cracking. Not advertising per se, you know, but subtle touches like using empty Golden Apples tins to stick wild plants in and making sure the labels show on camera. That sort of thing is done all the time on commercial shows, I'm told. Peter, you have such a charmingly devious mind, you won't mind thinking up a few schemes in a good cause, will you?"

"Not at all," Peter assured her. "How long should it take to get a squirrel out of a bird feeder?"

"What? Oh, you mean Viola and Knapweed, I'd forgotten all about them. They do seem to be taking their sweet time, don't they? Heavens, you don't suppose they've been netted?"

"I sincerely hope not. An alternative explanation might be that they've found themselves a comfortable nest of leaves somewhere and are engaging in—er—pastoral pursuits."

"How astute of you, Peter. That possibility, I confess, would not have entered my mind. The disadvantage of having been reared by a maiden aunt, I suppose. Perhaps we should stroll over to the edge of the woods and converse in raised voices on the beauties of nature."

Thorkjeld Svenson offered no conjecture, he was already out the door, galloping toward the woods. Winifred was startled.

"Does he really think they may be in danger?"

"No," said Peter. "He's afraid he himself is. Sieglinde Svenson has—er—decided views about canoodling on campus, and the field station counts as part of the college."

"I see. So if Knapweed has succeeded in getting Viola on her back, Sieglinde will soon get on Thorkjeld's. Dear me, how Rabelaisian. Come on, then, we'd better chaperone."

The two hurried out past the bird feeder, noting that it was now squirrelless and not much the worse for wear, though empty of seed. A little way into the woods, they came upon the president hunkered down beside a stump. On the stump sat a downcast young botanist, sniffing dejectedly at a sprig of fragrant bedstraw.

"The squirrel tried to bite me," Knapweed was telling the older man, "so I pulled my hand back and she called me a wimp. So then I grabbed it by the tail and hauled it out but I was trying not to hurt it so it got away from me and jumped on her shoulder and scratched her a little and she started yelling that I did it on purpose. So the squirrel jumped off and ran up a tree and then she—well, she wanted to and I said I wouldn't."

"Wouldn't what?" asked Miss Binks. "Oh, I get it. Pastoral pursuits."

"I just don't happen to believe a person should expect—and anyway, I didn't want to," Knapweed muttered sulkily. "I'm practically engaged, for Pete's sake! Well, sort of, in a way. My girlfriend's father's a casket salesman and pretty straitlaced, so I can't go around getting—but I wouldn't even if I did because I think such things ought to mean more than as if we were just a couple of squirrels or something. Not that I have any right to be knocking the squirrels, they're not my field. For all I know, squirrels are just as moral as casket salesmen. But Viola's so darned—well, I shouldn't be saying stuff about her, either. Maybe she was just trying to get a rise out of me."

"M'yes," said Peter. "No doubt. Which way did she go?"

"I don't know. I happened to notice this *Galium triflorum* here and tried to divert her interest, but she told me to stick it in my ear and flounced off in a huff."

"Well, these things do happen." Winifred sighed. "To some people, at any rate. Why don't you go back inside, Knapweed? We seem to be having rather a run on visitors today and we oughtn't to leave the station unmanned. We others may as well see where Viola's taken herself off to. This way, I think."

Winifred Binks could track like an Indian; she'd noticed some small derangement of a leaf or a dent in the forest mold and was plunging confidently through the undergrowth. As a rule, neither she nor the men would have been unwilling to let the young woman prowl at will, but today was different.

The spoor was not hard to follow, Viola was no Indian. "She's circling toward the road," Winifred announced after they'd gone a quarter of a mile or so. "Thank goodness for that. She ought to be out of the woods by now."

"Urrgh!"

Dr. Svenson could not have stated the position more succinctly. The trackers were in fact near the road by now, they could catch glimpses of asphalt through the trees. More than that, however, they could see directly in front of them a small area of torn-up ferns, scuffed-up leafmold, broken twigs, and a wisp of bright green cotton knit caught on the thorns of a blackberry vine.

Winifred was determined not to panic. "She could have stepped on a digger wasps' nest and got caught in the briers when she tried to run. That happened to me once, and it's no fun, I can tell you. One can't help dancing around, which of course is the worst thing to do. See, she's plunged through the bracken over there."

"Carrying a hundred-pound boulder?" said Peter. "Look at the depth of those footprints."

"Viola's a big girl and she's wearing heavy boots," Winifred insisted. "Anyway, those prints won't tell us much, too many pine needles mixed in. They do look rather ominous—look, they go straight to the road. Oh dear."

Streaks of black rubber on the asphalt told a story. "She must have been dragged out of the woods and taken away in a car, but why?"

"Phone," barked Svenson.

"Yes, the police. Hurry!"

Winifred began to run back toward the field station. Peter outstripped her this time, he'd been a miler in his youth and could still cover the ground when he had to.

Knapweed was alone in the lobby, putting his bedstraw in a flower press; he looked up and started to say something. Peter ignored him and rushed to the telephone. By now he knew the state-police number by heart and the officer at the switchboard recognized his voice.

"What's up, Professor Shandy?"

"I'm at the Balaclava College field station on the Whittington Road. We're missing a young woman employee named Viola Buddley. About five foot seven, stocky build, weight maybe a hundred and fifty or so, wearing hiking boots, khaki shorts, and a torn green jersey that reads 'Have you hugged a tree today?' across the front. Reddish-blond hair and a great many freckles. It appears from the signs we've found that she was captured in the woods a short way from the station during the past fifteen minutes or so, and taken away by car. Don't ask me what car, I haven't the foggiest idea. We're guessing that this may have something to do with last night's murder of Emory Emmerick. He'd been around the field station all last week and she'd gone out with him the night before he was killed. Please notify patrol cars in the area. If I get anything more, I'll let you know."

By the time Peter got off the phone, the president and Winifred had come in. "The state police are putting out an alert," he told them.

"Not enough," barked Svenson. "Shandy, car. Binks, stay."

"But I—" she began to protest.

"Hold fort. Answer the phone. Calthrop, guard."

"Yes, sir!"

The young botanist spoke up manfully, no doubt eager to redeem himself after his rather unfortunate showing with regard to the red squirrel. Peter gave Knapweed an encouraging nod and darted out to his car before Svenson could beat him into the driver's seat.

They'd judged from the direction of the tire tracks on the road that the kidnappers' car, if in fact it was one, had headed away from Lumpkinton toward the neighboring town of Whittington. That road was never well-traveled, Peter remembered miles of nothing but woods. "Let's try it," he said, and Svenson agreed.

They met only a few cars, mooching along at low speeds and carrying only leaf-peepers out to admire what was left of the autumn foliage. There was precious little of that by now, the searchers were able to see a fair way into the woods. It was Svenson who spotted the flash of bright emerald green.

"Stop!"

"By George!"

Peter pulled over to the side of the road, shoved the car keys into his pocket, and got momentarily snared in his seat belt. Svenson charged ahead into the underbrush like a wild boar spoiling for a fight. To his manifest regret, not a malefactor was in sight. Once they got her blindfold off, however, Viola was ever so glad to see them. She couldn't say so because she still had a gag over her mouth. Both had been ripped from the bottom of her green T-shirt; by now there was little left of the shirt and thus a great deal of Viola on view. She hadn't been able to remove either the gag or the blindfold because she was tied hand and foot to a tree.

A box elder, Peter noted. Choosing a smooth-barked tree might have shown a modicum of compassion on the part of her abductors, since a more rugose integument could have been tough on her mostly bare back and probably full of ants, but he suspected they'd picked the box elder simply because it was there. He went to work on the ropes and noted with scorn that the knots were all grannies.

"Look at this, President," he said. "This rope's just like the ones on the net that trapped Emmerick."

The president must have been thinking of Sieglinde, he didn't want to look. All he said was "Ungh," and went on studying the underbrush for possible clues.

"My sentiments exactly," snapped Viola, who by now had the gag out of her mouth. "Would you mind postponing the Sherlock Holmes routine till after you've finished untying my hands, Professor? If I still have any, that is."

"Oh, sorry. There, how's that?"

"I don't know yet. I can't feel a thing." She tried wiggling her fingers and they worked pretty well. "I guess I'll be okay. I'm just so mad!"

Peter removed his flannel shirt and gallantly assisted her into it. Fortunately he had a windbreaker in the car, so the President's sense of decorum didn't get too stiff a jolt. "Can you tell us what happened?" he asked Viola once they were both decently covered.

"All I know is, I was walking through the woods. Knapweed and I had gone to get that squirrel out of the bird feeder, remember?"

"Urr," said Dr. Svenson encouragingly.

"Well, Knapweed got kind of carried

away out there. God, these botanists! You wouldn't think it to look at him, I guess it must come from hanging around with the birds and the bees and the flowers all the time. Anyway, I belted him once or twice and told him where to head in; but I didn't feel like going back to the station with him and having to keep fighting for my virtue till Professor Binks got back, so I decided I'd take a little hike for myself. I figured I'd be okay if I stayed out near the road, but was I ever wrong! Here I am walking along minding my own business and somebody sneaks up behind me and pulls a sock over my head."

"A sock?" said Peter.

"I don't know what it was. It felt like a big knitted sock, the kind you wear with hiking boots. I tried to put up my hands and pull it off but he—I think it was a he—had me pinned. I couldn't do a thing. So the next thing I know, he's ramming a gun in my back and telling me to be a good girl if I didn't want to get hurt. Which I didn't, so I quit trying to kick his shins and he told me to start walking. How did you find me?"

"We noticed signs of a struggle in the woods and tire marks on the road, and—er—came looking."

"Lucky for me. I don't know what I'd have—" Viola swallowed a couple of times, pulled Peter's shirt more tightly around her and went on. "Anyway, he tied my hands and made me get into his car and we drove off. He kept poking the gun at me every so often and warning me not to get cute."

"Just one man did all this?"

"As far as I know. Maybe there was somebody else in the back seat. I couldn't see because I still had that thing over my head. You know, now that I think of it, I'll bet it was a ski mask put on backward. I could breathe fairly well, but there was no way I could peek out from underneath. It came down tight over my face."

"You couldn't recognize the person's voice?"

"Not at all. He talked funny, I think he might have had marbles or something in his mouth."

"But did he talk? Did he say why he'd taken you prisoner?"

"He kept yelling, 'What did he tell you?' I said 'He who?' and he said I knew damned well who and to stop trying to be cute or he'd plug me where it hurt. So then I thought of Emory and said was that who he meant and he said damn right he meant Emory and what did he tell me? He said, 'Did he say where he put it?' I said I didn't even know what it was and would he kindly tell me what the hell he was talking about? So we argued back and forth for a while, then he stopped the car and made me get out and pushed me into the woods and tied me up the way you found me."

"But you didn't have the—er—mask over your head when we found you," Peter reminded her. "What happened to it? Did you get a look at his face when he took it off?"

"No," said Viola. "He tied my hands and feet to the tree first, then he ripped the pieces off my shirt and got behind the tree and reached around. All I saw was the tail of my shirt coming down over my eyes. I tried to turn my head and bite him, but he slapped my face and told me not to get funny. Then he shoved the gag in my mouth and said maybe I'd be ready to talk after I'd had a couple of days out here by myself to think it over. Then I heard him crashing through the brush and the car start up and drive away and I—oh God! I thought I was going to die. I thought some animal would come and g-get me."

She was starting to fall apart. Svenson wasn't about to let her.

"Cry later. Talk now. What did Emmerick tell you?"

"He never told me anything!"

"Must have. Yammering type, saw you often. Job? Hobbies? Family?"

"Oh, that. Yeah, Emory did talk a lot. I thought you meant like secrets."

Svenson waited. Viola shrugged. "Well, he didn't go much for Chinese food but he was crazy about Italian. Is this what you want?"

"Go on."

"He claimed he was divorced, and more or less gave me to understand that he wouldn't be interested in getting married again but he was still interested, if you get what I mean. Only I've got this snoopy landlady—it's next to impossible to rent an apartment around here, so I'm stuck in a rooming house—and Emory was staying at the inn over in Balaclava Junction, which is about the same as boarding in a monastery from the way he described it, so it wasn't going to work out. Which was okay by me because I wasn't all that crazy about him anyway."

Peter weeded out the one salient fact.

"Staying at the inn, you say? I wonder whether Ottermole knows that. He'd better take a look at the room. Go ahead, Miss Buddley, did Emmerick discuss any of his alleged colleagues at the Meadowsweet Construction Company?"

"Not that I remember. He asked a lot of questions about Professor Binks."

"He never mentioned Mr. Fanshaw?"

"Would that be Chuck? Emory talked about this guy named Chuck, but never called him by his full name."

"Too bad. What did he say about Chuck?"

"He said Chuck owed him money."

"Really? How did he happen to tell you that?"

"Probably because he'd had a few drinks. Then he said Chuck was a swell guy and he wasn't worried about the money. I got the idea that it was quite a lot, but Emory might just have been trying to impress me. Look, do we have to keep standing here? What if that guy with the gun comes back?"

"Urrgh!" For the first time that day, Thorkjeld Svenson smiled.

7

"Do you want to go straight to your rooming house, Miss Buddley?" Peter hoped she'd say yes, but the ex-captive shook her head.

"Uh-uh. Take me back to the station, if you don't mind. I need to pick up my car."

"You're sure you feel up to driving?"

"I will by the time I get there. I'll just keep reminding myself how good it's going to feel to get into a hot bath and a whole shirt."

What would feel good to Peter would be not having to drive back to the field station; it was getting monotonous. However, noblesse obliged as usual. He got Viola safe inside while Dr. Svenson made a beeline for the telephone. While the state police were being informed that the lost had been found, and in what dire circumstances, Winifred Binks poured Viola a steaming cup of camomile tea.

"Drink this, then go home and stay there until you're completely over the shock. Don't worry about the station, we can manage without you for a few days. Peter, will you drive along behind her to make sure she doesn't get abducted again on the way?"

"Yes, of course." Peter had been planning to do it anyway, though he did think young Calthrop might have offered.

Knapweed wasn't saying much of anything, he'd seemed more surprised than distressed when Viola returned in such a state of disrepair. Peter was still wondering which of their stories about the squirrel incident to believe, or whether the truth lay somewhere in the middle, as was generally the case. Slumped over the worktable, gazing dully down at his flower press, Knapweed was hardly the prototype of the swashbuckling ravisher.

But one never knew. Peter shelved the problem and turned to Dr. Svenson. "Got straightened out with the police, President?"

"Yah. They're coming. Want to see where Miss Buddley was captured and where we found her. Pick up a clue, maybe. You get her home. I'll wait for them here. Bum a ride in the paddy wagon, give Sieglinde a laugh."

Give Sieglinde a fit more likely. Peter was relieved not to be stuck with showing the state troopers around, anyway. He was itching to get back to Balaclava Junction. He wanted a shirt even more than Viola did, she was still wearing his and he couldn't decently ask for it back. He wanted to collect Ottermole and a warrant and search Emmerick's room at the inn before somebody else beat him to it.

Unless somebody already had. Dolt that he was, why hadn't he thought of this sooner? Mainly because he hadn't known where Emmerick lived until Viola told him, he supposed. That was an explanation, perhaps, but hardly an excuse.

Anybody who'd delactified as many cows in his day as Peter Shandy knew there was no use crying over spilt milk. He switched his mind to the bird who called himself Fanshaw; had Ottermole managed to make him talk? The chief knew enough not to knock a prisoner around, but he could be awfully formidable in that black jacket of his, scowling down an the culprit and working his pocket zippers back and forth. Peter decided he might as well phone Ottermole while Viola was still steadying her nerves with camomile tea and rehashing her tale to Winifred Binks.

When he mentioned searching Emmerick's room at the inn, Ottermole laughed. "I'm way ahead of you, Professor. Ellie June

Freedom, that's the inn-keeper, was on my ear two hours ago. 'Chief Ottermole,' she says in that high-toned voice that sounds like a cat squeakin' a rubber mouse, 'one of my guests is missing. Mr. Emory Emmerick did not appear for breakfast and his bed has not been slept in.'

" 'Miz Freedom,' I says right back, 'you better go ahead and eat Mr. Emmerick's boiled egg yourself. You've lost yourself a guest.'

"So once she let me get a word in edgeways I told her what happened and she went right up in smoke. 'Fred Ottermole,' she says, 'you come right straight out here and take away the demised's effects. Respectable guests do not go stravaging around in the middle of the night getting hoisted into trees and having their throats cut. What, pray tell, do you think I pay taxes for?' "

Peter was charmed. "Did she really say 'pray tell'?"

"She sure as heck did. I didn't say anything back because she's a second cousin to Edna Mae's sister's mother-in-law and I figured I better not start anything, you know how it is. Anyway, somebody'd have had to do something about Emmerick's stuff anyhow, sooner or later, so I went and got it.

Come on down and look it over, any time you want."

"I'll be happy to. Who did the packing?"

"I did it myself. Didn't notice anything to get excited about, but I guess you never know."

"True enough," said Peter. "Is there any hope Mrs. Freedom hasn't yet got around to cleaning the room?"

"Are you kiddin'? She was following me around the whole time I was there, with the vacuum cleaner in one hand and a bucket of hot soapsuds in the other, yammering at me to hurry up so's she could get the place swabbed out and fumigated. I did manage to search under the bed and behind the dresser, pretending I was just making sure I wasn't leaving anything of Emmerick's behind to contaminate the atmosphere, but I didn't uncover any false beards or incriminating letters. I did find one of those sissy novels about a mean baronet with a terrible secret and a beautiful orphan governess who was really the heiress to a duke's fortune. Edmund ate a page or two when I brought it back. It made him sick to his stomach."

"M'yes," said Peter, "I can see why it might."

He glanced over at Winifred Binks. She

was an orphan, reared from an early age by a strong-minded aunt. She'd have made a rattling good governess; there was no doubt she'd have handled the most saturnine of baronets with finesse and aplomb had the opportunity ever come her way. She could probably have been beautiful if she'd put her mind to it.

Hers was already the true beauty of spirit and intellect, and then there was all that money. Might a tale of rival passions explain Emmerick's sudden demise? Peter thought not; but there again, one never knew. He bade the hypothetical siren an affectionate good-bye, threw a curt nod in the general direction of the sulky Knapweed, and prepared to take the still visibly upset Viola to her place of abode.

Fortunately the distressed damsel was boarding over in Lumpkin Corners, which was more or less on Peter's way home. He saw her safely to her landlady's presence, realized he was starving since he'd had nothing since breakfast except one daylily-pollen muffin, and debated the advisability of stopping at the Plucked Chicken for something to eat.

No, he'd wait till he got home. He wanted that shirt, he wanted the familiar hospitality of his own kitchen, most of all he wanted Helen. He was more than a little distressed to find Jane Austen in sole charge of the domicile and a note on the kitchen counter telling him that Helen was up at the college library doing some research for her paper.

Feeling bereft and exhausted, Peter fixed himself a salami sandwich and took a bottle of beer out of the refrigerator. He carried them upstairs for company while he changed into a somber brown-and-gray flannel shirt to match his mood and added a thick gray cardigan to warm him up. There was by now a decided nip in the air; running around in his underwear had raised a pretty fair crop of goose bumps, even though he'd kept the heater on in the car. He scribbled a PS to Helen's message saying he'd be in the hoosegow should she care to drop around with some hot soup and a file, and went on down to the police station.

Officer Dorkin, whom Peter had known as Budge ever since the days when he'd been the boy who mowed the Shandy lawn, was not supposed to be on duty now but didn't intend to miss out on the excitement. Fred Ottermole and the large tiger cat named Edmund who belonged to Mrs. Lomax up around the corner but like to hang out with the boys in blue were also waiting for Peter in the office, and welcomed him as one of their own.

"Fanshaw's in there with his lawyer."

Ottermole jerked his head toward the other half of the police station, another small room behind the office. As the town lockup, it boasted bars dating from the Civil War era. Indoor plumbing had been installed during the Coolidge administration. The interior and the exterior woodwork of the small brick building had been given fresh paint by a WPA work party under the aegis of Franklin D. Roosevelt. Thus the Balaclava Junction Police Station was not without historical interest; although Fanshaw's lawyer, when he was let out of the lockup, appeared to be unimpressed.

"I wouldn't keep a dog in this place," he remarked testily.

"I wouldn't either," Ottermole reassured him. "So what's your verdict? Are you planning to try for bail or do we bung your guy along to the county jail?"

"You have nothing on which to hold Mr. Fanshaw."

"The hell we haven't." Ottermole reached for a zipper.

The lawyer took a giant step backward. "This is harassment!"

"What's harassment? Me getting out my handkerchief so I won't sneeze in your face?" The chief did in fact produce a real linen one, exquisitely clean, freshly ironed, bearing his monogram in the corner, hand-worked by Edna Mae in blue with a little pair of handcuffs underneath. "Sorry, it's the cat, though I hate to say so in front of him. Edmund's sensitive."

"So is my client sensitive." The lawyer was a scrapper, Peter decided, you had to hand it to him. "What was the big idea, bringing every kid in town to gawk at him?"

"Those were my kids."

"All seventeen of them?"

"Only the first four," Fred admitted. "The rest are in my Sunday-school class. They came on a field trip to learn what happens to guys who go around bearing false witness, like your so-called Mr. Fanshaw in there. For your information, the Meadowsweet Construction Company's going to stick Fanshaw with a charge of misrepresenting himself as a member of their staff as soon as we get through sticking him with whatever we're going to stick him for, like maybe accessory to murder. I've got every right to hold him on suspicion and that's just what I'm doing. So shove that in your habeas corpus, mister!"

"Well, you didn't have to take away his belt and shoelaces."

"Sure we did. That's how we get all our belts and shoelaces. Save a penny here, a penny there, it adds up. Look, we've got work to do if you don't mind. Why don't you drop back tomorrow around noontime and bring some Chinese food? Edmund's partial to bean sprouts. Aren't you, old buddy?"

Ottermole rubbed the big cat's head, Edmund put out a paw and flexed his talons. The lawyer started to say something. Edmund hissed. The lawyer got a good look at his fringe of fangs and backed toward the door.

"I'll be back, all right," he snarled.

"Wear your shin guards next time. Edmund's hell on pant legs."

The door slammed. Fred Ottermole grinned. "Cripes, if I wasn't chief, I'd arrest myself for disorderly conduct. Help yourself to Emmerick's luggage, Professor, it's all right there beside my desk. Edmund'll keep an eye on you. Budge and I'd better check on the prisoner, he may need to go to the kitty box or something. Not that he'd tell us if he did, he's still not talking."

"Not even to the lawyer?"

"Oh, he talked to him, I guess. Budge and I weren't supposed to listen, so we switched on the TV and watched a demolition derby for a while. It was depressing as hell. There wasn't a car on the course that didn't look to be in better shape than our cruiser, not even the wrecked ones."

"Hey, Chief, how about if I enter the next race driving the cruiser and see if I can win us the price of a new one?" Budge Dorkin volunteered.

"Why not? It's our only hope. Turned up anything, Professor?"

"I don't know yet. Go ahead and tend to your prisoner, why don't you?"

Ottermole and his officer went into the lockup, Peter squatted on the floor and opened Emmerick's suitcases. They were crammed with what looked to Peter like pretty spiffy clothing for a soi-disant site engineer to be toting around. On top of a sumptuous Turkish toweling bathrobe bearing the monogram of a luxury hotel, Ottermole had dumped a bunch of papers, most of them building-trade publications intended, no doubt, to lend credence to Emmerick's role.

One loose sheet of paper caught Peter's eye; not because of its content, which was only an advertisement from an expensive gentlemen's outfitter, but because of a doodle in the margin.

Somebody, presumably Emmerick himself, had executed a sketch of a stemmed dish that Helen would have called a compotier and Mrs. Lomax simply a compote. He'd filled it with crudely drawn apples and carefully colored in each penciled circle with one of those yellow markers that Peter's students used to spotlight the paragraphs in their textbooks that they thought he'd be likely to quiz them on. Peter deplored the practice; in his undergraduate days, students had kept their textbooks clean in order to increase their resale value. Peddling your own last term's books was your best chance of having money enough to buy somebody else's leftovers next semester.

But such maunderings were beside the point. To Peter today, such a dishful of such a fruit could mean just one thing. What would a man who'd been passing himself off as an employee of a construction company have had to do with a food-packing firm called Golden Apples, run by a family named Compote?

Such hairs as were left on the back of Peter's neck began to prickle. Who was Emmerick, anyway? Could it possibly be only a coincidence that Sopwith should have taken time out of his weekend to raise a question about Miss Binks's majority holdings in Golden Apples on the very morning after the man who'd apparently made this doodle had been so bizarrely murdered? Or that the bird now caged in the next room had come looking for Emmerick, too?

One must not jump to conclusions. Maybe Emmerick had merely been a compulsive doodler of compotiers full of golden apples. People did have pet doodles. Peter himself was partial to fat rabbits. Rabbits were easy enough, one simply made a big circle for the body and a smaller one for the head, then added ears, whiskers, and two dots for eyes. Sometimes he attached legs, sometimes he didn't, depending on his creative mood of the moment. Sometimes he drew his rabbits back-to, omitting the eyes and scribbling a fluffy round scut in the appropriate place.

Helen drew daisies in the grass with fleecy summer clouds overhead, frequently adding butterflies with triangular wings and long, curly antennae. Occasionally Helen also added bumblebees, though she drew the bees disproportionately large in order to make room for googly eyes and horizontal stripes. Helen was always meticulous about the feelers with little knobs on the ends and the fuzzy legs hanging down. Helen really spread herself when it came to bumblebees, Peter thought fondly.

He reminded himself that compotes, not bumblebees, were the issue at hand. Further search of Emmerick's effects revealed no evidence that the man had been a frequent doodler of compotes. He didn't seem to have been any great shakes as a doodler, by and large; all the others Peter could find were prosaic squares, rhomboids, and equilateral triangles such as might reasonably have been expected from an engineer, even a fake one. Emmerick had drawn these with precision and shaded them in carefully, often using a different-colored pen. So his having used yellow on the apples would not have been out of character, Peter supposed.

However, the only pens Peter could find were a red one and a blue one. Red and blue were the colors most frequently used on the squares, rhomboids, and triangles, although a few doodles were red and black, along with one or two that were blue and black. Emmerick might have taken the black pen with him on the owl walk to make notes with. It seemed hardly likely, however, that he'd have carried a yellow marker, unless he'd picked it up by mistake thinking it was a roll of lemon-flavored Life Savers.

There was, as far as a determined search could reveal, no yellow marker among the stuff Ottermole had brought from the inn. No yellow had been used on any of the geometric doodles. One could deduce from this that Emmerick had drawn the dishful of golden apples before coming to Balaclava under false colors; ergo, that Golden Apples had been the real reason why he'd come. One might even be correct in one's deduction. Then again, one might be altogether wrong. It behooved one to get a line on Emmerick's true identity before one started deducing anything at all.

About all Peter could say of Emmerick so far was that he'd taken his wardrobe seriously, that his tastes had been expensive, though, by Peter's standards, somewhat outré, and that he had in fact indulged a secret passion for Life Savers. However, the flavor he'd fancied was not lemon but root beer. Peter had excavated no fewer than eighteen rolls, these from sundry pockets, most of them opened and more or less depleted. Emmerick had kept a bottle of bourbon, no doubt for medicinal purposes; Peter didn't see anything outré about that.

Emmerick had lied about the car he'd been driving. He'd claimed it belonged to the Meadowsweet Construction Company and was a perquisite of his position. Documentary evidence now revealed that he'd rented the vehicle from the Happy Wayfarer rental car service over in Clavaton only one day before he'd arrived at the field station.

How Emmerick had got to Clavaton was a question but would not have been a problem. He could have flown to Boston or the Hartford-Springfield Airport and taken a bus or a taxi from there. He could have bummed a ride from some easily gulled motorist, or hijacked a motorcycle with a sidecar for his luggage. He could have been ferried under cover of darkness in an unmarked van by a sinister accomplice with one eye and a nasty scar. He could have been let down on a rope from a hovering helicopter. He could have paddled up the Connecticut River in his little red canoe and made an overland portage to the Clavaclammer, which was Balaclava County's one truly navigable waterway; though Peter doubted he had.

The car-rental place listed New York City as Emmerick's place of abode. Peter assumed the state police must still have his driver's license along with whatever else they'd taken from his pockets when they'd carted him off in the ambulance. Perhaps they also had that yellow marker. Ottermole had better deputize Professor Shandy to go and collect these effects, they ought to be kept with the rest of this stuff until it could all be turned over to the next of kin, or the county district attorney, or whomever protocol decreed. Monday would be time enough for that, unless Ottermole got sick of tripping over the suitcases.

Speaking of Ottermole, what in tunket were he and Budge doing in there all this time? Giving the prisoner a flea bath? Peter stood up, eased the kinks out of his legs, and poked his head around the corner. The door to the lockup stood wide open, as did the bathroom window. Side by side on the iron cot that was its sole furnishing sat Fred Ottermole and Budge Dorkin. They were playing cat's cradle with a piece of string, and making a thorough mess of it. The prisoner was nowhere in sight.

8

"What the flaming perdition do you two clowns think you're up to?"

"Huh?" Fred Ottermole looked up at Peter, his face blank as a new police blotter. "Oh hi, Professor. What's cookin'?"

"Where's Fanshaw?"

"Who?"

"Your prisoner, drat it."

"What prisoner?"

"Great balls of fire! Ottermole, do you know what you're doing?"

"Sure, playin' checkers. We often do. No harm in it, is there?"

"This is checkers?"

"Isn't it?" A note of doubt had crept into the chief's voice. He stared at his hands, snared in the string that Budge Dorkin was still patiently and senselessly winding in and out through their wildly conjoined fingers. "What the hell? Budge, what do you think you're doing?"

"Huh?"

The young officer had the same blank look on his face as Ottermole's had shown. He quit trying to do whatever it was he'd thought he was doing, but didn't do anything else. Peter reached down and began trying to disentangle their hands.

"I don't believe this. Don't you two realize what's happened to you?"

"Huh?"

"You've been hypnotized, damn it! Wake up! Abracadabra! Presto, change-o! Snap out of it, for God's sake!"

"Huh?" said Budge Dorkin.

Fred Ottermole was a fraction less befuddled. He began trying to help Peter get the string off, thus creating a Gordian knot that had to be dealt with in Alexandrine fashion by Peter's jacknife.

Peter had nursed a fleeting hope that cutting the knot might constitute some rite of exorcism, but it didn't. Ottermole was still half-befuddled, Budge was completely out of it. Peter supposed the spell would wear off in time; maybe coffee would help.

The interior of the station percolator was stained a deep brown by the accumulations of years. Trying not to look, Peter filled it with water at the bath-room sink, which was also fairly well antiqued. He spooned in as much coffee as the basket would hold and set it on a hot plate that didn't look as though it could possibly work but, for a wonder, did. When the brew had perked to the color and density of molasses, he filled two mugs and took them into the lockup.

"God, that's awful stuff!" After a few sips, Ottermole sounded almost like himself. "What'd you do, Professor, lace it with battery acid?"

"I made it extra strong in the hope of waking you up," Peter told him. "Ottermole, can't you remember anything about what happened?"

"Sure I remember. What's eating you, anyway? You came in here and asked me about that guy Emmerick's stuff that we'd brought over from the inn. I told you to go ahead and look it over, then Budge and I—we came in here and—" He stared down at the tangle of string in his lap as though he'd never seen it before. "What's this string for? What the hell am I sitting on this cot for? We never sit in the lockup. It's bad luck."

"And well you may say so. Ottermole, pay attention to me. You know who I am and all that."

"Hell, yes. You're Lizzie Borden. What's the matter with you today, Professor? You're acting mighty strange, even for you. What happened, you get kicked on the head by an owl last night or somethin'? Hey, did I tell you our group saw—"

"Ottermole, shut up and listen. Late this morning, while you were still at home, I brought in a prisoner from the field station. He'd gone there claiming to be Emmerick's boss at Meadowsweet Construction Company and giving his name as Fanshaw. Do you remember anything about that?"

"I remember Emmerick. He's the guy who got offed last night while we were owling. But this Fanshaw—you trying to kid me, Professor?"

"Ottermole, I am not trying to kid you. Ask your wife. Ask Cronkite Swope. He met us at your house and came here to the station with you. He took pictures of you stowing Fanshaw in the lockup."

"He did? How'd I come out?"

"I don't know, I haven't seen the prints yet. The point is, Ottermole, that photographs were taken. They'll prove beyond any shadow of doubt that you did in fact put Fanshaw, though that may not be his real name, right here in this very slammer. Fanshaw was still here about half an hour ago when his lawyer, or somebody representing himself as a lawyer, came to see him. The lawyer was already in here with Fanshaw when I arrived at the station. You told me so. You and Budge were sitting out in the office with Edmund, waiting for the lawyer to come out."

"Edmund? Cripes, is Edmund okay?"

"He's curled up in your file basket pounding his ear as usual. Never mind Edmund, Ottermole. Try to concentrate on what I'm saying. The lawyer came out and had some sharp words about his client's accommodations. You put him in his place with a bit of snappy repartee."

"I did? What'd I say?"

"Let me finish. You then told me to go ahead and search Emmerick's luggage while you and Budge came in here to check on the prisoner. I became engrossed in my search; then I realized that you and Budge were taking a long timc in here and being awfully quiet about it. So I looked in and found the two of you alone here on the cot trying to play cat's cradle with that hunk of string. And making a damned poor fist of it, I may add. I asked what you were doing and you said you were playing checkers."

"So what? Maybe I was giving you some snappy repartee."

"Ottermole, you were not engaging in snappy repartee, you were zonked out of your skull. That bastard hypnotized you and Budge and turned you into a couple of zombies. Temporarily, I hope. You seem to be coming out of it, more or less, but look at Budge. Budge, do you know who I am?"

"Huh?" said Budge.

"There, Ottermole, see what I mean? Drink your coffee, Budge. Maybe it will jolt you out of your trance. Here, take a sip."

"Ugh!"

Could this be a glimmer of intelligence? Peter coaxed him to take another.

"Do I have to?" The words came slowly and mournfully, but at least they came.

"Yes," barked Ottermole. "That's an order, Dorkin."

Shuddering, the young cop obeyed. His eyes glazed over, then snapped to awareness. "Police brutality! My mother keeps telling me I ought to apply for a job at the box factory. The hours are better and so's the pay. What are we sitting in the lockup for, Chief? And what happened to Mr. Fanshaw? Did the lawyer bail him out?"

"Fanshaw?" Ottermole looked blank again, then made a brave attempt to cover up. "Tell him, Professor."

Peter told. Budge was awed.

"Wow! A real master criminal. Hey, I remember now. Fanshaw took this shiny thing out of his pocket and started waving it back and forth. You couldn't help looking at it, it was so shiny and—I know! It was a gold coin, a great big gold coin with an eagle on it. It was on a gold chain with a little ring to hang it by. And it kept going back and forth, back and forth, back and forth, back and—"

"Budge! Wake up!"

"Huh? Oh. Gosh, Professor, for a second there I felt as if I could still see that—back and forth, back and forth, back—"

Peter leaned forward and gave Dorkin a fairly determined slap on the cheek. "Budge, you are not going back to sleep. You are awake, do you hear me? Awake, drat it!"

"Ouch. Okay, Professor, if you say so. See, I'm awake. Which way did Fanshaw go? We've got to get him back. Back and forth—"

"Budge!"

"Finish your coffee," growled Ottermole. "God, I can't remember a damned thing. How long were we in here before Fanshaw started with the back and forth, back and—"

"Cut it out, Ottermole, you'll put Budge to sleep again," said Peter. "Budge, can you answer the question?"

"I think it must have been right after we went in. I sort of remember he had the—the you-know-what, I better not even say it—in his hand. He opened his hand and it hung down and started to swing and—and I want to get out of here."

"Good idea."

Peter took Dorkin and Ottermole by an arm apiece and pulled them up off the cot to which they'd been rooted. Fanshaw's orders must still have had some power, he thought, but getting them out into the office seemed to break the spell. Ottermole checked his daily report and found it filled in with the details concerning a man calling himself Francis Fanshaw, who'd been brought in under arrest by Acting Deputy P. Shandy and detained in the lockup pending further investigation in the death of Emory Emmerick.

"Okay, Professor, this report's in my own hand-writing, so I guess I've got to believe it. We might as well put in the rest of the story. How may *P*s in 'hypnotized'?"

"I know, Chief." Budge Dorkin had recently came across a cache of old Charlie Chan and Dr. Fu Manchu paperbacks in his grandmother's attic. He was reading them to improve his policing skills and had become surprisingly erudite as a result. "Let me write up the report this time. Shall I put in about Mrs. Ottermole bringing the beans and hot dogs?"

"Sure, why not? Let the public know we treated that bastard right even if he did turn out to be a lousy ingrate," the chief replied bitterly. "Anyways, I bet we're the only cops in Balaclava County who've ever been hypnotized by a master criminal."

"Think of it as another anecdote for your memoirs, Ottermole," said Peter. "Let's see, it's now—good Lord, it's half-past five. Where has the day gone? My wife must be home from the library by now."

"Oh gosh," cried Budge, "and my Aunt Maude's coming to supper with her new boyfriend. Mind if I take off now, Chief? My mother'll kill me if I don't show up."

"I thought you were all gung-ho to catch the master criminal."

"Well, yeah, but my mother—"

"Fanshaw's over the hills and far away by now, I expect," Peter interposed. "Like as not, that lawyer was waiting on the corner with a getaway car while I was horsing around with Emmerick's haberdashery. Speaking of cars, Ottermole, Fanshaw left one at the field station when I ran him in, and Emmerick must have had another parked here somewhere. He drove Miss Binks in from the field station yesterday afternoon, as I recall, but they met me at Charlie Ross's garage and we all drove out to our territory together. I was damned annoyed about his coming, I may add. I hadn't expected Emmerick to invite himself along on the owl count. Aside from his being a total loss as a counter, it meant we three had to squeeze together in the front seat. Dan Stott and the president took the whole back, needless to say. Didn't Mrs. Freedom mention anything to you about Emmerick's car?"

"Come to think of it, not a yip," the chief replied. "Go ahead home, Budge. Frank Lomax ought to be along any minute now. I'd better give Mrs. Freedom a buzz and see what she has to say about the car."

What Mrs. Freedom had to say was short and shrill. She didn't know anything about Mr. Emmerick's car, nor did she want to. She had guests to feed. She'd thank Fred Ottermole to run his own business and leave her to do likewise.

"That means the car is not in her parking lot," Ottermole interpreted. "If it was, she'd still be bending my ear about getting it out. I'll try Charlie Ross."

Charlie was home eating his supper, according to a minion who'd been left to run the gas pumps. Several cars were in the lot. Most of them belonged to Peter's neighbors because parking was restricted on the Crescent; there wasn't one whose owner the minion couldn't name.

"I don't s'pose you'd care to cruise around town and see if Emmerick's car is parked on the road anywhere?" Ottermole asked Peter. "Or I could go myself after Frank comes in. The cruiser's makin' those awful noises again and I was kind of hopin' to eat supper with Edna Mae and the boys, but . . ."

Peter suppressed a sigh. "I get the picture, Ottermole. All right, I don't mind going." Like hell he didn't. "Just let me make one more call first."

The call was to the field station. Knapweed Calthrop answered and was, if not happy to be of service, at least willing. Yes, Mr. Fanshaw's car was still in the lot. Yes, it was a 1989 gray Chevy. Yes, the license plates corresponded with the numbers Professor Shandy had read off to him. What did the professor want him to do about the car?

"Nothing, thanks. I'll see that it's taken care of."

Peter turned to Ottermole. "Here's an interestirng development. According to this invoice I found in Emmerick's luggage, the car Fanshaw drove out to the station this morning is the same one Emmerick rented last week from the Happy Wayfarer in Clavaton."

"Yeah? So, why not? They were both workin' for the same company, weren't they?"

"Er—not according to Meadowsweet, but I expect it's fairly safe to assume they were working together one way or another. I was thinking about the transportation logistics. As you know, there's no direct train or bus service into Balaclava Junction. Taxis from Clavaton are damned expensive and scarce as hens' teeth, but it looks as if Fanshaw must have taken one unless there's another accomplice in the woodwork. You'd better ask the Clavaton police to find out whether any of the local drivers brought a fare over here any time yesterday or this morning."

"Couldn't Emmerick have picked up Fanshaw sometime yesterday?"

"He'd have had to do it early in the morning. He spent the whole day making a pest of himself at the field station, Miss Binks told me, then drove her here and invited himself along on the owl watch. If he did collect Fanshaw, then Fanshaw would have had to hole up somewhere overnight, which is another point that must be checked out."

"Maybe he stayed at the inn and that's how come Emmerick's car wasn't in the lot when I went over."

"He could have stayed at the inn, but that can't be where he got the car. Emmerick drove straight to Charley Ross's, dropped Miss Binks off, then parked a little way up on the street and got into my car. So how would Fanshaw know where to find the rental car? Furthermore, how did he get hold of the keys? Emmerick surely didn't know he was going to be killed, he was cavorting around like a blasted monkey last night. Either he'd made a prior arrangement with Fanshaw to leave the car and the keys on the road, as he did, or else the keys were taken from his pocket while he was up in the tree getting himself murdered."

"Unless the Wayfarer gave him a spare key," Ottermole suggested.

"M'yes, a point to consider, though rental agencies aren't usually all that accommodating. Emmerick could have had one made, I suppose. Did you get the rest of his effects from the state police, by the way?"

"Not yet, but they gave me a list over the

phone. Raise up a little, Edmund. There you are, Professor. Sorry about the pawprints."

"Quite all right, I'm used to Jane's. Let's see: wallet containing credit cards and a New York driver's license made out in the name of Emory Emmerick, cash in the amount of—well, well! Why do you suppose he was carrying two thousand dollars around when he had all those credit cards? Pocket comb and mirror, egad. Two rolls of rootbeer Life Savers, one full, one not. Pocket compass, waterproof match safe, collapsible hunting knife, battery-operated hand warmer, fish scaler, folding telescope, desalinizing pills—where in tunket did he think he was going? No keys, car or otherwise. I think we'd better call Mrs. Freedom again."

"You call her," said Ottermole. "She's already mad at me."

Peter called. He was not well received. Certainly Mrs. Freedom had seen Mr. Emmerick's car in her parking lot yesterday morning. She kept careful tabs on her parking lot, she wanted him to know. No, she hadn't seen the car this morning. Why should she have? Mr. Emmerick hadn't been there, had he? He wasn't ever coming back, was he? Her waitress hadn't shown up, either, but a fat lot anybody cared about Ellie

June Freedom's problems. She didn't bother to say good-bye, and Peter couldn't say he blamed her much. A new thought had struck him.

"Ottermole," he said, "how would you describe Fanshaw?"

"Huh? What do you mean, how?"

"Height, weight, age, complexion, eye color, clothing, the usual. Would you say he was a tall man?"

"Not specially, I mean not what you'd really call tall. More tall than short, I guess. How about average?"

"Um. Was he heavy or slim?"

"Gosh, I didn't notice. Sort of in between, wouldn't you think?"

"I expect I would, because I wouldn't know what else to say. Was he light or dark or in between?"

"Kind of—I don't know. Average?"

Peter didn't even try for eye color. "Can you recall any distinguishing features?"

"Well, he didn't have a bushy red beard or a big scar down the side of his face, I'd have remembered something like that. I think. You know, Professor, it's a funny thing. I remember Fanshaw well enough now that I've read my notes and all, but I can't seem to recall one damned thing about him. Do you think it's on account of him hypnotizing me?"

"I don't know, Ottermole, but he didn't hypnotize me and I can't seem to picture him, either. Let me call Miss Binks, she has eyes like a hawk's."

Winifred Binks was there, she had a clear general impression of Mr. Fanshaw, but when it came down to specifics, she couldn't quite put her finger on a single detail. She asked Knapweed Calthrop to help her out; he did no better than she. Winifred found the circumstances very provoking, and Peter could not but agree.

9

"Hypnotized?"

The conch shell on the whatnot vibrated audibly. Jane Austen, who'd been peacefully making bread on the president's knee, leapt two feet straight in the air, then rushed to Peter for solace. Being conversant with the courtesies due a sensitive feline, Dr. Svenson apologized.

"Sorry, Jane. Shouldn't have yelled. But Yesus, Shandy!"

"I couldn't agree more, President. Naturally one doesn't expect such melodramatic occurrences in one's own bailiwick. I was more than a trifle nonplussed, myself."

"And you don't nonplus easily, dear," said Helen Shandy. "Shall I mix you a Boomerang?"

"Sit still, my love. I'll do it."

"No, you've been up half the night and tearing around un-hypnotizing people all day. I haven't done anything more strenuous than flip through the library card catalog."

Helen set down her own glass, on which she'd made little progress so far. A Balaclava Boomerang is, as Helen well knew, not the sort of drink to be approached too boldly. Its principal ingredients are homemade cherry brandy and home-hardened cider. Only cherries and apples grown within the purlieus of Balaclava County produce the desired results in the manufacture of the ingredients, therefore Boomerangs are never served anywhere else and then only by those favored few who are able to obtain (a) the requisite ingredients and (b) the secret formula.

Helen's research into the annals of the Buggins family had confirmed that the Boomerang was an invention of Belial Buggins, a nephew of Balaclava Buggins, the college's founder. Belial had also been the reputed father of Hilda Horsefall, now married to Dr. Svenson's Uncle Sven; Dr. Svenson might be said thus to have acquired a family interest in the Boomerang. This could explain his expressed willingness to have another now with Peter. Since alcohol works on the human body in direct proportion to the body's size, Svenson could easily have managed half a dozen, but he never drank more than two. The president was fully conscious of his position and the responsibility incumbent upon him to set a good example to the young minds under his charge. If he hadn't been, his wife would have reminded him.

Sieglinde herself would normally have been among those present, for she and Helen were close friends. This weekend, however, she was baby-sitting her Olafssen grandchildren while daughter Birgit and her husband Hjalmar were off to collect a trophy awarded them by the National Raspberry Growers' Association for their outstanding contributions to the field of rubiculture. Since both Birgit and Hjalmar were Balaclava graduates and former students of Peter Shandy, this ought to have been the prime topic of conversation, but today Peter had too much else to talk about.

"I called Cronkite Swope to see about the photographs he took of Fanshaw, and he says there isn't one where the man's face shows clearly. He managed somehow to keep his head turned away from the camera every time. And the eeriest part of all is that when we tried to get up a description of Fanshaw for the state police to track him down, not one of us could remember what the bugger looked like."

Peter shook his head. "The best Swope could come up with was that Fanshaw reminded him of a statistic. Forty-two-and-a-half-percent-of-the-population sort of thing. He said Fanshaw looked like half a percent. All I can think of is that chap who played tennis in *The Thirty-Nine Steps* and showed up again in *Mr. Standfast.*" Peter was a keen student of the works of John Buchan. "You know, the one who was always turning out to have been somebody else. He had that same sort of bland, characterless face which can resemble anybody at all or nobody in particular. Change his clothes, slap on a false mustache—"

"People like that don't have to resort to artifice," Helen argued. "They just think themselves into the role and Bob's your uncle. What you'd better do is find out whether Count von Schwabing sired any illegimate sons during his early period, while he was committing all those unnameable crimes he got thrown out of Germany for."

"This would have to be a grandson," said Peter. "Anyway, members of the nobility didn't get thrown out for siring bastards. He'd have had to do something really unnameable, like cheating at cards or shooting a fox."

"Ungh," grunted Dr. Svenson. "Sounds to me more like The Shadow." The second Boomerang never made Dr. Svenson garrulous, but it did tend to loosen his vocal cords a little. "Power to cloud men's minds. Not women's, though. Women's minds don't cloud."

"Sometimes they do," Helen told him kindly, "but I can't imagine that Winifred Binks's ever does. And you say she doesn't remember either, Peter? That really is uncanny. Unless it's just that you were all tired out from what happened at the owl count?"

"Ottermole wasn't in our group," Peter argued, "though I grant you he stayed with the owl count straight through to the finish. But Budge Dorkin didn't participate, and he can't remember, either. In his and Ottermole's cases, it could be post-hypnotic suggestion, I suppose, but that wouldn't account for the rest of us. Drat, it's humiliating to realize one's faculties are so easily numbed."

"Bemused, I should say," Helen modified. "Like when the magician holds out the hat and it looks empty to you but the bunny's in there all the time. I wonder whether they use he bunnies or she bunnies?"

"I expect they choose dumb bunnies, so the critters won't know enough to put up a squawk when they get crammed into the false bottoms. Can't you look it up somewhere? Librarians are supposed to know all this stuff."

"That's right, embarrass me in front of Thorkjeld and get me kicked off the staff so I'll have to stay home and darn your socks. I see through your chauvinist machinations, Peter Shandy, and you needn't think I don't. Thorkjeld, you'll stay and have a bite to eat with us?"

"Sorry. Gudrun and Frideswiede are cooking supper. Wish me luck."

Dr. Svenson finished his drink and took his departure. Realizing how hungry he was, and how enticing was the scent of pot roast wafting from the kitchen, Peter went to set the table. Helen took the hint.

"Poor darling, you must be starved. Did you get any lunch?"

"A moldy crust and a sip of water. Brackish, with tadpoles."

"Ah, good. There's a lot of nourishment in tadpoles, I believe. Shall we turn on the evening news?"

Peter groaned. "Let's not. I don't feel up to any more catastrophes today. Drat, I wonder if we should have left Miss Binks to stay out there by herself tonight."

"But Winifred's not by herself, is she? I thought that young botanist was parking in her spare room as a perquisite of office."

"As an alternative to being paid a living wage would be the more accurate rendering. We don't aim to palter away Grandsire Binks's millions on lavish stipends for weedy post-graduates. Calthrop will get his doctorate out of us if he keeps on the way he appears to be going, and maybe a full-time teaching position if he shows enough of the right stuff. So far there's been barely a glimmer, but one never knows. Miss Buddley claims he attempted to force his attentions on her this morning."

Helen elevated an eyebrow. "Did he really?"

"Good question. Calthrop maintains it was Miss Buddley who made the running. In any event, the denouement was that she stalked away in a huff and got herself abducted."

"Peter! You didn't tell me that."

"Sorry, my own, I assumed the president would have."

"A specious excuse if ever I've heard one; you know what a prude Thorkjeld is. Actually he hadn't been here all that long before you came home. We were still talking about Emory Emmerick. So what happened to Miss Buddley? Is she still missing?"

"No, we found her." Peter filled in the details of the kidnapping and its aftermath. "She was in a state of considerable disarray, having been gagged and blindfolded with strips torn from her upper garment. I had to lend her my shirt in order to spare the president's blushes."

"Noble soul! I hope she has the decency to give it back. Had Miss Buddley any idea why they snatched her?"

"She's of the opinion that there was only one snatcher. He appeared to think she was in possession of some piece of information

Emmerick had given her, and insisted she divulge it. She was unable to do so, having no idea what he was talking about. He remained of the opinion that she was just being ornery, and left her tied to a tree out along the Whittington Road for rumination and reflection."

Helen shivered. "The poor woman, she must have been scared stiff. Is she all right now?"

"She complained of ant bites and nervous strain but seemed little the worse for her adventure, barring the shirt."

"You know, Peter, it strikes me as more than a bit remarkable that Miss Buddley should go strolling or flouncing, as the case may have been, through the woods just as a kidnapper happened along. Doesn't that make you wonder a bit?"

"This whole affair makes me wonder more than a bit," he replied. "One conjectures that the kidnapper did not in fact just happen along, but had been lurking nearby in hope of an opportunity."

"But how would he have known where she was going to be?"

"Maybe he planted a tracking device in her hiking boots. Would there be perchance another morsel of turnip in the pot?"

"Of course, dear. Allow me."

"With pleasure." Peter pulled the horseradish jar closer and ladled another dollop on his plate. "In point of fact, my love, it's not outside the bounds of possibility that Miss Buddley may be telling the exact truth, as she sees it, about her adventure. She'd been on friendly terms with Emmerick. He'd taken her out to the Bubble night before last. They danced up and down the bowling lanes, she told me. If this other chap had been there spying, he could easily enough have got the impression that Emmerick was seizing the opportunity to whisper something other than sweet nothings into her shell-like ear."

"Are her ears in fact shell-like?" As a librarian, Helen always preferred to be sure of the facts.

"Don't digress, my love. We may be getting somewhere here, though I can't imagine where. Emmerick must have been involved in something fairly dire, wouldn't you think? Otherwise, why should anyone go to all that trouble to kill him? Why it happened the way it did is more than I can fathom, but there has to be some kind of explanation."

"Such as that whoever pulled him up in that net was someone who wouldn't have been able to get close to him any other way?" Helen suggested.

"Gad, I hadn't thought of that angle. Somebody with a horrendous case of halitosis, you mean? Or someone who was allergic to Emmerick's dandruff and would otherwise have given himself away by sneezing before he'd had his chance to plunge in the fatal weapon, whatever it may have been?"

"Of course, dear. That's the only reasonable explanation."

"Which is?"

"Whichever you prefer," Helen conceded generously. "I was thinking more along the lines of a prosthesis or a sprained ankle."

"As well you might, but how would a person with a prosthesis or a sprained ankle have climbed down from the tree and made his getaway before Winifred and I could get to him? Why wouldn't they just shoot Emmerick from a distance, or sneak into his room and load his toothpaste with strychnine?"

"Because the murderer couldn't shoot straight and was fresh out of strychnine? Or because he had a consuming hatred for Emmerick and wanted the satisfaction of killing him hand-to-hand? Or hand-to-neck, in this case. Peter darling, I know you've been tootling back and forth to the station all day and you must be sick of it, but do you think we might just buzz out there one more time and see whether Winifred might like to come back with us for the night? I know I'm being fluttery and feminine, but—"

"I'm feeling fluttery, too, if you want to know," Peter admitted, "and since when did I raise any objection to your femininity? Shall we go right now?"

"Unless you want dessert? It's only fruit and cheese."

"Then let's save it for Miss Binks."

"Darling, why can't you bring yourself to call her Winifred? She'd much rather you did."

"I know that, Helen. It's just that she reminds me so much of my fourth-grade teacher. I'll gird up my loins and try to remember not to be intimidated."

"Do. You're a big boy now, you know. Come on, let's get these dishes cleared up."

Working together, they had the kitchen tidy in next to no time. Jane Austen expressed justifiable displeasure at the prospect of being left alone again, so they invited her along for the ride. This time Helen drove and Peter gave his full attention to Jane, who'd developed a taste for motoring. She liked best to sit on Peter's shoulder with her tail across his face like a ringed mustache, making comments about the scenery as they went along.

"I suppose we ought to have called to say we were coming," Helen remarked as she was turning out of the village onto the Lumpkinton Road.

"She'd only have told us not to bother," said Peter. "You know how independent Winifred is. How's that for bravado?"

"Excellent, darling. You must try saying it to her face sometime. I know Winifred's independent but she's also a great deal more vulnerable at the station than she was where she lived before. And there's been so much hoo-ha about all that money of her grandfather's, people may think she keeps it stacked in the corners like firewood. I do wish she'd get herself a great big, ugly watch-dog. Or at least a yappy little one."

"She's afraid a dog would scare off the local fauna," Peter objected.

"Then that must be about the only thing she is afraid of, as far as I've been able to make out. Winifred has this theory that being afraid is the most dangerous thing you can do."

"She's right, you know."

"I suppose so." Helen sounded a trifle irritated. "But it's awfully hard on her friends. And it certainly didn't work today for Viola Buddley. She's seemed intrepid enough, the few times I've met her. Goodness knows what she'll feel like after this. I hope you're not going to have problems keeping your help out at the station."

"So do I, now that you—phoo! Jane, please try to keep your tail out of my mouth. Now, as I was trying to say, that you mention it. We'll just have to wait and see what develops. I expect if we had to, we could put a squad of students out there as bodyguards or caretakers. It would mean building them some kind of bunkhouse."

"Two bunkhouses," said Helen. "One for the hims and one for the hers. You know what Sieglinde's like."

"I do indeed. Maybe we could tack a couple of wings on the television station. That would probably be cheaper than putting up a whole new building, though I dread the thought of messing about any longer with those confounded blueprints. Tell me, Helen, how do you think Emory Emmerick worked up enough chutzpah to pass himself off as an employee of the Meadowsweet Construction Company? How did he know the real site engineer wasn't going to show up some morning and crab his act?"

"The question, I assume, is rhetorical. Obviously Emmerick had inside information about when the real man was due to appear. As to how he found out, that's another and tougher question. Didn't you and Thorkjeld know?"

"No, my love, on these lengthy construction projects one tends to develop a sense of kismet. If the job keeps moving forward, as opposed to coming to lengthy and unexplained halts, one gets to feeling that's all a reasonable person can expect. Precisely how and when things happen is the responsibility of the people who are being paid to run the show. So far, the Meadowsweet crew have kept on showing up and making a decent show of diligence, so we haven't been sweating the small stuff."

Jane was now evincing a desire to move from Peter's shoulder to his knee. He assisted her descent and got her adjusted to their mutual satisfaction.

"All set now, Trouble? I don't suppose, Helen, that it would be an earthshaking task for somebody bent on skulduggery to worm a piece of information that would hardly be considered top secret out of some Meadowsweet employee who has access to the scheduling. One merely strikes up an acquaintance and plies her or him with booze, blandishments, or baksheesh, depending on the circumstances and the persons involved. I could do it if I had to. You could do it better and faster, no doubt."

"I'm sure I could." Helen didn't believe in false modesty. "But why?"

"Aye, there's the rub. Drat. I just wish we could waltz into the station and meet Winifred rushing up to us with a mysterious black notebook written in code by the late Emory Emmerick and containing a nice, fat, juicy clue."

"Shades of Franklin Scudder! Dream on, General Hannay."

Peter took his wife's suggestion literally and joined Jane in a catnap. He woke slightly refreshed and in some measure restored just about the time Helen turned off the road into the station's parking lot.

They'd rather expected to find Winifred Binks and Knapweed Calthrop over at the house drinking dandelion coffee or perhaps one of Winifred's more potent potations. In fact, the lights in the station lobby were still on and the two of them could be seen at the table, studying something that lay before them. They looked up as the car's headlights shone in the window. Winifred Binks rose and came to the door. Knapweed was right on her heels, clutching the gavel.

10

"Why, Peter! Haven't you had enough of us for one day? And Helen and Jane, too? What a pleasant surprise. We're delighted to see you, I hope it's not a duty call. Do put that gavel down, Knapweed, the Shandys aren't going to attack us. Knapweed and I have committed a breach of the peace, Peter, though I'm not sure what we're guilty of. Breaking and entering with intent, perhaps. We knew we ought to leave that car for the police to search but they didn't come and they didn't come. Finally we couldn't stand it any longer, so we put Baggies over our hands in case of fingerprints and went rummaging. And what should we find slipped down behind the driver's seat but somebody's little black notebook. It appears to be written in code, but perhaps that's just our ignorance. Want to see?"

"Need you ask?" said Peter. "This may

be just what we've been praying for. You—er—kept the Baggies on while you turned the pages?"

"We didn't have to. Knapweed got the inspired thought of turning them with those big tweezers he uses for arranging his botanical specimens. I couldn't manage the tweezers, but he handles them like a surgeon."

The young graduate student blushed. "It's only a matter of practice. Bedstraws are such ticklish little dickenses. But they're good company when you get to know them. Hi, kitty."

Jane, who'd been rubbing against his left pant leg, took the "Hi, kitty" as an invitation to climb it. Knapweed set down the gavel and picked her off his jeans, then settled her comfortably in his arms. "Jane? Is that your name? Hold still, can't you? I want to count your whiskers."

"Great Scott, Helen, he's one of us!" Peter exclaimed. "I should explain, Calthrop, that both my wife and I also have the habit of counting things. Jane has—er—, sorry, Calthrop. I shouldn't deprive you of the pleasure of finding out for yourself."

"Your count may be off anyway, dear," Helen cautioned. "I found a stray whisker on the livingroom sofa yesterday while I was tidying around, I can't imagine why I bothered. Mrs. Lomax always—why on earth am I driveling on about Jane's whiskers? Let's have a look at that notebook."

"By all means," said Miss Binks. "We can't make head nor tail of it, but you're the expert at this sort of thing.* Here, sit down. Is that light strong enough for you?"

"It's fine, but I can't say it's doing much good. Knapweed, would you mind turning the pages for me? Peter, what is this? Not shorthand, at least not any system I've ever seen. Not Greek or Arabic or Hebrew or Sanskrit or Cyrillic or demotic Egyptian, and certainly not hieroglyphics. I suppose we could fall back on the old relative-frequency system for starters. I do wish I'd brought volume five of the *Encyclopaedia Britannica* with me."

"But how were you to know you'd want it?" said her hostess. "What do you think we should do?"

"I think we ought to put this notebook right back where you found it," Helen told her. "But first, why don't we just run it page by page through your copy machine? Using

**Vane Pursuit,* 1989.

Mr. Calthrop's tweezers, of course, so we won't smudge the pages. I hate to keep making you work, Mr. Calthrop."

"Heck, I don't mind a bit, but I wish you'd call me Knapweed. Everybody else does. Everybody who calls me anything at all, anyway. Would it be okay if I made two copies instead of one? I'd love to have a stab myself; I've never tried to unravel a code."

"Nor have I," said Winifred Binks. "That's an excellent idea, Knapweed. The more of us who try, the likelier somebody is to succeed. Don't you agree, Peter?"

Peter didn't know whether to agree or not. As Knapweed had already tweezed on to the notebook, however, and was carrying it over to the copy machine, he saw little point in raising a fuss. Knapweed could always get it back again, and make himself as many copies as he wanted after Miss Binks had gone to bed. Peter wasn't about to sit out here with the skunks and raccoons all night, keeping watch on that rented car. He doubted very much that Fanshaw would try to sneak back here and pick it up. The man would be a fool to come anywhere near the station again, unless the notebook was his own and he didn't dare leave it for somebody else to unravel.

"I wish I knew which of those two dropped this thing," he told Miss Binks. "We have to assume Emmerick and Fanshaw were a team, but what the—er—dickens were they working at?"

"Good question," she replied. "In view of what happened to Viola this morning, we must further assume that the work is going on regardless of the fact that Mr. Emmerick is no longer with us. What bothers me most, Peter, is the way these impostors keep popping up. First Emmerick comes along pretending to be what he obviously wasn't. Then Emmerick dies and Fanshaw appears, apparently not realizing Emmerick is dead. We get him nicely disposed of, then some third person kidnaps Viola. Then that lawyer shows up and gets Fanshaw out of jail. I ask myself, where's it going to end?"

"And well you may, Winifred." There, by George, he'd done it! "I did tell you Fanshaw was out of the lockup, but I don't believe I filled you in on the details. What happened was that the lawyer was with him in the cell when I arrived at the station. He came out and Ottermole had a few—er—words with him, then he went off and Ottermole and Dorkin went to see whether Fanshaw might need to be—er—taken out of his cell. I was searching through Emmerick's effects for possible clues at the time and didn't pay much attention. After a while, though, I realized things were quiet in the lockup, so I thought I'd better check. I found the coop open, the bird flown, and Ottermole and Dorkin sitting together on the cot playing cat's cradle and thinking it was checkers."

"But why?"

Peter shrugged. "Your guess is as good as mine. As best we could piece the story together, Fanshaw had hypnotized both of them at the same time by waving a gold coin on a chain in front of their noses."

"That is simply incredible. You're quite sure they weren't shamming?"

"No question. I know Fred and Budge well enough, they were completely out of the picture. It took some doing to bring them around and I'm not at all sure some kind of post-hypnotic suggestion mightn't still have been in force after I left them. Such things can happen, I believe. The subject coasts along for days behaving just as usual, then all of a sudden he starts walking on his hands or eating peas with his knife."

"Ugh! What a dreadful thought. Then do you think it was safe to leave them alone?"

"I didn't. The night officer came on and they went home, Budge Dorkin to meet his aunt's new boyfriend and Ottermole to play his nightly game of cops and robbers with his children. We'll simply have to wait and see what develops."

"Like Cronkite Swope with his photographs."

"Good thinking, Winifred." There, he'd done it again. More smoothly this time, it was really quite easy. "I called Swope and he says there's not one decent likeness of Fanshaw in the lot. He's either out of focus or turned away from the camera."

"How uncanny!"

"Or canny, depending on how you look at it. My opinion is that Fanshaw must have had plenty of experience in such matters to have shown that much presence of mind. How's it coming, Calthrop?"

"Done, I think. I'm just checking."

The botanist was still tweezing pages, but drawing only blanks; it wasn't until the last page that he came across anything else. This was not more of those odd symbols, but merely a rough drawing of a stemmed dish bearing a few roundish doodles that might have been meant for apples.

"Well, well," Peter exclaimed.

"Well what?" Helen demanded.

"See this?"

He pointed to the drawing Knapweed had just copied. Helen sniffed.

"Artistically undistinguished, in my opinion. Am I to gather that it has some kind of symbolic significance?"

"You might wish to consider that Winifred is, as she just learned today, a major stockholder in a firm called Golden Apples, which is owned and managed by people named Compote. What interests me particularly is that I found a similar doodle on one of Emmerick's papers."

"Then you think we can assume this notebook belonged to Emmerick?"

"I don't think we're in a position yet to take anything for granted, but at least it's something. Good work, Calthrop. May I have a set of those copies?"

Knapweed handed them over. "So now you want me to put the notebook back where we found it?"

"If you'd be so good," Peter replied. "Still handling it with your tweezers, though I'm sure I don't have to remind you."

"But if that man Fanshaw is loose again, what's to stop him from coming to get it?"

"Firstly, if the notebook belonged to Emmerick, as we may infer from that doodle, Fanshaw may not even know it exists. Secondly, if he does know, he may not be aware that it's not among Emmerick's effects, which he hasn't had a chance to examine. Ottermole's collected some of them from Emmerick's room at the inn and the state police took the rest from his pockets at the morgue. Thirdly, if the notebook's really Fanshaw's and he runs the risk of coming to look for it in the car, we'll know for sure that it's important."

"Hey, you're right! Maybe I ought to keep watch overnight in case he shows up."

"Rather you than I, young man. It won't much matter if Fanshaw does steal the thing back, now that we have copies. You know, I'm wondering if this alleged code is in fact some kind of engineer's shorthand, it looks to have been worked out by a pipe fitter. I'll ask one of the chaps in the engineering department to have a look."

"You might also try to find out whether it may be some kind of computer language," Winifred Binks suggested. "Most things are nowadays."

"Too true."

Peter's reply was blurred by a yawn too big to choke back. Helen handed him the disreputable tweed hat and mackinaw he'd dropped on a chair when they'd arrived.

"Come along, darling, you're out on your feet. Winifred, you must be ready to drop. Would you like to drive back and spend the night with us again? You, too, Knapweed, if you don't mind sleeping on the living-room sofa."

"Thanks, Mrs. Shandy. I could sleep on a hat rack if I had to, but I think I ought to stay here and man the barricades in case there's any trouble. Besides, we have people coming tomorrow."

"Nobly spoken, Knapweed," said Winifred. "You're a dear to offer, Helen, but we'll do quite all right in our own downy beds. We did expect a troop of Boy Scouts from Lumpkin Upper Mills to be bivouacked out here tonight doing their own owl count, but the scoutmaster called to say it was too cold. Translated, I expect that means their parents are afraid to let them come because of what happened to Mr. Emmerick."

"And who could blame them?"

"Not I, surely. However, we do expect them first thing in the morning. I'm supposed to show them how to leach the bitterness out of acorns, then roast them over an open fire. They were supposed to gather their own acorns, but Knapweed and I collected a bucketful this afternoon to speed things up. With no untoward incident, I'm relieved to say. We've got them shelled and leaching in the brook."

"Viola phoned a while back to tell us she's feeling better and could come in for a while tomorrow if we needed her," Knapweed put in, "but I said we could manage, so she's going to wash her hair instead."

"So you see we're more or less back to normal," said Winifred. "I'd offer you a cup of camomile tea for the road, but you don't look to me as if you need any. Good luck with the code, or whatever it is, and thank you for thinking of us. Nighty-night, Jane dear. Come again soon."

Peter said, "Good night, Winifred," just to keep in practice. Jane gave Knapweed's hand a parting lick, which pleased him greatly. Helen fished out the car keys and got them back on the road, Peter and Jane both had to be waked up when they pulled into Charley Ross's parking lot. Jane showed an inclination to walk the short way home. Helen protested.

"No, you don't, young woman. You're

not going to start roaming the streets downtown like your cousin Edmund."

Edmund was in fact only a sixth cousin once removed, but relatives were relatives in Balaclava County. Peter ended the matter by scooping up the cat and letting her work out her irritation on his mackinaw, which was long past hurting anyway.

"Now, we're all going to have a nice, quiet Sunday," Helen decreed as they walked up the hill. "We'll sleep as late as we like and I'll make us a nice big breakfast whenever we feel like eating."

"Too bad we didn't think to bum some acorns off Winifred," said Peter. "We could sit around the backyard roasting them over a campfire."

"Yes, dear." Helen glanced up at the moonless, starless firmament. "I have a hunch those Boy Scouts aren't going to get many acorns roasted tomorrow, unless they do it over the station fireplace. I don't care what the weatherman said, I predict we're in for a real rainstorm."

As so often happened, Helen was right. Sunday morning never quite arrived. The sky stayed leaden; the rain lashed against the windows, drummed on the roof, and no doubt leaked around the bulkhead into the cellar. None of the Shandys got up to look; they were content to laze and drowse until Jane decided it was tummy time and Helen's conscience got the better of her. Peter was the last one down. He found his wife at the kitchen table with a cup of coffee in front of her, sausages in the frying pan, a pitcherful of pancake batter ready for action, and Knapweed's copies spread all over the place.

"Any luck, Mrs. Holmes?"

"Not a glimmer." Helen gathered up the sheets and parked them on the cutting board with a can of cat food to hold them down. "I've phoned Winifred. The Boy Scouts aren't coming, so she and Knapweed are going to wallpaper her living room. She'd been putting it off for a rainy day, and she's not likely to find one rainier than this. She's been out to check the rain gauges, there's already upward of half an inch. They haven't had any luck with Emmerick's code. I had to tell them we haven't, either. Maybe I'll feel smarter after I've had something to eat."

"Yes, pet. Want me to do the flapjacks?"

"Not if you're planning to flip them in the air and try to catch them in the pan. You know what happened last time."

"There's gratitude, forsooth! Which of us

had been nattering for three years about getting the ceiling done? And who provided the ultimate impetus?"

"I grant you the impetus, but what about the stove? I don't know when I've seen Mrs. Lomax more upset. And that was after we'd scraped most of the batter off the burners. Go see if the Sunday paper's come, since you burn to be helpful. I hope that child didn't simply dump it on the doorstep and gallop off, the way he usually does."

"If he did, what we have now is papier-mâché," said Peter in a voice of doom. "Gad, what a down-pour! Jane, get your nose out of that frying pan and come help Papa brave the elements."

Jane made it clear that she felt her first duty was to the sausages, so Peter went alonc. He managed better than he'd expected; the Boston paper was so wrapped around with circulars and classified ads, thanks to somebody's having got it assembled the wrong way around, that the relatively meager news and editorial sections were damp only halfway through. Today, moreover, he found another quite unexpected, far less ponderous journal propped up against the front door, enclosed in plastic and dry as a bone.

The latter's front page featured an exclusive, on-the-spot photo of a cadaver being toted down a woodland path by two well-groomed stalwarts in state-police uniform. There was another showing Chief Ottermole, looking even handsomer and groomier, thanks to Edna Mae's fond attentions, arresting a medium-sized man who had his head turned away from the camera. Peter dumped the bigger and wetter paper in the umbrella stand and carried the other back to the kitchen.

"Look at this, Helen, the *Fane and Pennon*'s finally got around to putting out a special Sunday edition. Another milestone in history! Ottermole's made the front page."

"As when does he not? My stars and garters, Edna Mae's going to run out of wall space. Isn't there a picture of you anywhere?"

"Gad, I should hope not. Swope knows better."

"Well, I think it's discriminatory. We have walls too, you know."

"Then why don't you hang up that photograph of me at the county fair, judging the twenty-seven-pound Balaclava Buster that old coot from Outer Clavaton dragged in."

"Yes, with your back to the camera and a rip in the seat of your pants."

"Merely a snag. I happened to sit on a splintered rail at the cattle pens that some bored beast had been chewing on. You must admit the rutabaga came out well, though."

"I grant you the rutabaga. Give those sausages a turn, will you? Gently, without histrionics." Helen added two pancakes to the stack she was keeping warm in the oven and poured more batter. "I may as well finish the batch, we can have tea and crumpets this afternoon."

Helen and Peter had been amused while in Britain to learn that crumpets resembled American batter cakes closely enough to make no great difference; this would be a good day for a high tea by the fireplace. They ate their excellent breakfast, read each other snatches of Cronkite Swope's lively reportage, turned down the telephone so they wouldn't hear it ring after they'd got one too many calls from neighbors who'd also been reading the *Fane and Pennon*, and tried not to think about various tasks they too had been putting off for a rainy day.

Every so often, one or both of them would take another whack at the code. The encyclopedia up at the college library would have given them the relative frequency of the various letters of the alphabet; but that would have meant a slog through the rain and this really was too beastly a day to bother.

About two o'clock in the afternoon, Timothy Ames slished across the Crescent with his cribbage board under his raincoat. His house was directly across from the Shandys', which was about as far as anybody cared to go. Tim and Peter played. Helen retired to the kitchen to make fudge, not that they needed the extra calories but just because it was that sort of day. Once the nutmeats were in and the fudge set to harden, she picked up Knapweed's copies again.

11

Peter was in the act of pegging out when he heard the cry from the kitchen.

"Dolt! Dizzard! Double-dyed dunderhead! How could I have been so blind?"

"Excuse me, Tim. I'd better see what's up." He dashed to the kitchen. "Wherefore the wailing, woman?"

"It's toothpick letters, that's all. Didn't you play with them as a kid?"

"When I was a kid, one whittled one's own toothpick out of a burnt match."

"And carried it around in a little gold case, I suppose? Here, let me show you."

"While Tim stacks the deck? I'll get him in here. Wait a minute."

He went back to the living room, but returned alone in a couple of minutes. "Tim says never mind, he'll read the paper instead. The rain got into his hearing aid on the way over and he has a static problem. So what's with the toothpicks?"

Helen had brought a box of toothpicks from the tiny pantry and was arranging them in geometric patterns on the table. "See, I've duplicated a set of symbols from Emmerick's notebook."

"Or Fanshaw's."

"Whichever. You'll grant that I've got them right?"

Peter nodded. What Helen had achieved was

"Featly formed, my love. Now what?"

"Now we add a few more toothpicks. Here, I think. And here, and—darn, I wish they wouldn't skitter around like that. Here, and I think we just move this one down a little, and here, and what do we get?"

"Good question. Oh, I see now. I'll be switched!

"CWBOUTGA. What's that supposed to mean?"

"Well, 'bout' refers to boxing. Maybe CW is supposed to fight somebody in Georgia. Perhaps if we go through the rest of the notes—"

"Wait a second, could this be the key?"

As a boy, Peter had always enjoyed working out the rebuses in the family almanac. He shuffled through the notes and found the drawing from the back of the notebook. "Suppose, for the sake of argument, C stands for Compote and GA for Golden Apples?"

"Of course, darling! Then could WB stand for Winifred Binks? You say she practically owns that company."

"According to her lawyers, she has controlling interest. So Compote Winifred Binks out Golden Apples. Or maybe the W means something else; it could stand for worried, or warning."

"Or wanting or wishing or simply waiting. Waiting, perhaps, to see what Winifred's going to do about her shares."

"Or worried about what she might do. Or wanting to buy her out so she can't do anything."

"Sopwith, the trust officer, claims the Compotes can't buy her out. They don't have the money."

"How does he know?"

"He damned well ought to, it's his job to know. Well, this looks promising, unless we're deluding ourselves. Let's, as you suggest, press on. We don't have to keep on with the toothpicks, do we?"

"Oh no, it's just a matter of adding one more straight line to each of the symbols, you see. There's a pencil beside the telephone, unless Jane's been playing with it again."

"That's all right, I have one. What's next?"

Working directly on the copies, Helen made light strokes. VBOKKCRED. "Could that mean Viola Buddley's all right but Knapweed Calthrop is a Communist?"

"Could mean he's red with embarrassment if Calthrop's version of what happened out by the bird feeder is the true one," said Peter. "Unless it's some key word like red for stop or red for danger? Drat it, Helen, this is getting too thought-provoking for comfort. Why couldn't the bastard have been more explicit?"

"Since he wrote them in code, he obviously didn't want them to be easily understood," Helen pointed out quite reasonably. "They could be just Emmerick's reminders to himself of things he ought to tell Fanshaw when they got together. Or he could have left the notebook in the car for Fanshaw to find when he picked it up last night. And Fanshaw didn't find it, which might explain why he showed up looking for Emmerick this morning. I do think it must have been Emmerick who made the notes, don't you? He was the only one in a position to make judgments about Knapweed and Viola. Fanshaw had never been near the station before, had he?"

"After what happened to Ottermole and Dorkin, who knows? He could have gone disguised as a Boy Scout. My primary concern is why Emmerick was there in the first place. Unless the FBI or the CIA had got a notion that the college is planning to use the television station for broadcasting subversive propaganda about getting down to cleaning up the environment instead of just talking about it, as in fact we are."

"But why would they send somebody pretending to be a site engineer before the station is even being built, let alone ready to broadcast anything to anybody?" Helen argued. "I've heard of getting in on the ground floor, but that's carrying things a bit far. Unless Emmerick was planning to plant bombs in the concrete so that the place could be blown up at some later date."

"Or hidden microphones so the anti-environmentalists could broadcast their own propaganda on Winifred's juice? Maybe it wasn't the FBI, maybe he was a foreign spy."

"Where from?"

"Who knows? Upper Volta, perhaps? Or Amalgamated Industries?"

"You know, Peter, I've had another thought. You don't think Emmerick could possibly have been sent as some kind of bodyguard?"

"By whom?"

"How should I know? But Winifred does have such scads of money and apparently that kooky grandfather of hers was into all sorts of deals she may know nothing about. Take Golden Apples, for instance. She's in a position to make or break the Compotes and she wasn't even aware she had any connection with them until yesterday. She could be just as important to other companies, couldn't she? Why hasn't that lawyer of hers explained? You don't think he's grinding some ax of his own?"

"Don't ask me. Debenham seems like a decent chap. We have to realize, Helen, that Winifred's had an awful lot of information dumped on her within the past few months. She's not used to dealing with business matters. She may not have absorbed everything she's heard, or she may simply have refused to listen until she'd got her house built and the station under construction. Now that she's out of the woods and getting the bit between her teeth, it's a whole new ball game."

"And the hand that rocked the cradle kicked the bucket. You do have a rather cavalier way with metaphors, Peter. But I see what you're saying; what it boils down to is that she'd better go into a huddle with her lawyers pretty darned soon and find out which wheels are within which."

"Not to worry, pet, it's all arranged. The president himself is meeting with Debenham, the trust officer, and a gaggle of accountants one day this week. They'll be going through Winifred's affairs from stem to gudgeon, leaving her free to leach acorns with the Boy Scouts."

"Oh. Why didn't you say so in the first place? Where was I? This must be an R. Rich—Richard who, I wonder?"

"Richardson's, I expect. This next would be 'longeared.' Screech, barn—that's Emmerick's briefing for the owl walk. He jotted down a few names in an attempt to appear knowledgeable but had no idea how to apply them, so he made a jackass of himself instead."

"Yes, dear. What's a stick path?"

"Stick to the paths, I expect. That's one rule we hammer into everybody. We don't want people straying away and getting lost, mainly because they start blethering for help and scare away the owls. At least Emmerick managed to get that through his skull. So did whoever killed him, obviously. They knew the poor fish would be along there sooner or later, so they spread their confounded net and waited. Drat it, Helen, the more things happen, the less sense they make. Are you saving that fudge for anything special?"

"Just letting it harden." Helen picked up a kitchen knife and made an exploratory incision. "Here you are, love, take a piece in to Tim. I'll finish these notes and let you know if anything exciting turns up."

Nothing did. The remaining sheets were only a jumble of what Helen took to be engineering terms, no doubt selected to lend authenticity to Emmerick's role as a site engineer. She'd get somebody from the college's engineering faculty to sort them out for her tomorrow. They didn't look to be important, but one never knew. She cut a small plateful of fudge and took it into the living room. She was reading the paper at about five o'clock when Tim's daughter-in-law phoned.

"Is Dad coming home for supper any time soon? It's so awful out that Roy wants to walk him home. Don't tell him I said so."

"Then why don't you two come and have supper with us? You can go home together afterward so he won't feel overprotected. It's not going to be anything special."

There was enough pot roast left to warm over. She could eke it out with a package of frozen peas, warm up those pancakes she'd forgotten to serve for tea, and call it crepes à la Shandy. Dessert could be what was left of the fudge.

Laurie said did Helen really want them and what could they bring? Helen said certainly she wanted them and how about a salad? Laurie said no problem. Evidently it wasn't, she and Tim's son Royall blew in about half an hour later, quite literally, since the wind was by now blowing almost at gale force. Roy carried a big bowl covered in aluminum foil and had a bottle tucked under his arm. Laurie had a well-wrapped plate.

"It's cookies," she explained as Helen took the goodies and Peter the streaming rain gear. "I felt like baking this afternoon. It's been that kind of day."

"I know," said Helen. "I made fudge."

"Oh yum! With nuts?"

"Of course. We'll have it with the cookies. Or right now, if you'd rather, only I was thinking about offering everyone a drink. What can I give you?"

"We brought some wine." Roy peeled a soggy paper bag off the bottle he'd been carrying. "An amusing little vintage they were running a special sale on over at the Hoddersville Hoochery. God knows what it tastes like."

"There's only one way to find out. Come and work the corkscrew. Would you like to set the dining-room table, Laurie? Five people would be an awful squash in our dinky kitchen, we may as well eat in style."

Nobody was hungry yet, so they lazed around the fire cracking hickory nuts and sipping at Roy's bargain wine. If not distinguished, at least it was drinkable.

Tim was in one of the easy chairs, Roy and Laurie on the floor at his feet. The Ameses made an interesting picture, Peter was thinking. As far as size was concerned, Tim would have been right at home in Bilbo Baggins's Hobbit hole. He had no beard and not much hair on his head, let alone his feet, but his eyebrows were bushy enough to make up the difference. The old man had put on a little weight since Laurie learned to cook, but he was still lean, brown, and gnarled as an oaken root; and almost as tough. But not quite. Thank God, Roy had brought home a good-hearted wife.

Roy was a lot like his dad in personality and character but not in looks, which was probably just as well. He was fairly tall and big-boned. Took after his mother's side of the family; that had been the winning side as long as Jemima was alive. She'd been dead now for several years; Peter had come upon her body in this very room. It was Jemima's dying that had brought Helen to him, but he didn't regret having got rid of the sofa behind which he'd found Jemima lying.

Laurie leaned forward to poke the fire, sending up a shower of sparks. She was a sparkler herself, little and dark and quick to react, though she had the gift of stillness between times that Jemima had always lacked. Laurie was no fashion plate, she'd dressed for the occasion in a blue sweatshirt with a polar bear on the front, a baggy denim skirt still damp around the hem, and white sweat socks. She'd left her rubber boots by the door, out of consideration for the Shandy floors. Jemima would have kept them on.

Laurie and Roy had led one of the student groups on the owl watch. They'd bagged more sightings than any of the rest, though they were quite willing to concede that Peter's team of experts would have beaten everybody else if it hadn't been for Emmerick's getting netted. They'd known the bogus site engineer; he'd insisted on giving them advice about programming that they hadn't wanted and weren't about to take. As biologists, they were already working with Professor Binks at the field station developing formats for various broadcasts they'd be handling once the television station was ready for use.

One miniseries Laurie and Roy had in mind would be hosted by Captain Amos

Flackley, who'd performed their marriage ceremony on his ship in the middle of the Ross Sea. They'd all three retired to Balaclava, the Ameses to teach at the college and ride herd on Tim, the captain to snatch up a fallen torch as Flackley the Farrier; but the spell of the nethermost continent was still upon them. Their show ought to be superb; Roy had lots of wonderful filming to draw on, Laurie was a splendid scriptwriter, and Captain Flackley knew a zoologist who was willing to lend them some live penguins.

They were also planning a series on the care and feeding of sled dogs. This was expected to attract a considerable response from malamute fanciers, of whom there were a surprising number in Balaclava County, including Captain Flackley himself. So there was plenty to talk about, but it was inevitable that the conversation would work its way around to the *Fane and Pennon*'s reportage of the recent bizarre happenings. Tim was the one who started the ball rolling.

"What the hell's all this foofaraw about trees, Peter? First that jackass who was supposed to be the station site engineer got dumped out of one wrapped up in a fishnet, then that hired girl of Winifred Binks's gets herself kidnapped and tied to another. What kind of trees were they?"

"Gad, Tim, that's one question nobody else has thought to ask. Emmerick's was an oak and Miss Buddley's a box elder."

"That so? We've got lots of oaks on the station property but I don't remember seeing any box elder. Nor white ash. I was thinking about that the other day. Pete, I think we ought to plant a stand of white ash out there. To hell with the elder, nobody makes collar boxes nowadays anyhow."

"Good thought, Tim. White ash is a damn fine tree and too much of it's been lumbered out. The trouble is, where to put it? A lot of the Binks land's low and on the boggy side once you get away from Woeful Ridge. White ash likes high ground."

"Hey, you guys," yelped Roy, "could we scrub the forestry a moment and get back to the grue? How come Emmerick was hauled up in that net, then dropped like a hot potato? Did they bag the wrong guy or did the rope break?"

"I'm guessing it was cut. As to why, I'm not even guessing," Peter answered.

"But aren't there any clues at all?"

Peter glanced over at Helen. "Shall we?"

"Why not? The sheets are still on the

kitchen table. I suggest you turn on the gas under the pot roast while you're getting them. I don't know about the rest of you, but I'm beginning to feel a mite peckish."

"Me too," said Roy. "Hickory nuts are hard work. Anything we can do to help?"

"Open another bottle of wine if anybody wants it, since we appear to have finished the one you brought. There's some burgundy in the pantry. Cider in the fridge, if you'd rather."

Everyone opted for cider except Tim. He said cider gave him the gripes and he'd settle for plain water. Helen went to put on the finishing touches and Peter showed the Ameses the toothpick code. Roy was able to sort out most of the technical terms, also to certify that they were bona fide technical terms and nothing more, as far as he could see. Laurie didn't believe for one second that Knapweed Calthrop could be either a radical or a menace, except possibly to himself. He was so wrapped up in the bedstraws that he never noticed anything else unless he happened to trip over it.

"Even me," she pouted.

"But not the shrinking Viola," Roy insisted. "I've seen Knapweed giving her the old oogle-eye often enough."

"That brings up an interesting point." Peter told them the episode of the squirrel feeder. "So which of the two do you think was lying?"

The voting ran along purely sexist lines. Roy opted for Knapweed, Laurie said Viola. Tim abstained. Helen said they'd better come and eat while it was hot. So they did.

12

They sat longer over their potluck supper than they'd meant to, which turned out to have been just as well. By the time the Ameses were ready to go home, the storm had blown itself out. Peter saw them to the door, then stayed out on the stoop to watch Tim safely across and catch a few lungfuls of well-washed air. There were branches down on the mall that ran down the middle of the Crescent, and puddles everywhere, but no real damage that he could see. He went back to Helen.

"I think we ought to phone Winifred."

"It's rather late, dear," Helen objected. "She's most likely in bed by now."

"I suppose so. But, drat it, I can't help

feeling edgy. I don't like what happened to Miss Buddley, I don't like it one bit."

"I don't suppose Miss Buddley liked it much, either. Go ahead and call, then; you'll lie awake fussing half the night if you don't. Winifred has an extension in her bedroom, she understands well enough the difference between self-sufficiency and stupidity."

The number for the house was the same as for the field station, and Miss Binks was at home. "Oh no, Peter, you didn't wake me," she assured him. "President Svenson called about fifteen minutes ago, which made the third time today. So thoughtful of him. And I was on the phone with Iduna Stott for quite a while before that. Early this afternoon, Cronkite Swope and Budge Dorkin braved the storm, gallant souls that they are. Cronkite took some pictures of that car Mr. Fanshaw left here, and Budge drove it away. Then they both called me to assure me they'd got back safely. I told Budge about the notebook, Peter; it didn't seem quite the thing not to. Was that all right?"

"That's fine. You'll be interested to know Helen cracked the code."

"Oh good. I've barely had time to glance at it myself, I've been so busy on the telephone. What's it about?"

Peter explained how Helen had figured out it wasn't really a code at all, and what they'd got out of it. Winifred was not much impressed.

"I have no doubt you've drawn the right conclusions, but I can't say I'm overwhelmed by the result. That notebook strikes me as the sort of theatrical nonsense to which I found Mr. Emmerick during our brief acquaintance to be all too prone. What I can't help wondering, Peter, is whether his death could have been the result of an overelaborate practical joke that went wrong."

"M'yes, that's something to think about, but how would you then explain his getting stabbed in the neck?"

"That does seem to be carrying a joke too far, I grant you. Unless he thought it was going to be a joke and whoever pulled him up really meant all the time to kill him. I don't know, Peter, I'm simply no good at riddles. Perhaps I'll feel sharper in the morning. Shall we have the good fortune to see you here tomorrow?"

"Yes, I think so. I have classes all morning and a student conference at half-past four, but I expect I could run out for a while after lunch. If the woods dry out and he's not too tied up, I might bring Professor Ames with me. He had some thoughts about a new timber plantation."

"Excellent! I've been wondering about that myself. Bring him anyway. If it's too wet in the woods, we can at least have a good chin-wag about the possibilities. Good night, Peter. I do appreciate your concern, you know."

"Even though you wish we'd all quit clucking over you and let you get some sleep. Good night, Winifred."

Peter himself went to bed expecting a clear day after the storm. During the night, though, a fresh batch of clouds rolled in. By morning, the sky was again completely overcast and the weather man was talking ominously of more rain. His students were as glum as the sky. He snapped them out of their sulks fast enough; Peter was no Captain Bligh, but somehow or other nobody tried any malingering in Professor Shandy's classes.

Even so, by noontime he was glad to get away from the classroom. He escaped to the faculty dining room, sat down with Tim and Dan Stott, and ordered the Monday special, whatever that might be, with pie to follow. The student waiter didn't have to be told what kind, pie at this time of year meant apple unless otherwise specified. Peter never did figure out precisely what the Monday special consisted of, but it didn't taste too bad.

Helen wasn't coming to the dining room today, she was lunching with her friend Grace Porble, the librarian's wife. Tim couldn't go to the station because one of his students had brought in a fascinating glob of mud which they and a privileged few others were going to analyze together. Dan was tied up in a seminar on advanced swine management out at the college pigpens.

"Then I'll go by myself," said Peter.

"Spoken in the staunchly resolute manner of The Little Red Hen." Dan Stott frequently read stories with animals in them to his grandchildren, of whom he had, at current count, twenty-three, and one great-grandchild on the way. "Bon voyage, old friend."

On his way to the car, Peter detoured past the police station. Fred Ottermole was there, sharing a ham on rye with his friend Edmund.

"Hey, Edmund, take it easy with that ham. I've got a mouth on me, too, you know. Hi, Professor. Jeez, I wish Edmund liked mustard. About the car, I got the guys from the state police over and we combed it for clues but didn't find anything except that black notebook you already know about, so I had Budge take it back to the Happy Wayfarer. I figured they'd be sticking us with a bill if we'd kept it any longer. Did you ever find out what those chicken tracks in the notebook are supposed to mean?"

"More or less."

Peter gave the chief a rundown on the chicken tracks, left him puzzling over the explanation, picked up his car, and headed for the field station. He found Winifred Binks in a full-fledged snit, which was most unlike her.

"I don't know what's got into everybody today," she was fuming. "I called Mr. Sopwith a while back about those Lackovites shares I want to get rid of. He claimed the market was off, whatever that may mean, and he didn't think it wise to sell them today. So I got in touch with President Svenson. He said the market isn't off and Sopwith was talking through his hat. So I called Mr. Sopwith back and told him so and he was really quite unpleasant. I had to get a bit sharp with him."

"Good for you," said Peter. "What about Golden Apples?"

"That's another thing. Mr. Debenham was supposed to get in touch with the Compotes first thing this morning and arrange a meeting. I hadn't heard from him by about eleven o'clock, so I phoned to see what was happening. He told me he'd called Golden Apples as I asked him to, but the Compotes weren't available at the time. He'd left a message, but they still hadn't returned his call. So I gave them a ring myself and they haven't returned mine, either. And Viola's acting like a scared rabbit and Knapweed's having a fit of the sulks and I'm about ready to move back to my lair in the woods. I'm going to call those Compote people again, right this minute. Will you excuse me?"

"Go ahead."

Peter knew better than to offer to make the call for her; Winifred could handle her own affairs. It was interesting to watch her in action.

"Hello," she was saying, "this is Winifred Binks. I wish to speak to either Mr. or Mrs. Compote at once. Could you explain why they are not returning my earlier calls? They've been out in the factory? Is there no way for you to communicate with the factory? Then I suggest you go into the factory and find them. Have one or the other call me back as quickly as possible on a matter of utmost importance. You do have my number; I gave it to you earlier."

Nevertheless, Winifred gave it again. She was too much of a lady to slam down the phone, but it was a near miss.

"Peter, I cannot understand those Compotes. One might think they were trying to avoid me, but why should they? Unless they're in the midst of some major catastrophe over there, yesterday's rain having got into their soybeans or something. But why wouldn't that snippy minx have had sense enough to tell me so?"

"Because she does not in fact have sense enough, is the obvious answer."

"Then I shall make sure they get rid of her and find somebody who does. If they haven't called me back by the end of the day, I shall ask Knapweed to drive me to the factory in person. I gather it's too far to bicycle. Viola, get Mr. Sopwith on the phone, please, and find out what's happening to those Lackovites shares. I do not wish to speak to him myself, I merely want him to stir his stumps and do as he's told."

Viola reported that Mr. Sopwith was on another call and would call her back when he was free. Winifred took several deep breaths, and the fire in her eyes died down to a glow. "I see Timothy Ames didn't come with you, Peter. This, it appears, is not my day. Precisely what was it he wanted to talk to me about?"

In sober fact, Tim hadn't expressed any immediate yearning to talk with Winifred, but Peter didn't think that was the time to say so. He was well enough pleased to switch the conversation to white ash trees, and she was clearly relieved to engage in a topic that wasn't concerned with finance. Even she admitted it was too soggy underfoot to go looking for possible planting sites, so she got out a large-scale topographical map of the Binks estate that Winifred's grandfather had commissioned once when he was seriously considering the possibility of organizing llama caravans as a substitute for school buses, and they spent an agreeable hour or so poring over it.

Winifred knew every inch of the ground and virtually everything that was growing on it, she was able to give a tree-by-tree report. As to what should be left alone and what should be rooted out in the interests of a higher good, she was willing to defer to experts, or so she claimed.

"Needless to say, Peter, we also have to

consider what's best for the wildflowers and decide what endangered species might successfully be introduced. Furthermore, I think something might be done about inducing the indigenous raspberries and blackberries to produce more abundantly without turning them from wild to tame. Am I overhopeful in surmising that Dr. Svenson's daughter and her husband might be of assistance to us in this area?"

"Not at all. Birgit and Hjalmar are itching to get involved with the station, though I don't suppose there's a great deal they'll be able to do this late in the year. What do you think, Calthrop?"

"The Rosaceae aren't my field," growled the botanist.

"What's eating him today?" Viola wondered.

"Never mind what's eating him," snapped Winifred. "What's eating Mr. Sopwith? You said he was going to get back to us."

"I know. Maybe he's waiting for the New York Stock Exchange to close."

"Or for the Tokyo Exchange to open. I myself am thoroughly fed up with waiting. Try him again."

Viola tried him again. Mr. Sopwith had just stepped out of the office.

"Then get me Mr. Debenham. I want to find out how one goes about firing one's trust officer."

Mr. Debenham was with a client and would call her back as soon as he was free. Peter glanced at the clock and decided he'd better not wait for the explosion.

"I'll—er—leave you to it, Winifred. I have a student conference to get back for. Call me at home anytime after six o'clock if anything comes up that you want to talk about."

"Thank you, Peter. I expect I shall do so, if only to vent my spleen against the banking and legal professions, not to mention the Compotes. I cannot imagine what's eating those people."

"Er—you don't suppose the Compotes are ducking you because they're afraid you may be calling about something they don't want to hear?"

"How can I reassure them if they won't talk to me?"

"You do have a point there."

Peter glanced from the sullen Knapweed, huddled over the table mounting dried bed-straw, to the twittering Viola at her desk. She'd thrown him one terrified ghost of a smile when he'd come in, then stayed cowering behind her word processor, poking at its keys in a flurried, furtive way as though she feared they might poke her back.

"Tell you what, Winifred," he said, "if you haven't heard from the Compotes by the end of the day, let me know. I'll pick you up in the morning and take you there myself."

"Oh Peter, that's too much to ask. Your classes—"

"Lab sessions. My teaching fellow can handle them, she'll welcome the experience. If they do call, let's go anyway. Tell them you'll be there by half-past ten. I'll pick you up here at nine, that should give us enough time. The Golden Apples plant is in Briscoe, about twenty miles below Clavaton; I've checked the distance on my road map."

"That's extremely kind of you, Peter, but are you sure President Svenson won't mind your taking the time?"

"Why should he? This is college business, in a manner of speaking. See you in the morning."

Peter made it back to Balaclava with ten minutes to spare, got rid of his car, hoofed it up to the campus, hauled a few students over the coals, and then went home.

There'd be no tête-à-tête dinner at home

tonight. Helen was guest speaker at the Clavaton Historical Society, she wouldn't be back home till ten or so. Peter weighed the possibility of scrambling himself some eggs, then decided he'd flake out awhile before toddling up to the faculty dining room. He'd fed Jane, mixed himself a light Scotch and water, and settled himself with the evening newspaper when Dr. Svenson blew in looking for a progress report.

"What's up, Shandy?"

"The state police are trying to get some kind of line on Emmerick, there's no news on Fanshaw, and Goodheart's taking my classes in the morning. I'm driving Winifred Binks to Golden Apples."

"Why?"

"Because that appears to be the only way she'll ever get to talk with the Compotes. They're not answering her phone calls, or hadn't by the time I left there a couple of hours ago. And Sopwith's been giving her a hard time over those Lackovites shares she told him to unload. I gather you've talked to her about that."

"Ungh. Up two points, God knows why. Perfect time to sell. Damn fool, she ought to sack him."

"She was about to do so when I left. I

don't think we need worry too much about Winifred's ability to handle her affairs. I've never seen her angry before, it's an impressive spectacle. Can I fix you a drink?"

"Why not? Couldn't get one at home, Sieglinde locked up the liquor. Says I'm too fat."

"Nonesense, it's solid muscle. Scotch?"

"Fine."

By the time Peter got back from the kitchen with another drink and a plate of bread and cheese, Svenson had picked up Jane and the paper, put on his reading glasses, and settled himself in Peter's chair.

"By George, President, I ought to sue you for alienation of affections."

"Bigger lap."

Svenson might be rough on people at times, but he was always gentle with animals. He ran one enormous finger delicately down the black stripe between Jane's dainty ears, then picked up the cheese knife and whacked himself off a hunk. It was excellent cheddar, a product of the college's dairy management department. "Sieglinde says I can't have any," he mumbled through a mouthful.

"One might make an observation about the mouse playing while the cat's away, but it seems inappropriate in your case. What are you doing for supper?"

"Hoping to bum a meal off you. Where's Helen?"

"Being a celebrity. I was planning to eat at the faculty dining room. Where are your daughters?"

"Gone to Birgit's. Pick up their mother. I wanted to go too, damn it! Couldn't spare the time. Uneasy lies the head that wears the propeller beanie."

"Gad, that takes me back! I got sent to the principal's office once in sixth grade for wearing mine to class. Nowadays teachers are grateful if their kids show up wearing anything at all."

Svenson hacked himself another wedge of cheese. "Lot of sense in dress codes. Kept the kids reminded of where they were, and what they were there for. World's going to hell in a handcart, Shandy. Young ones get preached at about drugs, sit watching television commercials. Grown-ups bellyache about tension headaches, fallen arches, whatever. Swallow some damned pill or other, and whoops-a-daisy. Ought to hang the manufacturers and the advertisers up by their thumbs. Goddamn Lackovites! Had Yoad's classes run some chemical analyses today. Only thing their stuff's good for is to give you cancer of the colon. Want some cheese, Yane?"

"She's had her supper," said Peter. "Which brings up the question of ours. Shall we go, or would you like another drink first?"

"I'd like it. Sieglinde wouldn't. Better go."

But Svenson didn't budge, nor did he demur when Peter took his glass back to the kitchen for a refill.

"It's only half, President. I stuck in an extra ice cube to create the illusion of plenitude."

"Ungh." Svenson drained the glass at a swallow and set it down. "Tired, Shandy. Getting old. Kick the bucket one of these days."

"As will we all. What you need is a square meal under your belt. Did you eat this noontime?"

"Can't remember. Goddamn reporters bugging me all day, looking for fresh corpses. Told 'em read the *Fane and Pennon*. Yesus, there's your phone. Must have tracked me down. Don't answer."

"I'll have to. I told Winifred to phone me if—hello?"

"Oh, Professor Shandy!" For a moment, Peter couldn't sort out the voice from the wails, then he realized this was Viola Buddley. "They took her! Professor Binks! She's gone."

13

"Who took her? Where did they go? Get hold of yourself, Miss Buddley. Or let me talk to Calthrop. Is he there?"

"He's on the f-floor. I think he's dead."

"Oh my God! Miss Buddley, listen. President Svenson and I will be out there as fast as the Lord will let us. Have you phoned the Lumpkinton Police?"

"N-no."

"Then do so at once. Lock the doors till they get there and make yourself a cup of tea or something."

Thorkjeld Svenson was hacking at the cheese, slapping together big cracker sandwiches for them to eat on the way. Peter nodded, broke the connection, and redialed.

"Hello, Mrs. Swope. Is Cronkite home? Peter Shandy calling."

Mrs. Swope knew better than to ask why. She had her son on the wire in no time flat.

"What's up, Professor?"

"You're closest to the field station, you'd better get over there fast. Winifred Binks has been kidnapped. Viola Buddley's alone with Calthrop. He may be dead. The president and I are starting now. I told Buddley to call the Lumpkinton police, but God knows when they'll show up."

"I'm on my way."

Peter slammed down the phone and reached for the telephone pad. "Swope's on his way. No, Jane, you can't come this time. I'm leaving a note for Helen. When will Sieglinde and the girls get home?"

"God knows. Around nine, I hope."

"I've told her to call your house. Let's go. Damn shame I put the car away."

Peter was struggling into his mackinaw, running to keep up with Svenson's giant strides. He'd barely got buttoned up when they were at Charlie Ross's, into the car, and on the road. There would have been no point in alerting Ottermole, the field station was outside his territory.

Drat, he wished there'd been time to eat a decent supper, no telling what they were getting themselves into. Peter took some of the president's crackers and cheese to munch as he drove, snatching a bite when he hit a stretch where it was safe to take a hand off the wheel. At the rate he was traveling, that wasn't often. He prayed they wouldn't get stopped for speeding; it would be just like those Lumpkinton morons to waste time hauling him over instead of hiking their carcasses out to the station.

Luckily, they didn't. He smoked into the parking lot. Swope was waiting. The Lumpkinton police hadn't shown up yet. The ambulance from Clavaton had come and gone, Swope had called them the second he arrived. Calthrop had been bleeding from the nose and ears and having some kind of seizure. His scalp was lacerated and swollen, his color was awful. The paramedic was fairly sure his skull was fractured.

"What about Miss Buddley?" Peter asked.

"She's okay, more or less. I've given her about a bucketful of camomile tea. It calmed her down some, only she keeps having to—here she is."

Viola was able to talk coherently enough now. What she had to tell was horrendous but not all that helpful.

"Knapweed was at the table where he always sits, messing around with his weeds. Professor Binks was at her desk writing a nasty letter to Mr. Sopwith. He never did return her call. I'd gone out to check the bird feeders. I was on my way back when somebody jumped out of the woods, grabbed me from behind, and pulled some kind of blindfold down over my eyes. Then they rammed me against one of those maples beside the parking lot and tied me up."

"Was this the same chap who got hold of you yesterday?"

"How should I know? I couldn't see anything. I was yelling and kicking and trying to get away, but it didn't do any good. I think it was more than one this time. They ran into the station, I could hear the gravel scrunching and Professor Binks yelling 'How dare you?' That's the first time I ever heard her raise her voice. Then I heard them dragging her out to the parking lot."

"Exactly what did you hear?" Peter asked her.

"Well, I heard Professor Binks making noises. She was going 'mf, mf, mf,' as though somebody had a hand over her mouth. And there was a lot of gravel being scuffed around. She wasn't going without a fight, I can tell you that."

"I'm sure she wasn't. You said there were more than one. How many more?"

"At least three, I should think. Two for the rough stuff and one to drive the car. They must have had one close by, I heard it drive up as soon as they got her outside. Then they cussed and banged around awhile, getting her into it."

"They didn't hurt her?"

"I don't think so. I heard somebody say, 'Hey, take it easy. Don't damage the merchandise.' I heard the doors slam and they took off like a bat. Some gravel spurted up and hit my leg, that's how close they were to me. It didn't hurt because I had my boots on, but it scared the hell out of me."

"Ungh," said Dr. Svenson. "What then?"

"Once they were gone, I began struggling to get free. I gucss thcy hadn't tied me so tight this time; after a while I managed to loosen the rope a little and then it was easy enough. I was furious with Knapweed for not coming to help me, so I came charging in to blast him out and here he was on the floor, all bloody. I thought I was going to pass out, but I knew I had to get help, so I called you. Then Cronkite came and made me drink all that tea and—I guess that's it."

"Didn't you call the Lumpkinton police?"

"I don't know. I don't remember. Maybe

I did pass out. I'm just so damned sick and tired of being tied to trees!"

"I called the police right after I'd called the ambulance," said Cronkite. "They claimed they hadn't got any call, but you know them. They said half the guys were on their supper hour and they'd send somebody along when they got back. Doesn't that frost you?"

"Urrgh!" said Svenson. "Which tree?"

"The one with the rope around it," snapped Viola. "What the hell difference does it make? I never want to see another tree, all I want is to get out of Balaclava County and never come back. I'm resigning as of this minute."

"Can't. Nobody else to run the place. Assign you a security guard. Resign when we get Binks back here."

"And how long is that going to take? You don't know who snatched her, or where they took her, or what they plan to do with her. Look what happened to Knapweed! She and he could both be dead by now."

"Bah. Get me the college. Extension five."

Viola started to protest, swallowed her words, and obeyed. Peter wasn't surprised, he knew what the president was doing. Viola was working herself up to another fit of hysterics, understandably enough. Having a small task to perform would switch her mind back to the commonplace, help her to pull herself together. By the time she'd put the president's call through, she was calm enough to follow Peter's suggestion that she go wash her face and fix her hair, though he privately considered it unfixable.

While Viola was fixing, Svenson was making arrangements for two of the college security guards to come out to the field station, and Peter was wondering what to do next, a Lumpkinton police car finally showed up. Two uniformed officers came in, viewed with interest the bloodstains in the lobby where Knapweed had fallen, asked a few inane questions, took a few useless notes, poked around a bit, regretted the lack of clues, expressed their sympathy to Viola when she came out of the bathroom looking slightly more disheveled than when she'd gone in, had their pictures snapped by Cronkite Swope, and took their leave.

They did promise to put out a bulletin, though they were not sanguine of results since Viola hadn't given them any description of the kidnap car, its driver, or any of the other passengers except Winifred Binks; who was no doubt either lying under the rear seat rolled up in a blanket or else locked in the back of a closed van. They favored the van, or possibly a recreational vehicle of the smaller type.

"The hell of it is, those dolts are right," Peter groaned as the pair drove away exuding an air of duty done. "Confound it, there's got to be something!"

The police had turned up nothing in the parking lot except churned-up gravel and a piece of rope under one of the slim maples where Viola had said it would be. This piece matched the rope that had been used to tie her up during her previous abduction, but that didn't necessarily mean anything. It was ordinary nylon clothesline, the sort that could be bought in any housewares department or filched from somebody's backyard. Peter wondered where the blindfold had gone.

"Oh, I remember now," said Viola, "I carried it back into the station with me. It was my own bandanna, I'd had it twisted around my head and they shoved it down over my eyes. Then when I saw Knapweed all bloody I tried to—he—I think I used it to wipe my hands."

"All right, Miss Buddley, take it easy. Did

you throw the bandanna in the wastebasket?"

"I don't know. Want me to look?"

"No, don't bother. Not to be sexist, but could we persuade you to make some coffee? President Svenson and I never got any supper."

"Oh sure. I don't mind. It's only chicory and dandelion, though. Professor Binks's special mixture."

"That's fine with us."

Peter dropped to his hands and knees and began exploring the indoor-outdoor carpeting that covered the lobby floor. After yesterday's rain, it was filthy with tracked-in mud and gravel, but not the sort of surface to take clear footprints. Cronkite was crawling, too, but neither of them found anything except a few dried leaves of the northern bedstraw over by the table and a cheap disposable pen lying under Professor Binks's desk.

"Winifred must have dropped this when they grabbed her," said Peter. "She'd never have been sloppy enough to leave it here."

"Maybe it belonged to one of the kidnappers," Cronkite suggested.

Thorkjeld Svenson grunted a negative. "Standard issue. College storerooms.

Bought two hundred gross. Special price. Waste not, want not."

"M'yes." Peter had been investigating Winifred's desk drawers. "I don't see any other pen here; ergo, this is more likely than not the one she'd been using. Miss Buddley, you mentioned on the phone that she'd been drafting a letter to Sopwith."

"It's on her desk."

Ordinarily Peter wouldn't have dreamed of reading somebody else's correspondence, but this was no time for niceties. "Gad, she wasn't pulling any punches, This letter could make Sopwith a likely candidate as kidnapper, if it weren't for the fact that he hasn't yet seen it."

"But anybody could have kidnapped Miss Binks just for her money," said Cronkite Swope. "She's so darned rich."

"She's committed a major portion of her inheritance to the station," Peter objected. "That's been well publicized. You ought to know, Swope, you wrote the articles."

"Yeah, but people don't always believe what they read in the papers. Anyway, they may figure she's made a lot more since then."

"Ungh," said Svenson.

Peter caught his meaning. "Granted Winifred has quite likely accrued as much more by now as she'd given away, but how is the criminal underworld to know that?"

The president snorted.

"All right, President, I concede your point. Debenham may be less discreet than he appears. Sopwith is almost certainly either a knave or a fool or both, judging from the way he's mishandling that Lackovites business. Furthermore, I suppose all the Binks Trust dealings get fed into some confounded computer, which means they could be accessible to any electronic pirate who knows how to push the right buttons."

"So?"

"So if this is an ordinary run-of-the-mill kidnapping, we'll surely get a ransom demand fairly soon. Somebody will have to stay here at the station all night, just in case."

"Well, it's not going to be me," Viola burst out. "I'm in no shape to hang around here waiting for somebody to heave a brick through the window with a note tied to it."

Peter had an idea that such melodramatic methods were out of date, though from the way this lot went around lashing buxom wenches to trees, one couldn't be sure. "I expect they'll just telephone," he said mildly, "but we certainly wouldn't expect you to stay, Miss Buddley. Who's coming, President?"

"Bulfinch and Mink." These were two of the Campus Security regulars: capable, intelligent men who could handle anything short of an artillery bombardment without turning a hair. "Any chance of keeping this out of the papers, Swope?"

"Gosh, Dr. Svenson, I don't know. I don't have to call in now, anyway, we won't be going to press till early morning. But what with the ambulance coming out here and hauling Calthrop off with a fractured skull, the story's bound to leak in fifty-seven different directions. I bet that night nurse at Clavaton Hospital's already been on the phone to Aunt Betsy Lomax, and you know what that means."

"Urr."

"Well, I had to tell the ambulance guys what happened," Viola Buddley interrupted. "They were asking me all these questions, as if they thought I was the one who hit him."

"So it seems kind of useless for the *Fane and Pennon* to sit on the story," Cronkite went on, "unless we get a message from the kidnappers saying they'll do something awful to Miss Binks if we talk. They didn't say anything to you about keeping it quiet, did they, Viola?"

"They never said anything at all to me, just grabbed me and blindfolded me and t-tied—"

She was working herself up to another fit of hysterics, it was high time to break up the meeting. "Swope," Peter said, "why don't you take Miss Buddley home?"

"I can drive myself," she protested. "I'm all right, honest. I'll need my car in the morning anyway; either I'll come to work or go home to Mother. I don't know, I suppose I'll show up. Maybe I'll feel braver by then."

"That's the ticket," Peter approved. "Then why don't you drive along behind her, Swope, and make sure she gets home safely? The president and I will stay here till Mink and Bulfinch show up."

"But what about filing my story?"

Peter looked at the president. Svenson heaved a mighty sigh. "How early?"

"Six o'clock?" Cronkite was beginning to sound hopeful.

"We'll let you know."

"What if I walk in the house and my mother already knows?"

That actually fetched a chuckle out of Svenson. "If your mother knows, print."

"Thanks, President! Ready to go, Viola?"

Miss Buddley snatched up a bright green vinyl raincape and slung it across her shoulders. "I've been ready for hours. I just hope it doesn't start to pour the way it did yesterday."

"By George," said Peter, "I hadn't noticed."

In fact, it must have been raining for a while by now. The cars in the lot glistened with moisture and small puddles were beginning to collect where the gravel was most deeply rutted. Viola and Swope both got off after some preliminary chugs and gurgles, their headlights dazzling and their windshield wipers flapping madly. The pole lights in the parking lot had turned themselves on when it got dark but didn't seem to be making much of an impression on the night. Peter began to realize what an isolated place the station was, and also what a less-than-satisfactory supper he'd had. Why hadn't Svenson told Mink and Bulfinch to bring along a few more sandwiches?

It occurred to him that he'd stashed a bar of chocolate in his glove compartment a while back, the giant economy size. There'd be enough for both himself and the president. Enough for him, anyway; the president had eaten the lion's share of the cheese. Peter made up a fresh batch of dandelion-root coffee, set it to perk, and went to fetch the chocolate.

Svenson had plunked himself down in the one chair big enough to hold him and was reading *The Amicus Journal*, his granny glasses halfway down his nose. Peter poured out a couple of mugfuls, took his over to Winifred's desk, and sat down in her chair. The ersatz coffee tasted better this time, either he was a better cook than Viola Buddley or else he was getting used to the stuff. The chocolate hadn't melted or gone stale, it was stuffed with nuts and raisins, just what the doctor ordered for a hungry man expecting a ransom call from an unknown kidnapper.

He was beginning to feel drowsy. How much time lay between him and the conjugal couch? Helen must be home from her meeting by now, covered with glory and wearing a corsage. Chrysanthemums, most likely. She always hoped her hosts wouldn't give her one, but they generally did. It wouldn't hurt to give her a call, but he was reluctant to tie up the line. What if those bastards were trying to get through?

14

By George, they were! Peter jumped a foot when the telephone rang, and grabbed the receiver on his way back down. A strange, raspy, breathy voice came through.

"We have Professor Binks in custody. She will be unharmed as long as you do exactly as we say. And what you do is nothing. Make no move, talk to nobody. Go home and sleep. Further instructions will be telephoned to this same number when we choose to give them."

"But listen." Peter's voice probably sounded as peculiar as the one on the other end of the line. "We may not be able to keep the story out of the newspapers. It's already been leaked."

"We expected that. It doesn't matter. Just wait."

"Wait for what? Why should I believe you? How do we know Miss Binks is alive? Is she there? Let me talk to her."

No answer came, but the phone hadn't gone dead. Peter waited. At last, to his infinite relief, Winifred's voice came over the line.

"Hello, is somebody there?"

"It's Peter, Winifred." Now he knew he sounded peculiar. "Are you all right?"

"Relatively speaking, yes. However, I am instructed to inform you that I shall be summarily dealt with if my captors' instructions are not followed to the letter. As I speak, some person who is built much like my Uncle Horatio—or possibly my Aunt Annie, the sex is indeterminable—is pressing a large firearm against my rib cage."

"My God!"

"Now, Peter, you mustn't be unduly alarmed. I get the impression that I'm worth far more alive than dead. If I find myself being too brutally mishandled, I shall simply make them shoot me and thus defeat their—"

The connection was abruptly broken. Incredibly, Peter was smiling when he put down the receiver. "President, where can we find a tugboat?"

"Huh?"

"I think we have a clue. Do the names Horatio and Annie mean anything to you?"

"Yesus, Shandy, what a woman! Yumping Yiminy, yes. Captain Horatio Bulwinkle and Tugboat Annie Brennan. Binks must mean the Clavaclammer. Southern marshes. New marina, water-treatment center, some damn thing. Tugboats, barges, dredges. Let's go."

"Our orders are to sit tight and do nothing at all."

"Huh!"

"I quite agree, but we've got to be cagey."

"Call Sieglinde first."

Svenson reached for the telephone, but Peter stopped him. "Wait a minute, let's have a look."

Peter was good with his hands. In a matter of moments, with the help of his trusty jack-knife, he had the mouthpiece off. "Ah, here we are. See that little jigger in there?"

"Yeepers creepers, we've been bugged. Take the damn thing out."

"No, I think we ought to leave it in. Go ahead and make your call, but talk in Swedish. Ask Sieglinde to get hold of Helen and tell her the game's afoot."

"Which foot?"

"We'll know in a while, I hope. Tell her that if anybody phones asking for you, she'd better say you're on your way home and ask for a number where you can call back. They'll just hang up. Ask her to pass the word for Helen to do the same. We're going to have to be damned circumspect, President, we don't want Winifred to get hurt."

"Huh!"

"M'yes, I appreciate the force of your argument. She's got them over a barrel, let's hope she can keep them there."

Peter had the telephone back together now. "There you go, President. Give Sieglinde my best regards and be sure she calls Helen."

Peter absented himself from the lobby while Thorkjeld Svenson made his call. He wasn't being scrupulous about not listening in on the conversation, the only Swedish words he knew were *skoal* and *smorgasbord;* he just wanted to look at the weather.

His grandfather's metaphors had tended to be on the earthy side. One was "It's raining pitchforks and dungballs," and that, Peter decided, was pretty damned close to what was happening right now. He wished it weren't.

He wasn't too concerned about his driving, the caffeine in the chocolate had given him a surge of energy. His car was in first-class shape and had been refilled with gas during its latest brief stay at Charlie Ross's. The distance from here to Clavaton wasn't great, the roads were good, barring a possible washout somewhere. He wasn't sure where the dredging was taking place, but he knew how to reach the Clavaclammer Road. Presumably all they had to do was follow the river along until they spied a likely-looking tugboat.

Would the boat be docked where they could climb aboard easily? Or would they have to swim out with daggers between their teeth, pirate-style? Where would they get the daggers? What if it wasn't actually a tugboat? No matter, it must at least look like a tugboat, or Winifred wouldn't have given that clue. Whatever it was would likely be hell to find in pitch-dark and pouring rain, particularly when they'd have to be careful in their movements out of regard for Winifred's sternal cavity. Not to mention their own.

President Svenson was winding up his phone call with a fervent burst of Swedish. Sieglinde must understand the words, the meaning would have been plain enough in any language. What a time for a lonesome husband to have to heed the call of duty!

Mink and Bulfinch ought to be heeding the call any time now, Peter decided it would be an act of kindness to have a potful of coffee waiting. Winifred would have to grind up more dandelion root when she got back; he'd measured out the last scoop from the canister before headlights shone briefly through the lobby windows, a car motor shut off, and two middle-aged but still wiry men dashed in from the rain.

"How's the driving?" Peter asked.

"Could be worse." Purvis Mink wasn't much of a talker.

"Like, for instance, a sleet storm on top of a blizzard. Going to rain all night, we heard the weather forecast on our way here. Seems a high front's met a low front coming through the Rye." Alonzo Bulfinch was chatty enough when he got the chance, which he frequently didn't, since he was boarding with Cronkite Swope's Aunt Betsy.

Peter would have liked to ask Bulfinch whether Mrs. Lomax had filled him in on how Knapweed Calthrop was doing, but there was no sense wasting time on matters he could do nothing about. The sooner he and Svenson got cracking, the likelier they were to succeed. The weather was actually in their favor, Winifred's guards wouldn't be expecting a sneak attack on a night like this.

Or so Peter tried to convice himself as he threaded his way around fallen tree limbs and through puddles the size of millponds. His windshield wipers were doing their utmost, but they couldn't sluice off the water anywhere near as fast as it was pelting against the glass. About halfway to Clavaton, they were stopped by a good-sized elm fallen straight across the road; but not for long. The president got out of the car and tossed the tree aside like a broken blossom. He wasn't even panting when he got back in.

According to the clock on the dashboard, they'd taken an hour and thirty-two minutes to reach the river road. It felt to Peter more like twenty years. As Svenson had predicted, they soon came upon evidence that big things were happening there, though of course no work was being done tonight. Sundry silhouettes of a nautical nature could be seen drawn up to docks that Peter couldn't recall having seen before; perhaps the docks had been built on purpose to accommodate this new flotilla of workboats. Some of the shapes showed riding lights bright enough to be a nuisance to anybody trying to sneak aboard, but probably not adequate for the sneaker to read the boats' names by.

Peter drove on past the docks so they could get some notion of the layout. It wouldn't matter that he'd slowed to a semi-crawl, nobody in his right mind would be driving any faster on a night like this. Once around the bend and out of sight, should anybody be looking, Peter found a place to stash the car on a concrete loading platform behind a low building that sat up from the road on the landward side. This might be some kind of storage warehouse, he surmised, he didn't waste time trying to find out.

"Flashlight?" growled Svenson.

"In the glove compartment," Peter told him. "The batteries and bulb are fresh, maybe we ought to use a dimmer."

Helen had left a silk scarf in the car, it seemed a shame to ruin the pretty thing, but she'd understand. Folded and wrapped over the lens, the thin cloth diffused the beam into a hazy glow giving them light enough to see a short way ahead.

"Won't use it till we have to," Svenson growled low in his throat. "Come on."

The two men picked their way across the road and around the docks, sliding on mud and splashing through puddles they couldn't avoid. Rain beat into their eyes, ran down their faces, inside their collars. Their situation was so awful that Peter began to find it funny; he had all he could do to keep from chuckling aloud.

Once down on the docks, they realized how high the boats were riding, and why.

The Clavaclammer, normally a sedate river content to flow gently among its green braes, was giving a fairly convincing portrayal of a raging torrent, already splashing right up against the edges of the docks. "By George," Peter muttered, "I've never seen it like this before."

He himself had always related more to Mole than to Ratty. A creature of the fields and hedgerows, Peter didn't know what to make of so much water all at once. He just wished to God the dratted boats would quit bobbing around long enough to be identified.

Some of them, the open scows and floating dredges, could be eliminated out of hand. There appeared to be no place aboard where a middle-aged woman could be hidden without the risk of drowning or pneumonia. One dock was evidently reserved for pleasure boats, sleek damsels of the deep with tarpaulins over their cockpits and curtains at their cabin windows. Any of these would no doubt offer a viable hiding place, but how would they relate to Winifred's dropped clue about the tugboat? Peter and Thorkjeld wasted a little time reading names, which told them nothing, and passed on.

Then they came upon three tubby workboats festooned along the gunwales with worn-out rubber tires. Svenson gave Peter's shoulder a squeeze that would have laid out a lesser man for weeks. "Which?" he breathed.

Peter pulled his sopping tweed hat farther down over his eyes to keep the rain out and looked the three over. Two were cluttered with all that stuff tugboats appear to accumulate; their cabin windows showed bare, black, and shiny in the rain. The middle one was relatively uncluttered, its paint was fresher, its windows had curtains pulled tight across them. Not a chink of light was showing, but Peter had a hunch that light was there. Feeling like Carruthers sneaking up on the treasure hunters' lair in Memmert, he doused the flashlight, sat down on a soaking-wet bollard, took off his boots, and hung them by their laces around his neck. Divining what he was up to, Svenson followed suit.

The sides of the tugboat were a good height above the dock, but getting aboard was no problem. Peter merely stood up on Thorkjeld's shoulders and walked across. Once aboard, he found a rope ladder lying ready, flipped it over the gunwale, and Svenson climbed up much in the manner of King Kong ascending the Empire State Building.

With catlike tread, upon their putative prey they stole. There was, of course, the chance that nobody else was aboard. There was a better chance that they might come upon some authentic crew member enjoying a peaceful evening with his book, his pipe, his dog, or his doxy; that was a risk that had to be taken. Peter tried the cabin door and found it locked. He stepped aside with an over-to-you gesture. Thorkjeld put his shoulder to the lock, and shoved. They were in.

"Why, Peter and Dr. Svenson," exclaimed Winifred Binks. "How good of you to come."

For the moment, the two were too preoccupied to respond. Even as they entered, a hulking fellow of uncouth appearance had been reaching for his M-1 rifle. In a matter of seconds, Peter had the gun and Dr. Svenson had wrestled the guard to a fall. Unfortunately, the pair continued to thrash around the tiny cabin's floor while Svenson was in the act of removing the fellow's belt and trussing him up with it, thus preventing Peter from reaching the door to the inner cabin. He very much wanted to do this, as instinct told him no sensible kidnapper would have left Winifred Binks here with only a muscle-bound oaf to guard her.

Instinct was right on the button. Peter was still trying to thread his way among the thrashing legs and writhing bicepses when a figure appeared at the inner door.

"By George!" he ejaculated.

Here stood Tugboat Annie in the flesh: a dumpy figure bundled into rubber boots, a heavy dark-green cardigan full of pulls and snags, and a much-bedraggled black skirt. Her face was red and weather-beaten, her wispy gray hair straggled out from under a man's old felt hat, the type that Peter's father used to wear.

"What the hell do you guys think you're doing?"

Her voice was somewhere between a squeak and a squeal. That did it for Peter. He raised the rifle to his shoulder and squinted amiably along the barrel.

"We just dropped in for a visit," he replied. "It's the custom around these parts. I don't believe you've met President Svenson of the college? President, this is that chap Fanshaw I was telling you about. Nice to see you again, Mr. Fanshaw, we wondered where you'd gone to after your ingenious jailbreak. Congratulations on your Tugboat-Annie getup, but I'm afraid you flubbed the voice."

"Oh?" Fanshaw was trying to fix Peter with a glittering eye. "Perhaps you wouldn't mind telling me what I've done wrong?"

"Quite a number of things, since you ask. To begin with, Annie was more a basso than a soprano. Secondly, it's not considered the done thing to hypnotize police officers while they're in pursuit of their duty. Thirdly, kidnapping heiresses is frowned upon in the best of circles. And fourthly, you've set yourself up for a murder rap."

"I've what?" There was a noticeable pause. "You don't know what you're talking about."

"Ah, but I do. I'm talking about the young botanist out at the field station whose name is Knapweed Calthrop and whose skull you fractured while you were in the process of abducting Professor Binks."

Peter could have sworn this was news to Fanshaw. He wasn't really surprised; Fanshaw had impressed him as being a conniver, not a hit man. God knew how many accomplices he had, or who was the ringleader. This hulk whom Svenson had just laid low was a more likely type to have slugged Calthrop and to have roughed up the luscious Viola. Fanshaw himself couldn't have been involved in yesterday's tree-tying episode, he'd been in the Balaclava Junction hoosegow at the time, hypnotizing Ottermole and Dorkin. That alleged lawyer who'd shown up at the station, no doubt with the real purpose of providing Fanshaw with a getaway car, could have been in on Viola's abduction, though. Or could he? Peter was cogitating when Svenson became restive.

"Shandy! Move."

"Er—yes, President, by all means. Winifred, I'm afraid we didn't think to bring you a raincoat. Perhaps you'd care to hold this rifle on Mr. Fanshaw while I see if I can persuade the Clavaton police to come out and make a pickup. Shoot him if he tries to reach for his hypnotizing apparatus. How does one work this telephone, I wonder?"

"The instructions are right there on the wall," said Winifred. "I noticed them while I was talking to you earlier at Mr. Fanshaw's behest."

"Ah yes, I see. Quite simple, really, if I could just get at the confounded thing. President, I'm sure you won't mind taking that other chap out on the dock so we'll have room enough to move in here? It'll save the police the bother of unloading him."

"Probably get the longshoremen's union on my back, but what the hell?"

Glad of a little more action, Thorkjeld Svenson dragged the recumbent knave to his feet and frog-marched him out of the cabin while Peter plumbed the mystery of ship-to-shore telephoning.

They were in luck; a Clavaton police boat was patrolling the river nearby on flood watch. Minutes later, it tied up alongside the tugboat.

The officer in charge was quite willing to take Fanshaw and his accomplice aboard, but reluctant to hang around for statements. Things were getting fairly brisk out on the river; they were worried about the Upper Clavaton Dam, which had been built during the administration of Ulysses S. Grant and was beginning to show its age.

Peter said that was quite all right, he and President Svenson were anxious to get Professor Binks home as soon as possible. They'd stop by the Clavaton police station in the morning, assuming they could get there, and give a full report. Svenson helped one of the officers to get the as yet unnamed accomplice aboard the police boat while two others attended to Fanshaw, who was still wearing his Tugboat Annie getup, supplemented by shiny new handcuffs.

Fanshaw didn't go peaceably. Peter and Winifred heard a scuffle on the dock, but it didn't last more than a moment. Svenson ducked back into the cabin looking pleased with himself. The police boat revved its engines and took off up the river. The tugboat rolled and pitched in the swell from its wake, the wind howled louder, the rain lashed even harder. It was high time they got out of there.

15

"That wretched, wretched man!"

Staring out at the fast-widening gap between the tugboat and the dock, Peter thought Winifred could have pitched her evaluation of Fanshaw in somewhat less decorous language. "That scuffle on the dock we heard just now must have been Fanshaw kicking the mooring loose from the bollards."

"But why?" Winifred demanded.

"Pure spite, I suppose. I can't see what he thinks he's gained by setting us adrift.

I'm just wondering why the river police didn't notice what he was up to."

"Black as the inside of a witch's pocket out there," Svenson grunted. "Rain hitting their eyeballs like flying rivets. Who gives a damn why Fanshaw did it? Got to get this craft under control or we'll be swamped. Back inside, Binks. Batten the hatches. Pilot house, Shandy."

Peter gathered that the president was talking about the small glass-enclosed structure perched on top of the cabin. He fought his way up the few steps that led to it, Svenson at his heels, and was using his flashlight to inspect the instrument panel when Svenson reached over and flipped a light switch.

"Batteries, Shandy."

"Oh, thanks, President. I should have thought of that myself."

"Yes. Know how to start this thing?"

"No, but I've started enough farm machinery in my day, it can't be all that difficult. What if we pull this? And turn that? By George, she's started. Now what?"

"Now get out of my way. This is a job for a Swede."

Peter gulped in ill-concealed terror as Svenson grabbed the wheel. The president was a menace on the highway, what would he be like in this raging maelstrom?

He was magnificent. The tugboat still bucked and pitched, but Svenson had put a stop to those sickening side-to-side rolls. He was neatly avoiding the increasing number of floating objects that were cluttering the river. The only thing he wasn't doing was the one thing Peter most urgently wanted.

"Er—President, shouldn't we head back to the dock?"

"Can't. Current's too strong. Get swamped. Head inshore, get wrecked. Stay in the middle, keep going, find a safe place to pull over."

"I see. Any idea how long that might take?"

"No. Quit bugging the captain. Food."

Peter himself was not eager for food at the moment; quite the reverse, in fact. However, he didn't argue but let himself out of the pilot house and fought his way below to the cabin. Winifred opened the door for him.

"Is there a galley aboard this floating bathtub?" he asked somewhat reluctantly after he'd mopped his face and shed his sopping mackinaw.

"Yes, in there." She indicated the cabin, which Peter still hadn't gone into. "I filled a kettle, but I was afraid to light the stove. Can you figure out how it works?"

The forward cabin was tiny but well arranged. This was really more a yacht than a working tugboat, Peter decided. There was a narrow table down the center with benches on the sides that could double as bunks. There was a work area with a small sink and running water, the stove that had intimidated Winifred, and cupboards containing dishes, tableware, and a few cooking utensils, along with tins of soup, luncheon meats, and other quick-fix edibles.

"At least we shan't starve," he remarked. "Is there any bread?"

"No, but there's almost a full tin of pilot biscuits," Winifred told him. "I can't find any vegetables or fruit, though, not even a jar of jelly. Do you suppose tomato soup has any value as an antiscorbutic?"

"Open a can and we'll give it a shot."

Peter gave the galley stove a once-over, decided it must work much like the portable camp stoves with which he had a fairly extensive acquaintance, and tried a match he'd fished out of another closed tin. It worked like a charm.

"There you are, Winifred, hand me your kettle. I trust this is bottled water coming out of that faucet, but I suppose we needn't worry so long as it's boiled. Er—I ought to mention that the president isn't sure how soon he'll be able to set us ashore. The high winds and strong current are creating—er—navigational problems. He seems to know what he's doing."

"Oh, I'm sure he must." Winifred was still exploring the cupboards. "The Viking blood, you know. Would you fancy some of this liver pâté with your soup? It doesn't seem to be quite so loaded with chemicals as the pressed ham. We could make sandwiches with pilot biscuits."

"Sounds good to me. What's to drink?"

"There's a bottle of whiskey and scads of beer. Ah, tea bags. I'll have tea. And a fresh-opened jar of instant coffee but no milk. They're well supplied with the nonessentials."

Nonessentials were a matter of opinion; Peter mixed himself a medicinal tot while Winifred operated on the soup tin. "We ought to take something up to the president, don't you think?" she remarked.

"Definitely," Peter agreed. "Soup, sandwiches, and coffee. We'd better skip the whiskey, it might be too heating for the Viking blood."

"Yes, I expect it might. Could I trouble you for that saucepan?"

"My pleasure." It was amazing how quickly he'd overcome that temporary repugnance toward food, Peter decided his stomach must be getting its sea legs. He hoped it wouldn't be needing them much longer, though, he was getting pretty fed up with this pounding and pitching.

He wished he'd tried to get Helen on the phone back at the station even if the dratted thing was bugged; at least she must have heard from Sieglinde long before this. He could try her now, he supposed, but what was the use? In the unlikely event that he managed to get through, what would he tell her? That he was bucketing down a maddened river in a tarted-up tugboat with Thorkjeld Svenson at the helm?

Not that the Viking wasn't doing an acceptable job; they were still afloat and hadn't hit anything that mattered. Not yet, anyway. Peter opened the pâté while Winifred stirred the soup and set about assembling some sandwiches.

"Is there any mustard, Winifred?" Maybe mustard was an antiscorbutic.

"Yes, I believe so." She handed over a half-empty jar crusted around the lid. "It doesn't look very appetizing. But then neither does the pâté."

"Beggars can't be choosers." Peter broke off an edge of pilot biscuit and ran a taste check. "Not too bad. Better than a boiled boot, anyway."

"Goodness, I hope we shan't get down to that. Actually, we could be in far worse straits than we are now," Winifred reminded him.

Peter hoped they wouldn't get to them. The soup was hot now, the kettle was boiling. He improvised a tray from a flattish tin, found a couple of mugs, filled one with soup and the other with strong black coffee, added a few of the biscuit sandwiches, and covered the lot with a plastic garbage bag. A clean one, fortunately.

"I'll take this up to the president. Go ahead and eat," he said.

The wind was no gentler nor the rain less wet, but Peter made it to the pilot house without spillage or dilution. Svenson was either glad to see him or, more likely, glad to see the provender. He finished the chorus of "Blow the Man Down" he'd been shaking the windows with—tugboat glass must be sturdy stuff, Peter decided—reached for the soup mug, and drained it in one mighty draft, Viking-style. Peter set down the tray on the chart table and turned to leave; by now the growls in his own stomach were almost overcoming the noise of the storm.

"What's your hurry, Shandy?" Svenson demanded through a mouthful of biscuit.

"I'm starving to death. I haven't eaten yet."

"Urgh." Svenson thrust the empty soup mug at him. "More. If there is any," he was considerate enough to add.

"There's more, but you'll have to wait till I heat it. We do have a galley and a fair supply of canned stuff. And, God knows, no lack of water."

Peter was able to rinse out the president's mug on the way back to the cabin by the simple expedient of holding it out to the rain. He found Winifred sitting up to the galley table like a proper lady, finishing her soup. She'd set a place for him and rigged a low rail to keep the utensils from slipping off.

"Well, Peter, how is our dauntless captain?"

"Still undaunted and in good voice, relatively speaking; he's having a whale of a time. He wants more soup, but I'm going to eat mine first. Gad, this tastes good!"

"Quite surprisingly good," Winifred

agreed. "Aunt always did say hunger was the best sauce. I've been trying to remember when I ate last, this has been such a long day. After we've done the dishes, I believe I'd like to lie down for a while. Those benches out in the main cabin, or saloon, as I believe it's called, convert into bunks. Or you could go first if you'd like. I expect one of us should stay alert, but we can sleep in rotation."

"Gyration will be more like it."

The boat was doing strange things again: jerking, wobbling, rushing forward as though it were being pushed by some giant hand. Had the president got carried away and opened the engine to full throttle? No, Svenson wouldn't be fool enough to try a stunt like that at a time like this. Peter downed the rest of his soup before it slopped out of the mug.

"Not to be an alarmist, Winifred"—he had to shout, the noise around them had risen to total pandemonium—"but I have the feeling that the Upper Clavaton Dam has just let go."

"I shouldn't be at all surprised."

Somehow or other, Miss Binks was managing to keep from spilling her tea, taking a genteel sip whenever it was possible to get the mug within range of her mouth without whacking her nose. "The force of the current is quite remarkable, it feels like riding the rapids in a canoe. Or so I fancy; I've never even been in a canoe, but it's something I've always wanted to try. Do you suppose President Svenson would appreciate our help in steering the boat?"

The teakettle hurtled through the air; Peter fielded it neatly. "No, he'd get sore if we offered. I expect he'd like that soup, but I'm scared to light the stove again. It might fetch loose and set fire to the boat."

"Then we'll just have to wait till things settle down. I expect this current will slacken once the initial impetus of the suddenly released water is spent, don't you think?"

"I should damned well hope so. Undamned, I should have said. Sorry, Winifred."

"Now, Peter, this is no time to go Victorian on me. The fact that I was held captive for a few hours shouldn't disqualify me from counting myself an emancipated woman, should it? You know, I can't help wondering why I was kidnapped."

"I should say that was obvious enough."

"To get hold of Grandfather's money? Well, of course, but that's my whole point.

Why did the kidnappers wait until after I'd committed so much of the inheritance to establishing the college field station? Wouldn't it have made more sense to snatch me away as soon as I'd managed to prove myself the only true heiress? Goodness knows there was enough hoopla in the papers at that time," Winifred added bitterly.

"True enough," said Peter. "And there was plenty more when you announced your plans for the college, as well there should have been."

Many readers had inferred from the media reports that she'd turned over her entire fortune to Balaclava. In a sense, that was actually true. As far as Peter knew, the college was her sole legatee.

"The figures made so blatantly public when the news came out were based on those which had been published back when Grandfather got into the headlines with that last crazy experiment of his." Winifred shrugged. "Considering what the estimates for building the station came to, it did look then as if I'd wind up with nothing left for myself, not that I cared. It wasn't until Mr. Debenham and the others began digging into what had been happening with all those supposedly worthless investments Grandfather had made that we began to realize how much there really is. But by that time I wasn't news any longer, thank goodness, and we've been able to keep the facts confidential, as they should be. So if Mr. Fanshaw and whoever's been working with him were planning to extort some gigantic ransom, what made them think I'd be able to pay?"

"Because Fanshaw and his pals know a great deal more about your personal affairs than they have any right to."

"But how did they find out?"

"M'yes, I was wondering about that a while back."

"Well, I've been racking my brain ever since those hooligans put that sack over my head and shoved me into their car. I just boil every time I think of the way they mauled me about."

Winifred boiled in silence for a few seconds, then went on. "I'm assuming Fanshaw is in fact the ringleader, though I don't for one moment believe that's his right name. Do you?"

"I'm not sure I even believe Fanshaw's a real person. He's too blasted much like a character out of John Buchan."

"Ah yes, the one who came to such a well-deserved end in *Mr. Standfast*. Aunt approved of John Buchan's novels because he always took so high a moral tone. I must confess I liked them for the adventure. Life with Aunt was pleasant enough, but it didn't offer much in the way of cut and thrust. Except sometimes at her tea parties. Anyway, Fanshaw must be safely behind bars by now."

"Keep your fingers crossed. That fracas on the dock has me stumped. I can't for the life of me figure out how he'd have been able to cast off those heavy hawsers from the bollards unless he'd had free use of his hands."

"Then you think he managed to get out of the handcuffs?"

"Houdini used to do it. You bunch up your muscles while they're snapping on the gyves, I believe, then you go limp and Bob's your uncle. Or else you have a friend on the force."

"Now, there is a possibility I hadn't considered. I was brought up to look upon our public protectors as pillars of rectitude, as I'm sure most of them still are. Some more than others, no doubt, human nature being what it is. I must say it seems to me one would need an extremely far-reaching organization in order to have a member of the river patrol bribed to function as liberator in case of an unexpected arrest at night under extremely adverse conditions. Though the adverse conditions could be exploited in one's favor if one were the sort who could think and act quickly. Fanshaw certainly must be that, judging from the way he managed to escape from the lockup by hypnotizing two policemen while—" Winifred turned pink and shut up.

"While I was playing tiddlywinks in the next room," Peter finished for her. "That's all right, Winifred, my shoulders are broad enough to carry the burden of a lame brain."

"Don't cut yourself down, Peter. Aunt always maintained excessive humility was a form of reverse braggadocio. How could you have anticipated so bizarre a trick? If you hadn't spotted Fanshaw so quickly under that Tugboat Annie disguise, something really disastrous might have happened. I certainly didn't, and I was right here with him for longer than I care to think about. Gracious, what would Aunt have thought of my being in the clutches of a master criminal? Not much, I'm afraid. Aunt deplored anything that smacked of the sensational."

In the most prosaic way possible, Winifred got up from the table and went to the sink, carrying the few dishes they'd been using.

She ran water into the tiny sink and began rinsing them off.

"I'm being chary of the water because we don't know how much there is," she explained. "Do you think we should set out a bucket for rainwater?"

"I doubt if we'd manage to keep it upright long enough to gather any, the way the wind's blowing out there," Peter replied gloomily, "which brings up another happy thought. I wonder how much gas is left for the engine."

"Let's not even think about that. Here, you dry."

Winifred handed him some paper towels from a roll over the sink. Peter began swabbing off plates and cups, setting them back in the cupboard they'd come from. There were guardrails along the shelves; even so it took some doing to keep them from flying back out. Nevertheless, the homely task was comforting. For the moment, he could imagine himself back on the Crescent with Helen at the sink and Jane climbing up his pant leg.

They were most likely both asleep by now, little dreaming that he was somewhere on the Clavaclammer, or maybe the Connecticut, with no prospect of getting ashore till fate and Svenson decided the auguries were auspicious. Peter hoped Helen had got back from Clavaton without running into any trouble. At least she'd understand his predicament if he ever got the chance to tell her; it wasn't so long ago that she herself had gone for an innocent boat ride and wound up in a desperate situation. From now on, by gad, the Shandys were staying ashore.

He put away the last of the dishes and tossed his paper towel into a wastebasket attached to one of the bottom cupboard doors. They were riding a trifle less frenetically by now. That appalling first gush of the floodwaters must have spent itself, thank God.

"I wonder if it's safe to light the stove now? The president must be wondering why I haven't shown up with his soup."

"I'll take it this time," said Winifred. "It's my turn."

"No doubt," Peter conceded, "but I'm heavier than you, hence less likely to get blown overboard. After you've had your rest, you might be better occupied in searching the cabin for any clue as to who Fanshaw really is and who may be working with him. Getting off this confounded tugboat isn't necessarily going to mean we're out of the woods."

16

"I know," said Winifred, "you don't have to remind me. These soups seem to be all tomato."

"May we never have a worse misfortune," Peter replied. "Hand one over, I'll cope."

Better he than she to be battling a lighted stove and a runaway saucepan, although he hoped it wouldn't come to that. Peter made doubly sure the bolts that held the stove to the counter were well tightened, and decided to heat the soup in the percolator, which they wouldn't be using for coffee since they had nothing but instant and not much left of that.

Seeing that he really wasn't going to let her help, Winifred went into the saloon. The bunks had built-in lockers underneath; instead of lying down, as Peter had assumed she would, she'd opened one of them and dragged out a suitcase that had been stowed inside. Peter picked his way around her, carrying an empty mug and his percolator full of hot tomato soup.

As he stepped on deck, he could dimly make out that the river was a good deal wider now than it had been when they'd started out. He found this circumstance unnerving. Had they drifted on out into the Connecticut, or might they in fact be sailing down the main street of some flooded-out town? Peter had a disconcerting mental picture of the tugboat crashing through the plate-glass window of the local feed and grain store and landing in the cracked-wheat bin. He wished to God it were light enough for him to see the banks, if there were any, and get some sort of handle on where they were. On the other hand, perhaps he was happier not knowing.

The wind must have abated a trifle, the rain wasn't pelting against his face quite so brutally as before. The percolator had been an inspiration, he made it to the pilot house without spilling a drop.

Svenson greeted him with a snarl. "Took you long enough. Take the helm while I stretch my arms. Hold her as she goes. Yesus, Shandy, this is some river! Twists and turns, cross currents, floating yunk."

"I can imagine. Am I right in thinking the Upper Clavaton Dam went out a while back?"

"Felt like it to me. Big swoosh, hell of a current. Quieter now."

Peter was nonplussed by the president's

definition of quieter. His own ears were ringing from the noise. The wheel was shivering under his hands like a nervous plow horse in blackfly season. He felt pretty twitchy himself. These were not ideal circumstances in which to make his debut as a helmsman, though with Svenson at his elbow gargling soup, he didn't actually have to do much except hang on tight and keep a sharp eye out for floating debris. There was plenty around, some of it small enough to be pushed aside harmlessly by the sturdy tugboat, some of it dauntingly impressive. Like that blackish mass looming up on their starboard bow, for instance.

"Great Scott!" he exclaimed. "President, isn't that the roof of a house over there?"

"Chicken coop, maybe."

"I don't hear any hens squawking."

"How could you?"

That was a reasonable question. One of the many things Peter hadn't known about boating was how infernally noisy it could be. What with the engine's chugging, the wind's roaring, the rain's drumming, the insistent pounding of the waves, and the thuds from assorted flotsam hitting against the hull, he and Dr. Svenson both had to yell even to make the other hear inside this small pilot house.

Down in the cabin, where he'd been lower in the water, away from the wind, with the solid cabin walls around him, Peter hadn't been so fully aware of the racket. This high, glassed-in perch was getting the main force of the elements; he wished it weren't. He scanned the confusing array of gauges on the control panel, thinking he might as well learn what he could.

"How are we doing for fuel, President?"

"God knows. Gauge stuck. Have to keep up with the speed of the current or she wouldn't answer the helm. Means we wouldn't be able to steer, couldn't handle emergencies."

"Er—have there been any?" Jokery was the farthest thing from Peter's mind just now, he couldn't fathom why the president laughed.

"All the time. One right now. Yesus, Shandy, look out!"

Svenson grabbed the wheel with his left hand, gave it a quarter-turn, then quickly set the tugboat back on course. Peter hadn't the remotest idea what the flurry had been about, he wished he were back in the turnip fields. At least turnips weren't given to bobbing around.

They were abreast of the floating house now. It was in fact a house, Peter could see curtains flapping out through broken windows, being cut to rags by the jagged glass and the raging wind. A hex sign had been nailed up under the peak of the roof, which just went to show how much faith could be put in hex signs.

The scene made him think of Huckleberry Finn's pap, floating down the Mississippi sprawled on the dirty floor of another flood-borne house, with the empty whiskey bottles and the greasy playing cards strewn around him and the bullet hole showing in his naked back. Peter felt a wholly insane urge to pull alongside, crawl through one of the broken windows, and have a look around. He was relieved when they'd put the house behind them and he didn't have to keep wondering who or what might be trapped inside.

"Plenty of poor souls will be homeless by morning, I expect." He had to say something to work the misery out of his system. "You read about people being flooded out of their homes, watch them on the news trying to salvage what bits and pieces might be left, but to find yourself out in the midst—"

"Shut up, Shandy," barked Svenson. "What's Binks doing?"

"Rifling Fanshaw's luggage, looking for clues."

"Good. Go help."

Not at all hurt by being thus rudely dismissed from his post as steersman, Peter took the empty mug and coffeepot and went below. Winifred was pleased to see him.

"President Svenson must be exhausted. How is he doing up there?"

"Still the firm hand on the helm. I spelled him long enough to let him stretch his muscles and drink his soup, but he didn't think much of my performance."

"I'm sure you were admirable, whereas if we'd let Dr. Svenson into the galley he'd have spilled the soup and blown up the stove," Winifred replied loyally and no doubt accurately. "I've been busy, too. As you suspected, Mr. Fanshaw is a man of many parts."

"What did you find?"

"A fascinating collection of passports, stuck up inside the locker with masking tape. He must have had a glorious time posing for photographs, I particularly like this one of him as a geisha girl. Note that he calls himself Sayonara Atakuku and claims Japanese citizenship. I wonder how he manages to keep track of which identity he's using at any given moment."

"Fanshaw must have a mighty competent forger on his payroll," Peter grunted as he leafed through the spurious documents. "Or else he fakes them up himself, which wouldn't surprise me any. He may also do a little business peddling passports to other crooks; some of these look as if they've never been used."

"You don't suppose he just does them as a hobby?"

"I'm ready to suppose anything of that bird. This is a real find, Winifred. Have you turned up anything else?"

"A few mustaches and a pair of elevator shoes. Oh, and the boat's name is the *Lollipop*."

Peter snickered. "The good ship *Lollipop*, eh? That ought to tickle the president. In whose name is she registered?"

"You're going to love this. Commodore George Dewey, with a beard to match."

Peter thumbed through the passports. "Ah yes, here he is. Not a bad likeness from what I recall of the original, which isn't much except for 'Damn the torpedos, full speed ahead.' I like the yachting cap and blazer; did you find those?"

"No, but I found a slinky green satin negligee with lace trimmings. You don't suppose Fanshaw's really a woman?"

"By George, that's a possibility. You didn't happen to notice whether he was looking suspiciously unkempt about the jowls last evening?"

"Peter, what an odd question! Oh, you mean that if he was a man, his whiskers might have started to grow in by then. Yours are quite apparent by now, I see. No, I can't remember but it doesn't really signify, does it? Some men are less inclined to hirsuteness than others, whereas some women are quite hairy. Aunt had rather a dapper little mustache in her later years. Anyway, Fanshaw would have shaved when he put on his Tugboat Annie getup, don't you think? I didn't find a passport for Annie Brennan, by the way, though I don't suppose she'd be one of his going-abroad personae. And I certainly can't envision his taking *Lollipop* all the way to Seattle. Can you?"

"No, but the president might. We may have to mutiny unless his Viking blood simmers down or the gas runs out. Do you suppose daylight will ever come?"

"It always has so far," said Winifred. "What I'm wondering is whether this rain will ever stop."

"It seemed to be tapering off a little when I last went out," Peter was happy to reply. "I have a vague recollection of Bulfinch telling us at the station that the storm's supposed to blow out to sea sometime tomorrow. Come to think of it, this is tomorrow. Or ought to be. You don't happen to have a watch on you? I forgot to wear mine."

"I could tell the time by the stars if there were any. As a guess I'd say it must be somewhere around half-past two or three o'clock. And I never did get that nap, did I? Perhaps I'll try for forty winks now, if you don't mind."

"By all means do. Are there any blankets?" Peter hadn't dared to leave the galley stove running any longer than it had taken to boil the kettle and heat the soup; by now the chill had crept back into the cabin.

"Yes, we have blankets, though goodness knows when they were last washed. No matter, I've slept on worse in my camping-out days."

Winifred lay down on the bunk from under which she'd taken Fanshaw's many forged passports, covered herself with one of the blankets, and shut her eyes. Seconds later she was breathing steadily, peacefully, and deeply; and smiling in her sleep. Peter gave her a thoughtful look, picked up another of the tobacco-reeking blankets, and stretched out on the bunk opposite.

When next he opened his eyes, the wind was down from a roar to a whine. He pulled aside the cabin curtain; the rain had all but stopped and the sky showed medium gray instead of muddy black. He leapt out the door and up to the pilot house.

"President, are you—"

"Coffee?"

"Er—soon. How's she heading?"

"Urrgh!"

"Aye, aye, sir. Back in a trice."

Peter hied himself below, filled the kettle, and lit the galley stove. He opened a can of something or other—corned beef or a reasonable facsimile, he guessed—and sandwiched hunks of it between pilot biscuits. As soon as the water began to steam, he filled two mugs with instant coffee, extra strong, and returned to the pilot house bearing breakfast, such as it was.

"Can we talk now, President?"

"No."

Svenson attacked the meat and biscuits like a hunger-maddened malamute. Peter sipped gingerly at his coffee and decided he'd better snaffle a morsel or two for himself while there was still any food to be had.

There was no place for him to sit; he stood and looked out through the rain-streaked glass. Grayness was all he could see: gray water, gray sky, Svenson's gray flannel shirt, his iron-gray hair plastered to his forehead by dampness and sweat or some of each, gray whiskers sprouting from cheeks, and chin gray with exhaustion.

"God, President," he exclaimed, "you look like the ghost of banished hope. Want me to take the wheel while you go below and stretch out for a while?"

"Coffee."

"Here, finish mine. I'll go make some more." He swapped his mug for the one Svenson had emptied and yet once more descended the narrow ladder to the cabin. He should have brewed a potful in the first place. Fortunately he'd decided the boat had quieted down enough now so that he'd dared to leave another kettle heating on the stove in case Winifred should wake up and want her tea.

He found her serenely pounding her ear. Being kidnapped must have been a fairly exhausting experience for Winifred, now that he had leisure to reflect on the matter. He'd better let her sleep as long as she could. Svenson wouldn't be able to go on much longer without a rest, either, from the look of him. Furthermore, they were almost out of pilot biscuits and Peter didn't even want to think about what might be happening inside the gas tank.

They'd have to risk landing soon, that was all there was to it. His own brief experience at the helm, however, had convinced Peter that he was not the man to land them. Somehow he had to keep the president functioning until they could locate a safe place to dock. Even an only somewhat safe place would do; he'd settle for getting firmly stuck in a nice, squishy mud bank. Anything but this eternal water, water everywhere. He opened another can of meat, chopped it into three parts, balanced each segment on half a biscuit. He rinsed last night's soup out of the percolator, filled the pot with boiling water, dumped in what was left of the powdered instant coffee, and went topside.

"Best I can do," he said when Svenson

cocked an eyebrow at the half-biscuits. "As of now, we're on short rations. Do you suppose there's any hope of our getting ashore in the near future?"

Svenson had his mouth full of meat; he made some kind of noise and waved his coffee mug. Peter stood watching him chew.

"Damned if I don't think you're enjoying this, President."

The big man gulped and shrugged. "Why not? Have to do it anyway. Look over the side. See what's out there."

"I know what's out there, more dratted water. What the flaming perdition do you expect me to see?"

"Sea serpents, mermaids, telephone poles, street signs, how do I know? Shandy, I don't know where we are. I don't know how fast we've been moving, I'm not even sure in what direction. We could be on the Clavaclammer or the Amazon or in some farmer's back pasture. Find me a landing. Find me a lamppost. Find me any goddamn thing we can tie up to. And find it fast. Engine's started to cough. We're running out of gas."

17

Peter stared as he had never stared before, straining his eyes toward where he hoped the riverbank might be. The river was still foaming with crosscurrents, the rain had picked up again. How Svenson had managed to get them this far without bumping into anything catastrophic was a feat only a titan or a sorcerer could have accomplished; fortunately Thorkjeld Svenson was both. Now if he could pull off one more miracle—was that a building over to the right? Peter waved his own right arm frantically.

"That way, I hope."

Shut up in the pilot house, Svenson wouldn't hear him yell. God willing, he'd be able to see the signal and make the boat obey.

The president had seen, *Lollipop*'s bow was turning. Peter kept on pointing. Now he could make out a shoreline, and movement. People, by George! Definitely people carrying sandbags, adding height to a dike they'd built along the bank. Now, was there any place to land safely? Yes, that was surely a dock; boats were bobbing in the water, tethered to some kind of wharf or pier that was now under water but still holding.

They were gliding in toward the boats, less noisily now; Svenson had either cut the engines or was riding on the fumes. Peter moved over to the thick rope that the perfidious Fanshaw had cast loose so many eons ago, picked up the end that had the loop in it, and got ready to throw it over anything that looked to be even halfway stationary.

Now those on shore had spied the *Lollipop*. They were waving, those who weren't too encumbered with sandbags. Peter waved back desperately enough, he prayed, to make them understand the boat was in trouble. They were pointing down at something. A pillar or stanchion of some kind; he pointed to it, too. Svenson understood, he was bringing them in slick as a weasel. What a man! Peter balanced himself as best he could, summoned up every scintilla of skill he'd acquired in a lifetime of horseshoe pitching, and threw a perfect ringer.

Somebody behind the sandbags was cheering, or maybe Peter himself was making the racket; he was too benumbed with relief to know or care. The pilot-house door opened, Svenson came out. The yelling turned to an awed hush as the great man's feet sought the narrow ladder. He'd put his red cap with the white bobble back on; all the president needed were a double-bitted ax and a great blue ox to pass for Paul Bunyan, Peter thought proudly.

Svenson paused, he was scanning the sandbag dike with mild amusement. Peter could see why. Those above had built well and truly, there was no gap through which stranded mariners could climb up. He didn't care, they'd manage one way or another. For now it was enough to be at least comparatively stationary.

One of the spectators yelled something Peter didn't catch. Svenson evidently did, he cupped his hands to his mouth and roared.

"Out of gas. Been traveling all night. Going below to get some sleep."

He ducked through the cabin door. Peter stayed on deck and took over the bellowing. "Where are we? Still on the Clavaclammer?"

"Yes! Just barely!"

There was more yelling but Peter couldn't make it out. He was feeling wobbly in the knees, it must be from lugging all that coffee. He waved to the sandbaggers and staggered into the cabin.

Svenson would never have fitted on one of those narrow bunks. He'd wrapped himself in a couple of blankets and stretched himself out on the floor to sleep the sleep of the just, as he well deserved to do. Peter kicked off the wet boots he'd been wearing, tiptoed around the slumbering giant, and got back into the bunk he'd so recently left. Winifred was still asleep also, he might as well just lie here a little while and rest his weary bones.

Then, somehow, bright sunlight was streaming into the cabin. Winifred, washed and brushed and neat as a pin, stood just outside the door, surveying the flood scene and drinking tea. Svenson was sitting up, scratching his bristly cheeks. Peter realized that his own whiskers were itching.

"Was there a razor among Fanshaw's effects, Winifred?"

"I believe so." She stepped inside and set down her mug on the bunk she'd vacated. "If you'd just scooch over a little, President, so I can get this drawer open? Thank you. Ah yes, here we are. Razor, shaving cream, and a bottle of after-shave lotion."

"Sissy stuff," growled Svenson. "Any more coffee?"

"Is there, Peter?"

"Sorry, President. Want some tea?"

"No."

Svenson lay back down and gathered his blankets around him. Peter took the razor and shaving cream, spurning the lotion lest he be thought a sissy, and went into what he supposed he ought to think of as the head. This was a tiny place with no shower nor any room to put one. He didn't care, he'd been more than adequately showered on during the past God knew how many hours.

It did feel good, though, to get rid of the stubble and have a wash. He bethought himself of fresh clothing he'd spied in Fanshaw's luggage, reflecting that he and the man of many passports were fairly close in size, and committed an act of piracy. Clean underwear, a clean jersey, dry shoes and socks, and the suit Fanshaw had been wearing before he changed into his Tugboat Annie outfit did much to boost his morale. The shoes were too wide and the pant legs an inch or so too long, but those were trivia compared to the bliss of getting out of garb that felt as if it had been tailored from wet seaweed.

Now to call Helen. She might be phoning the field station, worrying because he wasn't there. Peter tried the boat's telephone, but it wasn't working. Too much pounding, he supposed. "Drat," he fumed to Winifred, "I've got to get on shore and find a phone."

"What an excellent idea." Winifred herself, of course, had stayed as dry as a bone since she'd been snatched aboard the *Lollipop* before the second storm hit and had barely stuck her nose outside the cabin door until after it blew over. In her trim gray slacks and neat light-brown pullover, with her short-clipped hair waving softly from all the dampness, the heiress looked pretty much the way she always looked. No stranger could have guessed she'd been through such a drawn-out ordeal.

"They've rigged a ladder for us to climb over the sandbags, and tossed a rope so we can pull the boat up to it," she reported. "I tied the rope to what I believe is known as the gunwale. Was that the right thing to do?"

"An excellent thing to do," Peter replied. "Shall we?"

"But what about the president?"

"He looks to be good for a few more hours' sacktime. We'll leave him a note. Assuming we can find anything to write with."

Peter fished in Fanshaw's pockets. He found a ballpoint pen, he found a business card carrying Fanshaw's name along with that of the Meadowsweet Construction Company. He found no wallet nor key ring, but he did find a handsome gold coin with an eagle stamped on it, regrettably drilled through at the rim and strung on a long chain that must surely also be of gold.

"A twenty-dollar gold piece!" Winifred exclaimed. "Aunt's grandfather used to wear one of those on his watch chain. She had a photograph of him sitting in a great carved armchair with his frock coat open to show his embroidered waistcoat and that big gold eagle roosting comfortably on his corporation. Is this what Fanshaw used to hypnotize Chief Ottermole and Officer Dorkin?"

"Unless he has one in every outfit, which hardly seems likely. Well, well. We may as well take it along with us, one never knows."

Peter transferred his own wallet and keys to his borrowed pockets, wrote on the back of the card "Gone to find coffee," and left it on the floor beside Svenson's head. Then he went out and pulled on the rope to bring them up to the ladder. He held the boat steady while Winifred got her feet on the rungs, waited till she was safely atop the sandbags, and followed.

Water was lapping against the lower rows of sandbags but the river had stopped rising. This town, at least, wasn't going to get flooded out. A few spectators were leaning up against the improvised wall, probably exhausted from a long night's labors but too keyed up to go home to bed. A couple of them moved to help Winifred, but she was down before they could get to her. Peter followed less gracefully. The ground felt strange, it wasn't moving.

The spectators were smiling diffidently at the newcomers, not quite ready to break the ice. Peter smiled back.

"Thanks a lot for the rope and ladder," he said. "It sure feels good to be back on land. Had much damage around here? You look to be in good shape."

As always, there was one member of the group willing to take the lead. "Yes, we come through pretty well. We'd known for a long time that rotten old Upper Clavaton Dam was going to let go before anybody got around to fixing it, so we had our contingency plan all drawn up and ready to put into action. You folks run into trouble, did you?"

"You could call it that," Peter conceded. "We were—er—visiting the boat's owner when it broke loose from the dock in the storm. Fortunately the third member of our party happens to be an expert yachtsman. He brought us safely down the river, don't ask me how, until we were lucky enough to find a safe landing. He's still asleep; is there a restaurant or a grocery store open around here where we can pick up something to fix him a decent breakfast when he wakes up? And are your telephones working? We need to let our people know where we are. Er—where are we?"

His new acquaintance seemed to find Peter's question mildly amusing. "You're in Wilverton. There's a public telephone just up the street in front of the Lugitoff Superette and the Golden Apples Café's been open all night to feed the sandbag crew. They put on a decent meal if you don't mind health food."

"By George! We certainly picked the right place to run out of gas."

"Indeed we did," said Winifred. "I'm interested to hear you say Golden Apples, sir. Is this restaurant in any way connected with the Golden Apples packing company, which I believe is around here somewhere?"

"That's right, in Briscoe. That's the next town over; you must have come straight past it in the dark. Half the people in Wilverton work there. I do, myself."

"Indeed? I don't suppose you'll be going to work today, however?"

"Oh sure, I will. Bill and Dodie have a

full crew on as usual, only we'll start at ten o'clock instead of eight. That's part of our contingency plan; gives us time to go home and get cleaned up, maybe grab a few hours' sleep if we need to. We don't use it much except for a blizzard or a hurricane or something when we've had to dig out or the traveling's bad. Bill and Dodie planned the whole thing."

"They must be remarkably compassionate and resourceful people," said Winifred. "Are you by any chance referring to Mr. and Mrs. Compote?"

"Well, sure only nobody around here calls them that. You know the Compotes?"

"Not yet, but I very much want to. I wonder whether I might possibly beg a ride over to the factory with you? I was planning to see the Compotes this week anyway, and it seems a pity to waste the trip since we're so near. My name, I should say, is Binks; and this is Professor Shandy. We're both members of the faculty at Balaclava Agricultural College. Perhaps you'd go with me, Peter; or would you rather stay with the president?"

"No, I'd like very much to meet the Compotes, assuming this gentleman would care to take us. Are you agreeable, sir?"

"Well, sure, I guess. Only how'd you get back to the boat?"

"Walk, thumb a ride on one of the Compotes' delivery trucks, ask Dr. Svenson to pick us up in Briscoe after he's had his sleep and got hold of some fuel for the engine, whatever. Er—we neither of us happen to be wearing a watch. How soon would you need to start?"

"It's a quarter past eight now, near enough as makes no difference. Usually it doesn't take more than fifteen minutes to get over there, but I thought I'd give myself a little extra time this morning, just in case. How about if you go get your food and make your calls, and I meet you back here at half-past nine by the church clock? You'll hear the bell. My name's Fred Smith, by the way."

"How do you do, Mr. Smith." Winifred was not one to ignore small courtesies. "We'll be here on the dot, and thank you very much. Now, Peter, shall we try the café first?" she added as they walked off foodward. "My tongue's positively hanging out for a pot of camomile tea and a bowl of granola. With a great big red juicy apple for dessert."

"Gad, Winifred, I hadn't realized you

were such a wallower among the fleshpots. Go ahead, I'll meet you there. I want to catch Helen before she goes to work. Order me a couple of eggs and whatever else looks good."

Peter had found some coins in the pockets of his borrowed suit. This call was going to be on Fanshaw; the thought gave him a modicum of satisfaction. Hearing his wife's voice over the wire was a far greater one.

"Peter! Are you all right? Where are you?"

"In Wilverton, with Winifred and the president. We came down the Clavaclammer by tugboat."

"By what?"

"Tugboat. *T* for Triphonius, *U* for Ulalume, *G* for Garibaldi, *B* for—"

"Beast! Peter, talk sense. What tugboat? How in heaven's name did that happen?"

"In our last thrilling episode, as you may recall, the president and I were out at the field station, about to set forth on the track of Winifred's kidnappers. You did get a call from Sieglinde?"

"Yes, of course I did. She was not happy. Neither, I may say, was I. Are you sure you're all right?"

"I'm in reasonable fettle, considering. And you?"

"Darling, will you please quit trying to be funny and tell me how you got on that tugboat before I go into a screaming fit?"

"I should explain that it's not really a tugboat, just a tarted-up imitation of one that apparently belongs to Fanshaw. He or some henchman of his put through a ransom call while we were at the station. We insisted on talking with Winifred herself, and she, God bless her, gave a clue using the names Annie and Horatio. For Tugboat Annie and her nemesis, Horatio Bulwinkle, in case your memory doesn't stretch that far back."

"Oh, she is fantastic! Who but Winifred would have had such presence of mind?"

"You, for one. Anyway, the only logical place to look for a tugboat was on the Clavaclammer; so we went and there it was, with some hired gorilla standing guard and Fanshaw dressed up as Tugboat Annie."

"Good heavens! What did you do?"

"I didn't do much of anything except call the harbor police after the president had finished mopping up the bad guys. Unfortunately, while the cops were lugging them away, the boat somehow got set adrift. We didn't dare try to get back to shore in the dark, so we just kept on going till we wound up here. Briscoe's the next town over; so Winifred and I are going to get some breakfast here at the Golden Apples Café, which she probably owns unbeknownst, then drop in on Bill and Dodie Compote at their office."

"But what about Thorkjeld?"

"He's still on the boat, catching some exceedingly well-deserved sleep. He was up all night steering us downriver, God knows how. Call Sieglinde, will you, and tell her the old man's a hero, as if she didn't know. I should warn you, by the way, that I have a hunch the reason our mooring line got cast off is that Fanshaw managed to break away from the river police. You'd better carry your bumbershoot to work so you can beat off any heavily disguised ruffian who tries to abduct you."

"Yes, dear. Anything else?"

"Mink and Bulfinch are probably still at the station. I wish you'd let them know what's happened and ask them to notify the Clavaton police. I should imagine they'll want to come down here and seize the boat, though I'm sure the president would be willing to run it back if we can find some gas. Anyway, we should all be home one way or another sometime this afternoon, God willing and the creek don't run dry; which seems hardly likely, present conditions being as they are."

Helen started to say something but was interrupted by an importunate computer. "Please deposit an additional twenty-five cents."

"Damn!" said Peter. "This is Fanshaw's money and I've run out. Take care of yourself, Helen. God, I miss you."

Hanging up was a wrench, but the prospect of fresh edibles was a consolation. Peter legged it to the café, found Winifred dealing happily with a large glass of fresh-squeezed carrot juice, the camomile tea for which her soul had been lusting, and a stack of toast made from a wide assortment of whole grains.

"Ah, there you are, Peter. I've ordered you orange juice, coffee, and the Log Driver's Special, which is basically a large omelet and a great many home-fried potatoes."

"Excellent." He opted for wild oat muffins with his meal, and sipped at the hot coffee. It tasted, as he'd fully expected, like chicory.

"How is it?"

"Adequate. Not so good as yours, one

misses the ground dandelion root. You might mention that to Bill and Dodie."

"I look forward to the opportunity. Do try this barberry jelly, it's quite delicious. I wonder if they've thought of adding wild crab apples. Tame ones would do as well, I suppose. Dear me, I find myself all agog at the prospect of a good long chin-wag with my partners. Do you suppose this café is connected with the business? Mr. Debenham hasn't said anything about it. Nor has Mr. Sopwith. I must confess Mr. Sopwith is not my idea of an up-and-coming trust officer, though I expect Dr. Svenson will have him whipped into shape by the time they've been over the books." Winifred smiled a bit. "Perhaps that was not quite the expression to have employed."

"Oh, I don't know," said Peter. "I shouldn't be surprised if that's pretty much what's going to happen. Miss, could you pack up half a dozen of these muffins and a quart of orange juice to take with us? We'll stop at the grocery store for ham and eggs and coffee and a few more odds and ends, Winifred. I've asked Helen to phone the station and let them know you're safe. She's also getting in touch with the Clavaton police. I expect they'll want to impound the *Lollipop*."

Winifred giggled quite girlishly. "Not with Dr. Svenson aboard, I hope! Why can't we sail it, or her, I should say, back to Clavaton ourselves?"

"I don't know what the protocol is in these matters. Anyway, we'll get back one way or another. My car's still parked over by the wharves, at least I hope it is. But that's the least of our worries right now. Would you like another noggin of carrot juice or anything? What about the big red apple?"

"If that clock over there is right, we have exactly twenty-one minutes to take the president his breakfast and meet Mr. Smith, so we'd better get going. Peter, I've had the most dreadful thought! I didn't bring one red cent of money."

Peter chuckled. "Not to worry, you probably own the restaurant. Anyway, I have my wallet with me. Go ahead and take the apple."

"Very well, then, I can eat it on the way. Thank you, miss, that was an excellent breakfast. And thank you, Peter. Here, let me run ahead with the muffins while you get the groceries. I can start the kettle boiling."

By the time Peter got back to the boat, Svenson was stirring. "Urrgh?" was his greeting.

Peter held out the bag. "Food."

"Sieglinde?"

"I've talked to Helen, she'll have passed the word by now that you're safe with us. She's called the river police, too. I expect they'll be along in a while to pick up the boat."

"Gas. Take her back myself."

"Er—that's a possibility," Peter replied carefully.

"How do you like your eggs?"

"In quantity."

Scrambled was the easiest. Peter dumped a dollop of the butter he'd brought back into the only frying pan, broke in half a dozen eggs, added a splash of milk, and stirred. The kettle Winifred had put on was steaming; he took down a mug and spooned in coffee.

Winifred gave him a worried look. "I hope the president's not going to want much coffee. I used the last drop of water in the tank to fill the kettle."

"That means it's time we abandoned ship. Get him started on the orange juice and muffins," Peter suggested, unwrapping the ham.

It was already cooked, fortunately, since there was no room left in the frying pan. He gave the eggs another stir, arranged the slices of cold ham more or less tastefully on the biggest plate in the galley, decided the eggs were adequately scrambled, and piled them on top.

"Voilà, monsieur. Bon appétit."

"Funny," Svenson growled through a mouthful of muffin. "What next?"

"For you, three more muffins. For Winifred and me, a visit to the Compotes."

Peter took it upon himself to explain their plans, since Winifred had nobly begun cleaning out the frying pan with paper towels and salt, there being no water left except in the river. The president nodded.

"Go with you."

"Sorry, Captain, but you'll have to stay here and go down with the ship. Or not, as I fervently hope the case will be." From above came one mellow bong of the church's bell. "The tocsin hath sounded. Enjoy your eggs. Forget the pan, Winifred, we're due on the sandbags."

18

Fred Smith was punctual. Two minutes later, Peter and Winifred were with him on the road to Briscoe. It was as well they'd left early; tree limbs were down, puddles were everywhere. The worst hazard was the mass of dead leaves, reduced by the rain to a dark-brown pulp slippery as ice and even more treacherous. They needed that full half hour to reach the ugly sprawl of buff-painted concrete which was, Peter judged from the gleam in Winifred's eye, about to get a thorough image-lifting.

"This used to be a brewery," Smith told them. He hadn't done much talking so far along the way, nor had his passengers tried to make conversation lest they distract him from his driving. "Bill and Dodie picked the place on account of its water, there are natural springs up on the hill. Why don't I let you two out here? Bill and Dodie must be inside, that's their old station wagon parked by the main entrance. Just walk right in and holler if the girl's not at the front desk. Watch your step getting out."

"Thanks very much, Smith. We really appreciate this."

Peter got out first and held the door for Winifred, who was emancipated enough not to take umbrage at small masculine courtesies. She was plainly thrilled by the prospect of acquainting the Compotes with her plans for Golden Apples; Peter felt a qualm. This business had been Bill and Dodie's dream, their own creation, even though they'd brought it into being with old man Binks's grubstake. How were they going to feel about having another Binks blow in out of the storm laden with the wherewithal to achieve what all their years of dedication and hard work hadn't been able to pull off?

But it wouldn't be Winifred's achievement. He hoped to God the Compotes would have sense enough to realize that. If they hadn't stuck to their guns on quality and customer satisfaction all these years, Winifred wouldn't be offering them a plugged nickel now, much less flinging open the bottomless Binks coffers and inviting them to dig in.

Anyway, the moment of truth was at hand. Winifred sailed through the door head up and tail a-rising. The lobby was large and somewhat barren-looking; its only point of interest was a quite ridiculously ornate desk that Peter guessed had been a housewarming present from Grandfather Binks. Behind it sat a youngish woman in a yellow coverall who reminded him vaguely of somebody or other, he couldn't think whom. Winifred was beaming at her like a fairy godmother.

"Good morning. I'm Winifred Binks to see Mr. or Mrs. Compote, or preferably both."

The receptionist did not beam back. "Do you have an appointment?"

"No, I found myself in the neighborhood unexpectedly and thought I'd take advantage of the opportunity to call."

"You can't see them without an appointment."

This wasn't sitting well with Winifred. "Nonsense, of course I can. I assume this is their office." She moved purposefully toward the door behind the desk. "If you won't announce me, I shall do it myself."

"No! You can't" The woman—by George, she was a big one—rushed in front of Winifred, spread-eagled herself with her back to the door, and began screaming. "Help! Help! Hurry!"

The door was hurled open from inside. A man's face appeared above her shoulder, long, tanned, thatched above with gingery hair.

"Pipe down, Elvira! What the heck's the matter?"

"She's trying to get in!"

"Who is?"

"Her!"

"Her, who? Stand aside, can't you?"

"No! No! No!"

Her shrieks had reached Wagnerian intensity. The man, even taller than she, gave the visitors a look that was angry, bewildered, and, above all, embarrassed.

"Elvira, what the hell's got into you? Dodie, come here! She's having a fit or something. I'm sorry, ma'am!" He was having to shout, the receptionist was hooting like the wreck of the Old Ninety-Seven by now.

Winifred spied a water cooler in the lobby, rushed over to it, brought back a cupful of ice water, and dashed it straight in Elvira's face. The woman blinked, but kept right on screaming. By now Dodie, as she must be, had grabbed her by the shoulders from behind and was shaking her like a dust mop.

"Elvira, stop it! Get out of this doorway. Bill, can't you shut her up somehow? Elvira, for God's sake!"

By brute force, the two Compotes managed to force their crazed receptionist away from the office door. This only made matters worse. Elvira sprang at Winifred like a lunging tigress and would have knocked her to the floor if the heiress hadn't been so nippy on her feet. The Compotes grabbed her, one by each arm, and held on like grim death. They were neither of them small, but she swung them around as if they'd been kittens.

"Slap her face," panted Dodie.

"Gladly." Winifred obliged. It hadn't the slightest effect.

Peter had been standing aside, taking no part in the struggle, doing some fast cogitating. Light dawned. He drew from Fanshaw's pocket the golden coin on its golden chain and began swinging it back and forth in front of Elvira's engorged, convulsed face.

"Watch the coin, Elvira. Back and forth, back and forth. Keep watching, Elvira. Back and forth, back and forth, back and forth."

Reluctantly, then avidly, Elvira's eyes followed the glittering disk. Her yelling died away, her muscles grew slack.

"Relax, Elvira. Go to sleep. Sleep, sleep."

She slumped to the floor, her mouth fell open, her eyes shut. She breathed slowly, deeply. She slept.

"Well, I'll be jiggered!" Bill was wearing

a yellow coverall, too; he wiped the left sleeve across his brow. "That's the cussedest thing I ever saw."

"Elvira seemed like such a nice person," moaned his wife. "Of course we don't know her all that well, she's only been with us a month or so."

Dodie was a head shorter than her husband but, from the set of her chin, she was in no way subservient to him or anybody else. There was gray in her hair but her skin was clear, her cheeks were rosy, her eyes bright blue and wide open. The yellow coverall became her nicely. She looked like the sort who smiled a lot; right now her attractive face was troubled. "What in the world do you suppose got into her?"

Peter was still holding the twenty-dollar gold piece by its chain. "I believe this may be the answer. It belongs to a man who calls himself Fanshaw, among other things. From the way she reacted just now, I'd say he used it on her before planting her here as his spy, to hypnotize her and program her to keep you apart from Winifred Binks at any cost. This is Winifred, by the way."

"Yes, and I'm delighted to meet you," said the major stockholder. "I assume you two must be the Compotes. As you perhaps remember, both I and my lawyer have phoned during the past couple of days, trying to make an appointment with you. I'm sure you had good reasons not to return our calls."

Dodie and Bill exchanged puzzled glances. "The only reason I can think of," said Dodie, "is that we never got the messages. So you're Mr. Binks's granddaughter! We've been wondering whether we'd ever get to meet you."

"The only reason you didn't is that I had no idea there was any connection between us until just this past Saturday, when I met with my trust officer. You might be interested to know that I'd already instructed him to divert some of my funds to your company. I was familiar with your excellent products, I'd made a careful study of your operation, and I'd come to the conclusion that you were precisely the sort of company that deserved my wholehearted support. It was and is a source of immense gratification to me that we are in fact associates."

"Us, too," said Dodie somewhat numbly.

Winifred smiled. "My reason for wishing to see you is that, while I have no wish to interfere with your actual operations even if I had the expertise to do so, which I certainly haven't, I do have some ideas on marketing and sales promotion that I'd like to lay before you. Along with the offer of sufficient funds to carry them out, needless to say. That's why I took the liberty of barging past your dragoness and setting off this dreadful row, for which I most humbly beg your pardon, but I don't suppose I'd ever have got to reach you if I hadn't. Do you suppose we ought to put Elvira on a couch or somewhere?"

"I'd be inclined to leave her as she is," said Peter. "If we try to move her before she's had a chance to sleep it off, she might go into another tantrum. I don't know anything about hypnosis."

"You sure had me fooled," said Bill. "I had you figured for an expert."

"No, it's just that I had the chance to observe a couple of other people on whom Fanshaw had worked the same trick. Fortunately I also happen at the moment to be wearing Fanshaw's suit and he hadn't got around to emptying his pockets. Look, we have a lot to talk about. Why don't we make ourselves comfortable?"

"Sure thing, come right on in."

Dodie led the way into what must be the executive office, it looked to Peter more like his late Aunt Effie's back sitting room.

Along with a flat-topped golden oak desk that still had some of its varnish, there were a swivel chair that probably squeaked, a maple spring rocker and settee covered in badly faded chintz, a goosenecked desk lamp, one of those spidery black iron floor lamps with a yellowed parchment shade that everybody who couldn't afford anything flossier used to have back in the thirties, a few rag rugs, and a great many photographs, some in frames, some thumbtacked to the walls. There was even a matronly black parlor stove with a coal hod sitting beside it and a kettle steaming on top. On the rug closest to the stove lay a Boston terrier, gray around the muzzle, wheezing gently as he slumbered.

"Tiger's our watchdog," Bill explained. "Haul up and set, folks. You take the rocking chair, Winifred, that's where your grandfather always liked to sit. He was an interesting old fellow, always had some new bee in his bonnet. We got a kick out of having him around. Gosh, it's good to see you in his place, Winifred. You too, er—"

"Oh, I'm sorry. This is my good friend Professor Peter Shandy from Balaclava Agricultural College. I'm also on the faculty there, as you probably didn't know," Winifred was adding with naive pride when the door opened and yet another woman in one of the yellow coveralls that were evidently standard wear at Golden Apples bustled in with a handful of letters. She wasn't young, but she bounced along like a ten-year-old.

"Nor rain, nor squish, nor standing around half the night holding up sacks for the boys to sling sand into stays this swift courier in her appointed rounds. Here's your mail. Oops, sorry, didn't know we had visitors. Say, did you know Elvira's stretched out on the lobby floor, snoring worse than Tiger? I suppose she was up all night working on the sandbags, poor thing, but it's not like her. Elvira's always acted so proper. Hadn't we better bring her in here and put her on the settee?"

"No," said Bill, "if she's that tuckered out we'd better just let her sleep. I guess we ought to put a blanket or something over her. Dodie, maybe you'd like to do that so Mae can get on with her work. Thanks for the mail, Mae. Hope it's not all bills this time."

"Mae's a great one for mothering everybody," he added after she'd left. "Nice woman, she's been with us ever since we started. Say, Winifred, here's a letter from your lawyer. Mind if I open it now?"

"No, please do. I expect that's merely a request for an appointment, since he hadn't been allowed to reach you by telephone."

Bill ripped open the envelope, using a somewhat prissy celluloid paper knife molded in the shape of a winsome tot with a bow in her hair, clutching an even winsomer pussycat with a bow around its neck. Catching Peter's cocked eyebrow, he grinned.

"Family heirloom. My grandmother brought it home from the movies one Bank Night back during the Depression. She was so stuck on Ramon Navarro that my grandpop tried to sue him for alienation of affections. Say, what's this?"

His eyes narrowed, his jaw turned to solid rock. "Winifred, it says here you want out."

"What? Let me see that."

Winifred was not, after all, too well-bred to snatch. "Why, this is outrageous. Whatever can he have been thinking of? Peter, you were there, you heard my instructions. I made myself perfectly clear, did I not?"

"Clear as a bell. This past Saturday morning," Peter explained to the Compotes, "Winifred had a meeting with Debenham, who's been her family lawyer for many years, and a man named Sopwith, who's the new trust officer for the Binks estate. President Svenson and I sat in on the meeting. Winifred is ceding a portion of her estate to the college in order to establish a field station which will also include a television station. Her financial concerns therefore are very much ours, aside from the fact that she's a personal friend and we don't want to see her taken for a ride."

"So?" Bill Compote was still wary.

"So, as they were going through her various holdings, she told Sopwith to sell some shares her grandfather had bought in a company called Lackovites, with which you're doubtless familiar, and invest the proceeds in Golden Apples."

"My reason, as I said at the time," Winifred added, "was that I had studied both companies' operations and found that Golden Apples has a superb record for quality and honesty but a rather feeble one in sales promotion, if you'll forgive me for saying so; whereas the Lackovites people are superb merchandisers but their products are trash and I want no part of them. When I learned how strong my financial interest in Golden Apples is, I resolved to become personally involved in implementing a more aggressive merchandising program. That's why I instructed Mr. Debenham to arrange a meeting with you. There was absolutely no question of my asking you to buy me out, even if——er—"

"Even if we'd had the money, which we sure as heck don't," Bill finished for her. "Then what's this letter all about?"

"I cannot imagine. Mr. Debenham, of all people! I—I'm shattered. Excuse me."

Winifred sniffled and searched frantically in the pocket of her slacks. Dodie handed her a box of tissues.

"Thank you, Dodie. I do beg your pardon. It's just that we've been so—tell them, Peter."

Winifred buried her face in a tissue. Peter cleared his throat, wishing to blazes he knew what to tell. Now that he'd met Bill and Dodie on their own turf, he found it hard to believe they were masterminding some evil plot; but why should he take them at face value when so many others were turning out to be shams? For all he knew, Tiger might not even be their dog.

Well, what the hell? If this pair were running the show, there was no point in not telling them what they must already know. If they weren't, then it was only decent to cue them in. One way or another, they were surely involved; those little compote sketches among Emmerick's effects, not to mention the sleeping beauty on the lobby floor out there, clinched the matter. He began with Emmerick.

A few minutes later, Bill was scratching his ginger mop like a cat with a flea. "Godfrey mighty! You mean to say this bird Emmerick just went up in the net *alive and kicking* and came down *dead?* Just like that?"

"Exactly like that. And next morning, when we telephoned to notify the company he was supposedly working for, they'd never heard of him."

"Or said they hadn't." This was Winifred's show and she wasn't going to be left out of it. "At this point, I feel disinclined to believe anything about anybody. However, it does seem unlikely that the Meadowsweet Construction Company would lie about having employed Mr. Emmerick just because he'd been killed in a bizarre fashion. One does hear rumors of strange doings in large corporations. Protecting their image, I believe it's called. But Meadowsweet isn't all that large a corporation."

"Size doesn't matter," said Bill. "We had a mighty strange thing happen right here in Briscoe a few months back."

"Now, Bill, Winifred doesn't want to hear about that silly business at the hardware store," Dodie interrupted. "What happened next, Professor Shandy?"

Peter did feel some curiosity about what happened at the hardware store, but what he wanted most was to get out of here and back to Balaclava. He plugged on, with a good many contributions from Winifred: through Fanshaw's appearance, his arrest, his hypnotic jailbreak; through the temporary abduction of Viola Buddley, the doodles that appeared to implicate the Compotes in one fashion or another; he thought they might as well realize they weren't being taken automatically as the good guys. Finally he got to Winifred's kidnapping, the return of Fanshaw in a different guise, and the smashing grand finale that had led to their mad ride down the Clavaclammer and this morning's visit to Golden Apples.

"By gorry," said Bill when they got through. "If that isn't the darnedest! What are you going to do now?"

"Good question," said Peter. "We've sent a message to the Clavaton police to come and collect the tugboat, which contains some interesting evidence, including a number of fake passports allegedly issued to Fanshaw under various names and guises. Unless he had another lot of passports stashed somewhere else, and assuming that he did in fact manage to break away last night as I've surmised, this should limit his ability to get out of the country."

Peter shrugged. "Not that it's going to make him any easier to track down, I don't suppose. A chap with his moxie could take some finding even in a phone booth. The big question, of course, is whether Fanshaw's actually the ringleader or just one of the crew. As to what in Sam Hill it's all in aid of, your guess is as good as mine."

19

"Well, by jingo, I bet I can give a pretty good guess." Bill Compote was hopping mad. His eyes flashed green as a cat's, his ginger hair flopped in the air as he leaned over the desk, pointing one long knobby finger like a pistol. "You been talking to anybody about dumping your Lackovites stock, Winifred? Before that meeting, I mean."

Winifred considered. "Now that you mention it, I suppose I may have hinted at it, in a way. Not in so many words, of course. But we've had people coming to the field station for classes on natural foods: what to pick, how to prepare them, their nutritional value, and all that. Inevitably we always get around to which of the packaged brands on the market are worthwhile and which aren't, and I've expressed my opinions freely on the merits of Golden Apples versus Lackovites. As I mentioned, I've also made a good many inquiries about the two companies, mainly by going around to different stores on my bicycle and pumping the clerks. I shouldn't be at all surprised if some of the Lackovites salesmen had got wind of my nosing around, and had some of my comments repeated to them. Anybody who knows or suspects that the Binks Trust has been holding shares in Lackovites must surely have brains enough to realize I was getting ready to dump them. Why do you ask, Bill?"

"Because they're trying their damnedest to buy us out, that's why. They've been pulling all sorts of dirty tricks trying to break us down, but we haven't budged an inch and don't intend to. What it looks like to me now is that they've given up on Dodie and me and started in on you. That would make more sense anyway, you being the principal stockholder."

"My dear Bill," Winifred replied, "surely you must realize, as I do, that it's been your hard work and firmness of principle that has made Golden Apples what it is today, and mere accident of birth that has caused me to become involved. With your permission, I shall this week instruct Mr. Debenham"—she winced—"I shall instruct my legal representative to sign over twenty percent of my holdings to you and Dodie. That will put us on an even fifty-fifty basis, so that we can work as equal partners for as long as I'm able to pull my weight. In the event of my death or incapacitation, my half will revert to you. I realize I'm still taking gross advantage of my position as Miss Moneybags, but I do feel that I have something besides money to contribute and I want my chance to try. Furthermore, if we're really having a knock-down fight with Lackovites, I jolly well want to be in on it."

"Oh, Winifred!"

Dodie was hugging Miss Moneybags for all she was worth. Bill was pumping her hand, Tiger was trying to climb up in her lap. Peter realized he himself was beaming like a proud father. If the Compotes were phonies, then he was the lost Dauphin of France.

"Well then, that's settled." Winifred nodded briskly to conceal her emotion and settled Tiger more comfortably on her knees. "Now let me explain what I have in mind with regard to our merchandising program."

She did so, lucidly and concisely, setting forth her plans, backing them up with facts and figures. Bill and Dodie listened as though they'd been hypnotized, interjecting a word now and then only to clarify or amplify. They were entranced by her scheme for free advertising on the Balaclava television station, somewhat flabbergasted by her suggestions for landscaping the grounds of the old brewery in order to project a new, more prosperous image for Golden Apples.

"But that will cost a mint," Dodie objected.

"I think not. Will it, Peter?"

"Not so you'd notice it. Balaclava has a policy of providing jobs for students. We'll turn this into a work project for our landscape-architecture students, using shrubs, trees, and seedlings raised in our college nurseries and greenhouses which we'll furnish you at wholesale prices, the proceeds to go to our Endowment Fund. The kids will do the work at reasonable hourly rates, various faculty members will supervise and grade them on the results. Cronkite Swope will do an ongoing feature series for the *Balaclava County Fane and Pennon*, no doubt your local paper will do the same. You'll hold a big open house when the work's completed, Winifred will make a nice little speech. It'll be a fine publicity boost for Golden Apples and help the participating students get launched into good jobs."

"Always provided those thugs from Lackovites don't invite a pack of skunks along to the party." Bill was too much a Yankee to count his chickens before they were hatched. "I'm a hundred percent in favor of everything you've said, Winifred, but what the heck are we going to do about this mess we're in right now?"

"Find the skunk who's running the show and put him out of business," said Peter. "There's got to be a mastermind somewhere, and I think you must be right about his working at Lackovites. What can you tell me about their operations?"

"Mainly that they're a bunch of highbinders, but I guess you already know that. Winifred's right about the merchandising, it's the only thing that's kept them going. Dodie and I aren't much for running down our competitors, but the best we can say about Lackovites products is that most of the stuff they sell isn't downright poisonous."

"Provided you don't try to live on it too long," Dodie put in.

Bill snorted. "If you did, you'd either starve to death or come down with scurvy. Lackovites is in trouble with the Food and Drug Administration right now, if you want to know, though they've managed to keep it hushed up so far. In my opinion, that's why they're busting their britches to get hold of Golden Apples. Not to be tooting our own horn, but we do have a reputation for top-quality products. That's the one thing now that might save their bacon: getting hold of our name and trading on it. Which isn't to say they wouldn't drag us down to their own level once they took over. I asked that last bunch of vice-presidents they sent over why they didn't try using real food and putting in some quality controls instead of just trying to think up new ways to hustle the suckers, and they laughed at me. Cripes almighty, rather than let those vultures get their claws into Golden Apples, I'd burn this plant right down to the ground."

"And I'd be with him, holding the matches," said Dodie. "We've done a little what I guess you might call research on Lackovites ourselves. From what we can make out, they've got so many so-called executives over there all running in different directions that most of 'em don't have any notion what the rest are up to. Furthermore, they don't seem to care, long as the money keeps rolling in. When they start losing customers, they just put together another big advertising campaign introducing some new so-called wonder product."

"Which is the same old stuff in a different box," growled Bill.

"Yes, dear, but people fall for the catchy commercials and come looking, so naturally the big chains figure they have to carry it, and so it goes. At least it's kept going so far, but consumers aren't quite so gullible as those hustlers think they are. The Lackovites gravy train's beginning to run out of steam, and if those umpty-zillion executives aren't starting to panic, all I can say is, they darned well ought to be."

"So Winifred's dumping her Lackovites shares might very well be a signal to other stockholders to do the same," said Peter. "In any event, her infusion of new capital into Golden Apples is bound to have a serious impact on Lackovites unless they change their ways in a hurry. How soon do you think you folks can get started enlarging your sales force and improving your packaging?"

Bill smiled. "About twenty minutes from now. We've realized for a long time what was holding us back in the market, and we've had our contingency plan worked out in case we ever got our hands on some spare cash. First thing we'll do is get our publicity department, namely me, to draft a news release about company expansion. Then we'll start scouting around for some more good salesmen."

"Most of whom will probably be women," Dodie put in. "Our chief of sales, who's also a woman, will run a training program so that they'll know exactly what they're selling and how to present it. With a big-enough crew and effective advertising, Janice will have us knocking the socks off Lackovites inside a month. As for packaging, we've already had a design studio work up some ideas. Want to see?"

Naturally Winifred wanted to see. She wanted to see everything about Golden Apples, right down to the plumbing. Peter did not want to see, he wanted to go. He could not, at the moment, recall many things he had ever wanted more. Neither did he want to leave Winifred alone here with the Compotes. He didn't know why, he just didn't.

"Er—Winifred, not to rain on your parade, but hadn't we better start thinking about getting back? We don't know who's manning the field station, or how Calthrop is doing, or where Fanshaw's got to, among other things." One of the other things being that crazy letter of Lawyer Debenham's, though he didn't like rubbing salt into Winifred's wound.

Aunt had raised her well, a Binks did not put pleasure before duty. Winifred hoisted Tiger gently off her lap and handed him to Dodie.

"You're right, Peter, we must buzz off and let Bill and Dodie get on with their day's work. I'll speak with Mr. Sopwith again about Lackovites as soon as I get back, and woe be to him if he hasn't sold those shares. Why don't I phone you tomorrow morning, Dodie, and set up a time for us to meet with the packaging people and our sales manager? And for me to have my guided tour, to which I'm looking forward with eager anticipation. It's been delightful meeting my new partners, and I can't tell you how happy I am to be associated with Golden Apples. I'm sure we'll have our problems solved very soon.

Oh dear, that reminds me, do you suppose Elvira's still asleep out there? If she's awake, perhaps she can call us a taxi. I suppose the thing to do is go back to the *Lollipop* and see what's happened to President Svenson. Don't you think, Peter?"

"You don't need a taxi," said Bill. "We've got to make a delivery to Wilverton today anyway; how'd you like to ride back in one of your own trucks?"

"How delightful! I hadn't realized we owned any, you must be appalled by my ignorance."

"But you'll find she's a pretty quick learncr," said Peter.

Bill was acting just a shade too eager to get them out of there, Peter couldn't help thinking. Maybe there was nothing in it; except that the employees had got in late today and they'd be running behind schedule, along with having to face whatever other problems might have been caused by the storm and the flood.

Too, the Compotes could be feeling a bit overwhelmed by having Winifred dump her horn of plenty on their heads all of a sudden. They might be wondering if she was as wacky as her grandfather, and whether it was safe to take her offering at face value. They must surely be concerned about that letter from Debenham. Who wasn't? Peter said good-bye to Dodie and the old terrier and followed Winifred and Bill out of the office.

Elvira had vanished; the blanket was neatly folded and laid on the desk behind which she ought to have been sitting if she'd finished her nap. Bill grunted.

"Mae must have got her into the lounge. Just as well, I guess. Bad for the company image to have the help sprawled all over the lobby floor. I still can't make any sense of this hypnotism business. How the heck could a person let some stranger walk up to 'em and do a thing like that?"

"The same way two cops named Ottermole and Dorkin let it happen," said Peter. "They just didn't realize what Fanshaw was up to. It's often supposed that only weak-minded people are susceptible to hypnotism; in fact, I believe it's the other way around. I assume Elvira is of at least average intelligence?"

"Oh yes, she's smart enough. She's been handling some of the telephone orders and hasn't made a mistake so far that I know of. Knows how to talk to the customers, too. I sure hope this business hasn't fried her brain or anything."

"Ottermole and Dorkin pulled out of it all right. I expect Elvira will, too."

Peter didn't say much more after that. Winifred had plenty of questions about the company's operations and Bill was answering them at what Peter considered totally unnecessary length. He was relieved when they got back to Wilverton and saw the tugboat still moored below the sandbags, with Thorkjeld Svenson bestriding the deck like the Colossus of Rhodes.

Winifred was still saying good-byc to Bill. Peter left her to it and climbed up on top of the sandbags. "Ahoy the *Lollipop!*"

"Yesus, it took you long enough," Svenson yelled back.

"Winifred had a good many things to talk about with the Compotes," Peter explained as he clambered down the ladder to the boat, "and, I had to dehypnotize the receptionist. Luckily I had the right equipment with me." He reached into Fanshaw's pocket and pulled out the golden talisman on its chain. "Look at it, President. Watch the birdie."

"Funny." Svenson sneered at the swinging bauble. "Seen the river police. Left me a deckhand."

"Oh? Where is he?"

"Below. Making coffee. Want some?"

Peter shook his head. "No, thanks. I'm still trying to digest my riverboat special. Did they bring you any fuel?"

"All set. I'm taking her back. Climb aboard."

"Er—is there any offer of alternative transportation?"

"Knew you'd say that," Svenson grunted. "Police car. Over there."

"Ah. Then, since you have somebody along to help with the cooking, I expect Winifred and I'd better go the fast way."

"Aloha."

"And the same to you. Happy tugging." With enormous relief, Peter jumped back off the sandbags and went over to the waiting police car.

20

"I hope my car hasn't floated away."

Peter had been growing steadily edgier as they drew closer to Clavaton; some towns that hadn't had any contingency plans were showing horrendous effects of the dam break. "Fortunately I parked well up from the road, on a concrete platform behind what appeared to be a warehouse over by the docks."

The policeman who was driving nodded. "I think I know the place you mean, you should be okay. The river road's in pretty bad shape, but we can get to your car by going down over the hill."

By George, so they could. Peter hadn't even forgotten to transfer his keys to Fanshaw's suit. The car had stayed dry inside and started after only a few tentative coughs. He got Winifred safely stowed aboard, thanked their kind driver, and managed to follow the somewhat intricate directions for getting back on the Lumpkinton Road.

"I'll drop you off first, Winifred. Unless you'd rather come along to Balaclava Junction with me."

"Oh, thank you, I couldn't possibly. I must find out what's happened at the station, with Knapweed out of commission and Viola in a state. She may not even have gone in today. One could hardly blame her for staying away, considering what happened to her. Goodness, was it only yesterday? I feel as though we'd been gone a month."

"Haven't we?"

Inland, the road was in no worse shape than usual; Peter fed the car more gas. He was tired. God, he was tired! Was he getting old, or was this just the normal result of too little sleep and too much Clavaclammer?

Last Thursday night, he remembered distinctly, he'd had his customary good night's rest. On Friday he'd been full of beans, handling his accustomed teaching schedule with aplomb, relishing the prospect of a brisk night among the owls. He'd eaten a hearty supper and gone forth boldly, as he had for the past twenty Octobers, clipboard in hand, binoculars at the ready, prepared to let not one of the Strigiformes in his bailiwick go unlisted.

Now that he had so many more interesting ways to occupy his time, Peter was no longer the compulsive counter he'd been in his bachelor days. Until Friday night, however, he'd still taken a quiet satisfaction in totting up a tidy total. Today, he had a melancholy, end-of-an-era feeling that he'd counted one owl too many.

Peter still hadn't found out how that trick with the bunch of white feathers had been worked. He didn't see that it greatly mattered; he evidently didn't even care, or he'd have done something about it before this. In any event, the heavy rains must by now have obliterated whatever evidence there might have been. He said as much to Winifred and she agreed.

"I don't see that it matters, either. Knowing how they worked the owl won't bring Mr. Emmerick back. Not that we wanted him in the first place, though it's cruel of me to say so. Surely the man must have meant something to someone. It does concern me a little that we still don't know who he really was."

"If the police haven't found out by now, they soon will."

"To be sure! You're such a consolation, Peter."

Winifred paused. Peter was aware of her pausing; how could he have missed a pause like this? It was the kind that felt as if it could be picked up and stored away in a box. Not knowing what else to do, he waited.

"Peter," Winifred said when she at last got done pausing, "you're going to think me silly for asking such a stupid question, but did it happen to strike you that, despite the cordial reception we got from Dodie and Bill, there was a certain reticence in their demeanor? Every so often during our conversation, I got this odd little feeling that what they were saying was something quite different from what they were thinking.

Nothing hostile or hypocritical, but—something. Do tell me I'm being ridiculous."

"If you are, that makes two of us. I've been trying to think of a tactful way to bring it up."

"Why should you want to be tactful with me? I thought we were supposed to be colleagues."

"In my experience, it's the people closest to you whom you have to be most tactful with. If you really want to know, what I think is that the Compotes were knocked for a loop, first by our charging in unannounced and sending Elvira into fits, next by your rather staggering offer to make them equal partners and pour in the new capital they've been praying for, and lastly by that crazy letter from Debenham. I couldn't help wondering whether, since the only Binks they'd dealt with before was your grandfather, they might be—er—"

"Wondering whether I'm another loony bird? One could hardly blame them for that, could one? Well, I expect it won't take long to convince Dodie and Bill that, while we Binkses may be a bit flaky in spots, our promises are good and so's our money. Of course the letter must have upset them, it certainly did me. I simply cannot believe, after all these years, that Mr. Debenham would . . ."

Winifred shook her head furiously and blew her nose into one of Dodie's tissues. "Anyway, I'll have to get straightened out with him before I can tackle anything else. Right now I feel as though I'd waked up in my own house and discovered the floor had been snatched from under me."

She paused again. Peter let the pause run on to become a silence. What was there to say? At least, thank God, Winifred was preparing herself to face the lawyer's treachery head-on. And P. Shandy was prepared to face it with her, by gum. Like Disko Troop, he hated being mistook in his judgment; he'd taken Debenham for a decent man.

"Not far from the station now," he grunted after a while. "It was along about here the president and I found Viola tied to the tree. Why do you suppose they keep tying her to trees?"

"Because she bounces so, I suppose." Winifred was trying to sound chipper. "Viola rather reminds one of a loose hot-air balloon. I've felt like tying her down a few times myself. I wonder if she came in today?"

"Somebody's here, at any rate."

Peter could see two cars in the parking lot.

He could swear one of them belonged to his neighbors, the Porbles. Dr. Porble was Helen's boss at the library, his wife was Helen's great friend; he parked alongside and charged into the station lobby. A familiar, welcome figure was indeed sitting at the desk; but it wasn't Helen.

"Sieglinde! What are you doing here?"

Helen would have rushed to hug them both. The Viking's majestic consort went so far as to bestow a hundred-watt smile and a gracious inclination of her golden-crowned head.

"Thorkjeld telephoned to me after you had gone to seek the Golden Apples. He mentioned a shortness of hands at the station, so I borrowed the Porbles' car and drove myself here. It is good to see you, Peter. And you also, Winifred. But where is my husband?"

"Somewhere on the Clavaclammer, bringing back the tugboat," Peter explained. "I don't suppose the president happened to mention that he hauled off a miracle last night, getting us safely downriver in the dark after we were cast adrift and the dam let go. If it weren't for him, we'd have been wrecked and drowned."

"No, he did not tell me that. He said only

that he had enjoyed the sail but would have enjoyed far more being at home with me, which I well believe. I am not surprised that he is bringing the boat back, Thorkjeld is not one to shirk a duty. Also he gets few chances to run a boat. Purvis Mink and Alonzo Bulfinch are gone to their well-deserved rest, but Silvester Lomax is here. He has fed the birds and searched for miscreants, of whom as yet he has not found any but he is still looking. Silvester also has a great sense of duty."

"I'm glad of that," said Winifred. "It's delightful to see you, Sieglinde, and most thoughtful of you to lend a hand. Evidently Viola isn't going to show up today."

"She has come," said the president's wife with a barely perceptible curl of the lip. "I sent her back to don more seemly garb. Shorts at this time of year are absurd and lead to problems with the kidneys. Furthermore, fat, red legs with bulges above have nothing to recommend them for public viewing at any time. Trousers I could have allowed. They are at least warm and practical, although not flattering to women of stalwart build, as I know myself to my sorrow, and to Thorkjeld's amusement. Also, tree-hugging jerseys of a size too small with nothing underneath do not set an elevating tone in a place of learning. I explained all this. Your Viola did not perhaps see the thrust of my argument, but she quite clearly felt the force of my position. Tell me truly, Peter, did Thorkjeld get a suitable breakfast?"

"Never fear, Sieglinde, we knew better than to leave him unfed. There's a policeman with him on the boat acting as galley slave. Anything else happened since you've been here?"

"There is a message from Mr. Debenham, who is most eager to talk with you, Winifred. In fact it is two messages, one earlier from his secretary, one a short while ago from himself in great perturbation. I have promised that you will return his call at the first opportunity."

"I shall certainly do so," Winifred replied grimly. "Did he say he'd be in his office all day?"

"He has insisted he will not stir from his desk until he has heard the sound of your voice."

"He'll hear it, but not on the telephone. Peter, may I impose on you yet once again?"

"It's no imposition. Would you like to change your clothes or anything before we go?"

Winifred looked down at her jaded slacks and slept-in jersey. "I suppose so. I shan't be long."

"Take your time. I want to let Helen know we're back, and also to find out how Calthrop is doing."

"Oh yes, by all means. Find out if he's allowed visitors. You did say in the car that he's at the Clavaton Hospital. Perhaps we might pop in and see him after—"

She didn't wait to finish her sentence, Peter could understand why. Sieglinde found the hospital's phone number and, after a bit of shunting around, got him connected with the Intensive Care Unit. Calthrop was conscious and able to take nourishment by mouth. His vital signs were good enough for practical purposes, he was having tests to determine the extent of his head injury. No surgery was being planned at this time, he was being closely monitored. Only immediate family were allowed to visit.

So that was good news. Peter tried the Clavaton police station. The man called Fanshaw had in fact escaped in the storm. That was bad news, but he'd expected it. He dialed the college library and asked for his wife.

By the time Peter had reassured Helen that

he'd be home to supper though hell should bar the way, Winifred was back wearing not her usual slacks and jersey but a well-cut gentian-blue coat and skirt with a flowered scarf tucked in at the neck. Navy-blue shoes, handbag and gloves, plus a blue felt hat with a fan of blue-jay feathers completed the ensemble. Sieglinde was enraptured.

"Ah! This is how a distinguished member of our faculty should look. You are a credit to the college, Professor Binks. Is she not, Peter?"

"In this and every other way," he replied gallantly. Winifred would never be hanged for her beauty, but she did look pretty darned classy in that outfit. Distinguished, that was the word. Why didn't more women wear hats?

Putting on the dog for her interview with Debenham had been a smart ploy, she no doubt realized that. She climbed resolutely back into Peter's car, fastened her seat belt, and sat bolt upright, staring straight ahead, both gloved fists clutching the new leather handbag that no doubt held the fatal letter. Peter couldn't see her face, he was too busy watching the road; but he had a general impression of flared nostrils and tight lips.

This was surely one hell of a position for

Debenham's long-time client to be in. It was going to be a damned sight worse for the lawyer who'd put in years of hard work on the Binks account without recompense. To lose Winifred just when she was beginning to pay off in a big way wouldn't be the worst of the matter. His professional reputation would be bound to suffer. If word got out that he'd disobeyed his client's direct orders and conspired against her with the Lackovites crowd, he'd be lucky not to get disbarred.

Debenham had impressed Peter as being a decent, sensible man. Could he really have been fool enough to let himself get sucked in by knaves like Fanshaw and Emmerick? Had they managed to convince him that Winifred was in fact making a terrible mistake in allying herself so wholeheartedly with the Compotes? Had he some quixotic notion of trying to save her from her own folly? Or did he honestly have bad news about Golden Apples that he hadn't yet been able to tell her? Was this the reason for his urgent phone calls?

Peter could think of a less creditable but at least equally possible reason for those calls. If Debenham was aware that Winifred had been kidnapped and hadn't learned she'd got loose from her captors, his leaving those messages might have been an attempt to establish his ignorance of her being missing.

Well, the moment of truth was at hand. Winifred was straightening her hat, dabbing at her lips with a stick of pale-pink salve; flicking, by George, a powder puff across her nose. Gad, she was really going in for the kill. He kept a respectful step or two behind as the heiress sailed into the lawyer's office with her gunports uncovered and her powder, indubitably, dry.

A young male clerk was sitting in the outer office, looking up torts in a stack of tomes. Disturbed as she was, Winifred did not forget her manners.

"Good afternoon, Frank. Don't get up, I'll announce myself."

She didn't have to. The lawyer burst forth, evincing glad surprise.

"Miss Binks! Come right in, how good to see you. But you shouldn't have put yourself out, I'd have come to you."

She didn't speak, Peter surmised that she couldn't; she walked straight into the office and headed for the chair closest to the desk. No doubt this was where she always sat. Thwarted of his efforts to beat her to it and get her settled, Debenham perforce contented himself with fetching another chair for Peter. He then went around behind the desk and sat down in his own swivel chair, looking a trifle fussed, as well he might.

"It's good of you to come," he began redundantly. "What we need to talk about—"

Winifred had herself under command now. Her purse was open, the fatal document in her hand. "I am all too aware of what we have to talk about," she interrupted. "Professor Shandy and I happened to be with the Compotes at Golden Apples this morning when their mail was delivered. Mr. Debenham, can you give me any rational explanation as to why you wrote them this iniquitous letter?"

She handed it across the desk with a haughty sweep of her blue-gloved hand. Debenham picked up his reading glasses, fumbled them into place, and scanned the paper. His mouth flew open. He snatched off his glasses, rubbed them frantically on his tie, put them back on, and read the page again.

"Good heavens! Miss Binks, surely you can't think I wrote this?"

"If you didn't, who did?"

"I don't know! I would never—Miss Binks, look."

He opened his top desk drawer and took out a piece of writing paper, blank except for the name and address printed in black ink at the top. "This is my office stationery, the kind I have used without change for the past thirty-seven years. Would you kindly run your finger over the printing, then tell me what you feel? Please, I beg of you."

Winifred hesitated, then drew off her right glove and ran a fingertip gingerly over the letterhead. "It's full of little bumps."

"Yes, mine's done in what they call raised printing because, as you see, it is. Now please be good enough to touch the printing on this sheet you brought with you."

Less reluctantly this time, Winifred did so. Then her face broke into a smile of ineffable relief. "No bumps!"

"Precisely. Now would you further oblige me by looking at the signature? Here, use this magnifying glass. I ask you to compare the writing with the signature on these checks I've just signed for our office expenses. Do you note any discrepancies?"

"Yes, yes! I note them! The signatures on the checks are firm and decisive. This on the letter shows hesitation and wiggles, and there's something awfully peculiar about the *ham*. Ergo, we deduce that the letterhead has been photocopied from a genuine letterhead and the signature is a blatant forgery."

The clouds had blown over, Winifred was radiant. "I should have known. I can only say in extenuation of my obtuseness that I don't recall ever having received a letter from you. We've always communicated in person or by telephone. And this iniquitous message coming just when it did—you know how it's been these past few days, Mr. Debenham, just one perfidy after another. We've been conditioned to expect the worst. Can you ever forgive me?"

"My dear Miss Binks, I honestly think I could forgive you anything. I'm all too aware of your recent tribulations. I must confess that I was seriously perturbed when I telephoned the station this morning and found a strange woman in your place."

"That was Mrs. Svenson, the president's wife. As it happened, I'd been abducted from the station late yesterday afternoon and imprisoned on a tugboat tied up at the Clavaclammer Marina. Fortunately Peter and Dr. Svenson rescued me from the kidnappers, one of whom was the Mr. Fanshaw whom I believe you've already heard about;

although he was at the time disguised as Tugboat Annie."

"Great Scott!" cried the lawyer.

"You may well say so," Winifred agreed. "As Fanshaw was being dragged off by the Clavaton police, he contrived somehow to set the tugboat adrift. Trying to land would have been too dangerous, so Dr. Svenson manned the helm, as I believe it's called, and we sailed all night down the Clavaclammer; which is how we wound up at Golden Apples this morning."

"Oh, Miss Binks, what next? Let me get you a cup of tea. It's only tea bags, I'm afraid."

"Tea bags will be quite acceptable, thank you."

It was, after all, the gesture that counted. Mr. Debenham plugged in his electric kettle and took a box of arrowroot biscuits from his bottom left desk drawer. A cozy air of domesticity was replacing the tension of so short a time ago. Peter gave himself a mental kick for not having caught on that the letter might be forged; but then he'd never had any correspondence with Debenham, either. He sipped his tea and ate his biscuit and let Winifred do the talking.

Mr. Debenham listened, leaning back in

his swivel chair and pressing the fingertips of his two hands together in traditional legalistic style, shaking his head from time to time at the more outrageous revelations. At last he offered his professional opinion. "Miss Binks, this cannot go on. Steps must be taken."

"I fully agree with you, Mr. Debenham. Peter, have you any thoughts on the matter?"

"I certainly do. What I think is that we'd better hotfoot it over to the bank right now and exchange a few words with Mr. Sopwith. Do you know whether he's unloaded the Lackovites stock yet, Debenham?"

"He may have done so by now. As of half-past ten this morning, he had not. That was what I wanted to discuss with you, Miss Binks. In my opinion, Sopwith's unconscionable procrastination in carrying out your instructions raises a serious doubt as to whether he is in fact qualified to handle the Binks Trust. It may behoove us to begin examining those books without further ado. Shall I give him a ring?"

"Is he likely to be in his office?"

"Almost certainly."

"Then I think we should do as Peter suggests, and call on him forthwith, in person."

Winifred drew on her gloves and pushed back her chair. "Lead on, Mr. Debenham."

21

They had not far to go. The bank where Sopwith allegedly worked was just around the corner, in one of those blocks of dark-red brick and gray granite in the Victorian style so often to be found in New England towns that have managed to avoid the curse of modernization, built back when banks were supposed to be imposing instead of chummy. Debenham led them past the door to a staircase of polished granite with a wrought-iron balustrade that had knobs and plaques of well-shined brass worked in among the curlicues.

The trust offices were along the upper corridor, behind oaken doors with frosted glass panels. The officers' names were engraved on brass plaques. Mr. Sopwith was the third plaque on the left. His secretary regretted that Mr. Sopwith was in conference.

"Then get him out," said Winifred. "How can he be in conference? I can hear him quite clearly, talking on the telephone."

"It's a telephone conference."

"Tell him to hang up. Better still, I'll tell him myself." She headed for the inner office.

"But you can't just barge in without an appointment."

"Of course I can. I'm quite strong and very determined."

Peter started fishing for Fanshaw's golden coin, but he wasn't going to need it. This secretary knew when she was licked, she shrugged and punched a button on her intercom.

"Miss Binks is here to see you, Mr. Sopwith."

They heard a gobbling noise and saw a dark shadow appear for an instant behind the inner door panel. Then Mr. Sopwith spoke more clearly. "I'll be with her in a moment. Please ask her to wait."

"I do not intend to wait." Winifred spoke loudly and distinctly. "Mr. Sopwith, unlock this door at once. If you don't, we'll break the glass."

"Miss Binks, you mustn't," hissed Mr. Debenham. "That would constitute breaking and entering."

"And what is the penalty for breaking and entering?"

"As a first offender, you would probably be fined enough to cover the damages and court costs, and possibly be given a short suspended sentence."

"Oh well, then."

Winifred slipped off one of her new leather pumps, clasped it by the toe, and took a lusty swipe with the heel. The glass made a satisfying tinkle; she put her gloved hand in through the hole and turned the knob.

"Voilà, gentlemen. Shall we? Watch out for the glass on the floor. Mr. Sopwith, whatever are you doing up there?"

These offices had been constructed long before a room with a view had become a sign of prestige. Ventilation had been achieved by transoms over the doors and high windows on inside walls that opened out into air shafts. Below one of these archaic ventilators lay a chair, tipped over on its side. Above the chair, two legs in respectable banker's gray with a faint pinstripe thrashed the air in futile agitation. Winifred looked up at them with amused interest.

"Mr. Debenham, do you remember that time you escorted Aunt and me to a performance of *Iolanthe* at the high school? Doesn't this remind you of Strephon complaining that, since he's only half a fairy, his upper half can slip easily through the keyhole but his nether half is left kicking on the wrong side of the door? Do quit squirming and flailing, Mr. Sopwith, you're only making a bad job worse. Peter, if you'll bring that other chair over here"—as she spoke, she was straightening up the one Sopwith had tipped over—"you and I can each get hold—"

"Please allow me, Miss Binks." Quite nimbly for a man of his years, Lawyer Debenham sprang up on the chair. Peter mounted the other, each seized one of the pinstriped legs. From the doorway, the trust officer's secretary stared, aghast.

"Ready?" said Winifred. "One—two—THREE!"

Sopwith didn't come without a struggle but he came, landing in a heap on the wall-to-wall carpeting and glaring up at his rescuers with crass ingratitude.

"This is assault and battery! Miss Ledbetter, call the police."

"But they were only trying to help you, Mr. Sopwith."

"Help me? Help me?" To everybody's embarrassment, the trust officer rolled himself into the fetal position, put both hands over his face, and burst into loud sobs.

Calming him down took quite a while. Winifred lamented the death of camomile tea, Peter recommended a stiff belt of something alcoholic. The secretary shook an assortment of pens and pencils out of a pottery mug that sat on Mr. Sopwith's desk, took a bottle of brandy from a file cabinet, and half-filled the mug. The brandy helped some, but it was the hint Lawyer Debenham dropped about plea bargaining that finally brought Sopwith around.

"Er—um. If I might just have another wee drop of—thank you, Miss Ledbetter. I—er—hope you people haven't drawn a false conclusion from my little—ah—misadventure just now. What happened was that I had one of my asthma attacks. They come upon me unawares, suddenly, without warning. Don't they, Miss Ledbetter?"

"Um—ah—oh yes. One minute Mr. Sopwith's bright as a button, next thing you know he's gasping like a blowfish. So he jumps up on a chair and sticks his head out the ventilator to get a breath of fresh air. I'm always having to haul him down."

"Ugh—er—" Sopwith shot her a baleful glance. "It's quite a joke between us. Miss Ledbetter, have we received that report yet on the sale of Miss Binks's Lackovites shares?"

"The—her Lackovites shares, Mr. Sopwith?"

"Certainly her Lackovites shares. I specifically told you to get hold of that broker again and demand to know why the sale had been held up. It's not like you to forget, Miss Ledbetter."

"No, Mr. Sopwith. I don't forget."

The words were not spoken with the subservient respect a trust officer of the old school might expect from his female underling. Sopwith winced. Winifred pounced.

"Miss Ledbetter, it does not appear to me that Mr. Sopwith is evincing any symptoms of asthma. What he is doing is trying to make you take what I believe is called the rap for his own derelictions. If you are not involved in his chicanery, it would be an insult to womanhood for you to let yourself be manipulated in this demeaning and underhanded manner. It would also, I should point out, put you in an extremely sticky position. Now would you care to tell us the truth, or do you prefer to take your chances?"

"What kind of chances?"

"That's rather hard to say. So far, we know of one person who was snatched up in a net while participating in an owl count and returned to the ground stabbed to death. Another is here in the Clavaton Hospital with multiple injuries, including a skull fracture. A third has been kidnapped twice so far and left tied to a tree both times, once in the woods along a lonely stretch of road and once near the parking lot at the Balaclava College Field Station. I myself was abducted yesterday afternoon and imprisoned on a tugboat. Subsequently, an attempt was made to drown me along with Professor Shandy and Dr. Svenson, the college president. There have been other incidents of a less violent nature which I shan't go into just now."

"But why?"

"That's another thing I won't go into just now. However, we have a very good idea why and also who's responsible. Mr. Sopwith is going to tell us a lot more. Aren't you, Mr. Sopwith?"

It was an order, not a question; but Mr. Sopwith's lips stayed buttoned.

"Ah," said Winifred, "then it appears that Mr. Sopwith is going to wait for the police to interview him officially. Will they do it here in the presence of us all, or do they haul him off to their grilling room? What is the usual procedure, Mr. Debenham?"

"A very good question, Miss Binks. My practice, as you know, has always been in civil law; however, I can easily find out. Miss Ledbetter, perhaps you would be so obliging as to get the Clavaton police headquarters on the telephone. Explain to them that we have someone here who has attempted to commit suicide by hurling himself down an air shaft in order to escape facing possible criminal charges."

"You also have someone who's deliberately and willfully smashed in a door," Winifred added with a hint of a twinkle. "Both guilty parties must face the due punishment for our malefactions, must we not, Mr. Sopwith? How would it be if, rather than waiting here for the ax to fall, we simply strolled over to the police station and turned ourselves in? That would save the bank a good deal of embarrassment and perchance induce the arm of the law to rest upon us a trifle less harshly. What do you think, Mr. Sopwith?"

"Miss Ledbetter, get me my lawyer."

"Excuse me," said the secretary, "but now I'm all confused. Which do you want first: the stockbroker, the police, or the lawyer?"

"Forget the stockbroker," said Peter.

"You know perfectly well your boss never gave any order to sell those shares. Mr. Debenham can arrange the sale as soon as Miss Binks has chosen a new trust officer. I'd suggest you get hold of the lawyer while Mr. Sopwith's putting his coat on. Ask him to meet us at the police station. You're coming too, of course."

"Me? What for?"

"As a witness to my act of vandalism," Winifred told her. "And to Mr. Sopwith's asthma attack. Please let's not shilly-shally, Miss Ledbetter. We'll all feel much better if we simply do what we must and get it over with."

The secretary licked her lips. "You said somebody got killed. Who was it?"

"We don't quite know. He called himself Emory Emmerick and claimed to be a site engineer for the Meadowsweet Construction Company, but they say they've never heard of him. I'm surprised you didn't read about the incident in the papers."

"Oh. Yes, I—I guess I did read something about that. But I didn't realize—I thought it was just—I'll get my coat on. Unless you'd rather I called the police, Mr. Sopwith?"

"No! Don't call them." Sopwith clambered wearily to his feet and slumped into his swivel chair. “Don’t call anybody. I’ll talk.”

He took another sip out of the pencil mug, shuddering at the bite of the brandy. He sighed. He rubbed his hands over his face, he took out a handkerchief and mopped his eyes. They waited. At last he brought himself to speak.

“Miss Binks, I owe you an apology.”

“Go on.”

“First, I want you to know that there has been no embezzlement from the Binks Trust. When you check our books, you’ll find they balance to the penny. I may have been a rotter, but I am not a thief.”

“That’s something, at any rate. Do get to the point, Mr. Sopwith.”

He heaved the grandfather of all sighs, and he went on. “It’s about Lackovites. I—have not been entirely straightforward with you on that account.” He licked his lips. “What I told you on Saturday was true enough, up to a point. They have in fact shot forward very quickly, they’ve opened up a vast new consumer market for natural food products. We must not overlook their contribution to the cause of better nutrition, Miss Binks.”

“What is there to overlook, Mr. Sopwith?”

"Er—yes. That's the problem." Sopwith chewed on his lower lip as if to test its value to the cause of better nutrition. "Their products in some cases have not been—ah—all that might be desired. As a result, certain—ah—difficulties have arisen. Sales have fallen off, customer dissatisfaction is—ah—rife. So far, the company has managed to maintain its facade of prosperity through—ah—aggressive advertising and possibly a little—ah—creative accounting."

"You mean cooking the books?" said Peter.

"Well—ah—that term is not generally used in banking circles. In any event, certain government agencies have begun to—ah—take an interest. Next quarter's earnings will inevitably reflect a sharp loss; this cannot but affect adversely the market value of Lackovites stock. Therefore, company executives have hit upon the expedient of taking over the respectable and well-established Golden Apples Company. They had, for your information, already been mulling over the possibility of a take-over for some time, the idea being that Golden Apples's impeccable reputation for quality and service would have a—um—purifying effect on the somewhat tarnished Lackovites image."

"Yes, we know that," Winifred told him impatiently.

"You do?"

"I did mention that we know a good deal, Mr. Sopwith. However, I suppose your confirmation is useful. Please continue."

Sopwith cleared his throat. "Being aggressive, not to say impetuous, in their policies, the Lackovites people wanted to take action as soon as the plan was conceived. However, the fact that your grandfather held the controlling interest in Golden Apples and was—ah—not available for negotiation made this impossible, unless the trust officers for the Binks estate could be bribed or coerced into acting on their behalf. My predecessor being a man of utmost probity and Mr. Debenham being a shrewd and incorruptible guardian of both the founder's and the prospective heiress's interests, this avenue was not open to them. So they waited."

"Until Grandfather was pronounced dead."

"And my predecessor, Mr. Allerton, retired. In point of fact, I'd just taken over the Binks Trust a few weeks previously when Mr. Binks was pronounced—ah—officially deceased. If Allerton had known how soon that was going to happen, the old coot would have stayed on and I'd never had got the chance," Sopwith interjected with some bitterness.

"Anyway, the Lackovites people now felt that their time had come, particularly when it became known that the heir to the trust was a spinster lady of—forgive me—eccentric habits and no business experience. Your impressive donation of land and money to Balaclava Agricultural College, Miss Binks, was seen by them as an act of reckless fiscal irresponsibility, which of course was just what they'd been hoping for; and your—ah—environmental proclivities appeared to offer the perfect opening wedge. I was, as one might say, approached."

"By whom?" Winifred demanded.

"Ah—I am not prepared to divulge that information."

"Why not? Come now, Mr. Sopwith, I may be eccentric but I'm not stupid. It's either us or the police."

"Well—ah—the fact is, I never did learn her name. She said just call her Toots, so I—ah—did."

"Indeed? And where did you meet this Toots? Here in Clavaton?"

"Heavens no! I was in Boston. On—ah—

business. I'd dropped in at a—um—restaurant."

"I assume you mean a saloon or gin mill. So she gave you the glad eye?"

"Ah—I suppose you could call it that. She made an overture."

"To which you responded without hesitation, one gathers?"

"After the tensions of the day, I was—ah—trying to unwind."

Meaning he was drunk but not yet incapable, Peter deduced. "Can you describe this Toots?" he asked.

"Well—ah—she was—um—"

"Was she indeed? I suppose with a wig and—er—padding and so forth, she could have made herself up to look like just about anything. You're quite sure Toots was in fact a woman?"

"Quite sure." For a fleeting instant, Sopwith looked smug as a cat in a cream jug. "Oh yes, quite sure."

"Did you subsequently get to know Toots better?"

"Ah—er—yes and no. That is to say, I regret for your sakes that I never did manage to learn her true identity. Anyway, she and I—ah—fell into conversation. When she got around to asking me what I did, I—ah—

told her. I realized later that she must have known all along and had actually been—ah—stalking me. I felt, since I may as well confess the full extent of my folly, somewhat flattered."

22

"Other men have felt so before you, no doubt," said Peter. "So this latter-day Mata Hari got you to admit that you were the trust officer for Miss Binks. Then what?"

"We exchanged a few inconsequentialities about the Binks saga, as she chose to call it. Then she, no doubt disingenuously, revealed that she was a close friend of one of the executives at Lackovites. She had, she said, learned through him that the company was—ah—eager to acquire a controlling interest in Golden Apples."

"In other words, planning a hostile takeover?"

"Ah—quite. Toots intimated that it could be lucrative for me, in my position as trust officer, to induce Miss Binks to sever her connection with Golden Apples. A willing buyer would come forward as soon as she agreed to sell. This person, needless to say, would be merely a straw man. Her equity would immediately be transferred to Lackovites, the subterfuge having been rendered necessary by the Compotes' expressed refusal to have any dealings whatsoever with their competitor."

"As well they might," said Winifred. "I have the highest opinion of the Compotes and am glad to hear it thus confirmed. Did Toots's friend have any further plans for my money?"

"I was to persuade you to invest the profits from the Golden Apples sale in Lackovites, and to make additional stock purchases out of your trust. The Lackovites people would thus get back the money they'd used to buy you out, and your further investments—heavy, it was hoped—would help to counteract the—er—dumping of shares by present disillusioned holders, which is accelerating at a dangerous rate. This would also buy them time to polish their corporate image through a massive public-relations campaign built around their acquisition of Golden Apples."

"How philanthropic of me."

"Oh, but your interests were being taken into consideration, Miss Binks. Golden Apples had made no substantial gain in its earnings, as you know, whereas Lackovites stock would have gone straight through the ceiling as soon as the deal was consummated. You stood, in short, to make a bundle. It—ah—seemed reasonable enough at the time."

"Did it indeed? Was it Toots who unveiled this ingenious plan to you?"

"No, I believe her role was chiefly to—ah—capture my interest. The details of the plan were spelled out in separate conversations, first with a junior vice-president of Lackovites whose name was Emory, later with a senior vice-president, Mr. Dewey."

Peter and Winifred exchanged glances. "Not George Dewey, by any chance?" Peter asked. "Fellow about my height and build, with a beard and mustache?"

"Why yes, that's the man. He was even dressed like you, come to think of it. Do you know him?"

"I believe Miss Binks and I may have met both of them. Was Emory a blondish, talkative, glad-hander type? Clean-shaven, snappy dresser, younger than Dewey? Very helpful about telling you what to do and how to do it?"

"That's right. Somewhat too breezy in his manner and not always clear in his explanations. He almost turned me off the deal,

I have to say; he really didn't impress me as the sort of person I'd feel comfortable doing business with. Mr. Dewey was quite different: older, more responsible, low-key in his approach but fully in command of his facts. I was impressed by Mr. Dewey. He had me fully convinced that the arrangement would be to nobody's detriment and everyone's benefit."

"He's a persuasive fellow," said Peter. "And what was to be your share of the benefits?"

"Professor Shandy, I sincerely hope you don't think I would have been so venal as to accept a bribe?" Now that he'd abased himself, Sopwith was making a pathetic effort to climb back up on his high horse. "I was to receive a hundred shares of Lackovites stock as soon as I'd achieved the sale of Miss Binks's interest in Golden Apples, a second hundred once the purchase money had been converted back into Lackovites shares and resold to Miss Binks. Further emoluments of a similar nature would depend on the extent of future stock purchases by the Binks Trust. In other words, I'd be getting merely the equivalent of a salesman's commission. At least that's how Mr. Dewey put it to me,"

Sopwith added less bombastically once he'd seen the looks on his hearers' faces.

"As of now, however, you've received nothing at all?" said Winifred.

"Nothing at all," Sopwith replied sadly. "Merely a gentleman's agreement with Mr. Dewey."

"I see. Then my telling you to get rid of my Lackovites stock and turn over the proceeds to Golden Apples must have come as a serious blow."

"It did."

"And your otherwise inexplicable procrastination about obeying my orders was in fact your attempt to avoid breaking this potentially lucrative gentleman's agreement."

"Ah—um—"

"But you realized just now that it wasn't going to work, and that's why you tried to hurl yourself down the air shaft."

"No, he didn't."

Miss Ledbetter hadn't spoken for quite a while, the others were a bit startled to be reminded that she was still standing in the doorway. "What he did was, he remembered. Mr. Allerton, who used to have this office, was an Eagle Scout."

"I see," said Peter. "That explains everything."

"Well yes, it does. Mr. Allerton was always prepared, and one of the things he prepared for was fire. Back when employees were allowed to smoke at their desks, every so often somebody would empty an ashtray with a burning cigarette into the wastebasket. The stuff inside would catch fire. As a rule you'd just dump in a mug of cold coffee or smother the blaze with a telephone book or somebody's coat or something."

"But Mr. Allerton got to thinking about what could happen if the fire got out of hand in the outer office and he or some other trust officer got trapped behind it. So what he did, he had steel ladders fixed to the airshaft underneath the ventilators and held calisthenic drills every morning so the officers wouldn't get too fat and flabby to climb out. Now that Mr. Allerton's retired, they've quit holding the drills and Mr. Sopwith's been going to pot in more ways than one. You forgot about all those extra calories when you tried to escape, didn't you, Mr. Sopwith?"

"I told you I was having an asthma attack!"

"Yes, Mr. Sopwith. You also told me to stall Miss Binks and Mr. Debenham with any lie I could think of when they called again about her Lackovites shares."

"I can well imagine," Winifred sniffed. "Mr. Sopwith, you are a most inefficient knave."

"Yes, I know," he mumbled, totally defeated now.

"What do you think I should do about you?"

"Throw me to the wolves, I suppose. What else can you do?"

"There are various possibilities. Mr. Debenham, what do you think? Is it better to switch to the rogue we know not or stick with the one we know?"

"Miss Binks, would you really wish to continue doing business with Mr. Sopwith?"

"Why not? I've gone to the bother of getting used to him, and what's the sense in having to break in another when we're so busy with more important matters? Now that he's learned what a washout he is at chicanery, I find it most unlikely that he'd be fool enough to try again. What do you yourself think, Mr. Sopwith? Would you like to continue handling the Binks Trust, omitting the hanky-panky, or shall we ship you out to the field station and put you to planting ash trees?"

"Naturally I'd rather stay here, but how can I? Miss Ledbetter—"

"No sweat, Mr. Sopwith," the secretary replied. "I'm not going to rat on you; I'm leaving anyway to take a new job as a steamfitter. It's what I always wanted to do, but my mother wouldn't let me. Now, thanks to Professor Binks's inspiring example, I've found the courage to cast off the shackles of conventionality."

"Then—then I'm saved? I can retain my perquisites of office? Oh, Miss Ledbetter! Oh, Miss Binks! I'll reinstate the calisthenic drills tomorrow!"

"A wise decision, Mr. Sopwith," said Winifred, "and bully for you, Miss Ledbetter. Before you leave, however, I beg of you to get that broker on the phone and tell him Winifred Binks instructs him to dump her Lackovites stocks immediately at any price he can get. I don't care what harm it does to their corporate image, those rascals deserve a sharp lesson. All good wishes for success in your future career, Miss Ledbetter, I'm sure you've made a wise decision. 'This above all: to thine own self be true' applies as much to steamfitting as to banking, don't you think, Peter?"

"No question about it. Allow me to add my felicitations, Miss Ledbetter. Now, Sopwith, since you're back on the side of the angels, let's get back to Toots for a moment. Was she a big, hearty woman, tall and—er—well-endowed?"

"She was all of that." And then some, from the fleeting gleam in Sopwith's eye.

"She wasn't by any chance wearing khaki shorts and hiking boots?"

"Professor Shandy, what an odd question. No indeed, she had on something frilly and feminine and—ah—snug-fitting. Green, as I recall. Bright green, just about the same shade as a crisp new fifty-dollar bill."

"Which contrasted attractively with her reddish-blond hair?"

"So it did. However did you guess?"

"Green is a color much favored by redheads. Was her complexion pale or ruddy?"

"Oh, ruddy. Very healthy-looking, as though she must spend a good deal of time outdoors. On the golf course, I remember thinking at the time, or perhaps riding to hounds. That was one of the things that attracted me to her, that and her jolly, one might almost say ebullient, manner. We don't get much ebullience around the bank, you know; trust officers are expected to maintain an attitude of subdued affability attended by strict decorum at all times. Except on weekends, of course, though even then we have to be circumspect in our pursuits. If our VP for trusts ever caught me out riding to hounds with the swells on a Sunday, she'd be in here Monday morning running an audit on my accounts. Not that I'm complaining," Sopwith added manfully. "Better an only moderately well-paid but scrupulously honest trust officer than a knavish and despicable though filthy rich tool of wicked corporate interests."

"Bravely spoken, Mr. Sopwith," said Winifred. "Peter, that information you have just elicited leads me to believe we should get back to the station without further ado."

"Me, too. Sopwith, you'd better come along. We may need you as a witness. Debenham, could you follow in your own car?"

The main thing they'd need Debenham for would most likely be to drive Sopwith back here to Clavaton; Peter was damned if he'd play taxi any longer. "Miss Ledbetter, have you got settled with the broker?"

"Yes, Mr. Shandy. He says Lackovites has dropped eight points already today and dumping the Binks shares should really cook their goose."

"Excellent. Then, if we could impose on your good nature for one last small task, will you call the Balaclava field station? If Mrs.

Svenson is still there, tell her we're on our way back. And—er—happy steamfitting."

23

The Porbles' sedan was still sitting in the parking lot; now Viola Buddley's little red doodlebug was drawn up beside it.

"That's funny," said Peter, "I wonder why Sieglinde's still here. I should have thought she'd be itching to rush home and start chopping herring for the Viking's return."

"She's all right, though," said Winifred. "I can see her in there, sitting at my desk, drinking tea. I assume it's tea. Gracious to Betsy, is that Viola? And who's that gray-haired woman, I wonder? Shall I go in first, Peter?"

"Yes, why don't you? Sopwith, can you see in through the window?"

"No, I seem to have come away with just my reading glasses." Sopwith was vainly patting his various pockets. "How vexing."

"Then we may as well join the ladies. Don't hurry, and keep your head down so they can't get a good look at your face."

Winifred was in the lobby now, greeting

Sieglinde and being polite to the gray-haired woman. Viola, Peter noticed through the glass, was standing back looking smug. She'd changed, all right; she'd put on a frilly, snug-fitting dress the same shade as a crisp new fifty-dollar bill. The meeting with her erstwhile acquaintance could fairly be described as electric: once they'd got inside and Sopwith was close enough to see her, he reacted as though he'd trodden on a live wire in his bare feet.

"Toots!"

"Oh hi, Malcolm. What are you doing here?" Viola was as shocked as he, but doing her best to carry it off. "Hi, Professor Shandy. I guess you know Mrs. Svenson. And this is my landlady, Genevieve. I brought her along to help out."

"Nice of you," said Peter.

He took careful stock of the landlady. She had on a freshly pressed black skirt and an emerald-green T-shirt turned back-to-front under a dark-red cardigan. Her hair was suspiciously luxuriant and her face more carefully made up than one might expect of an elderly woman wearing rubber boots. As she started to rise, Peter shoved her back into her chair, pulled the gray wig down over her eyes, planted one knee on her padded chest, and took a firm grip on both flailing arms.

"Nice try, Fanshaw. Hold still or I'll have to get nasty."

"Let go! Let go, damn you!"

Fanshaw was cursing and clawing, Viola was on Peter's back, trying to pull him away. Sopwith was wringing his hands and issuing formal protests. Winifred and Sieglinde advanced to the fray.

Peter couldn't see what they did to Viola, but it obviously worked. By the time he'd got Fanshaw quieted down with a clout over the ear, the two older women had the young one laid out on the carpet, trussed up like a Thanksgiving turkey in some of the rope Winifred had thriftily saved from Viola's previous two tyings-up. Working smoothly together, they did an even slicker job on Fanshaw. When Debenham joined them, it was all over but the shouting.

There was plenty of that. Now that the two on the floor had to realize the jig was up, each was eager to lay the blame on the other. With both yelling at once, it was impossible to make any sense out of either. With the rest of the group trying to shut them up long enough to put the meeting on a parliamentary basis, the decibel level had got pretty high before a Clavaton police car pulled up with Thorkjeld Svenson inside.

Peter went to the door. "President, come here, quick. Tell the cops to come too, we've got some business for them."

"Yeepers, Shandy! Not Fanshaw again?"

"None other. Also his boss, if I'm not mistaken."

"I'll be yiggered!" Svenson was out of the car and into the station. At the moment, he had eyes for only one member of the group.

"Wife!"

"Husband!"

The Svensons exchanged one reasonably chaste embrace, then Sieglinde got down to business. She didn't have to raise her voice this time. As soon as they'd caught sight of the two Clavaton policemen and the awesome figure of the president, the two on the floor had clammed up tight.

"It is good that you are come. We have here, as you see, unfinished business. On my right is a man; do not be misled by the skirt. He has many names and does many things, all of them reprehensible. On my left is she who has been assistant to our beloved Professor Binks. She has called herself Viola Buddley, but responds also to Toots."

"Excuse me," Winifred put in, turning to

the two Clavaton policemen. "Not to confuse you, I'm Professor Binks and the lady at the desk is Mrs. Svenson, as you've no doubt gathered. These gentlemen are my colleagues, President Svenson and Professor Shandy; my trust officer, Mr. Sopwith; and my dear friend and long-time attorney, Mr. Debenham. Go ahead, Sieglinde."

"Thank you, Winifred. It is certain that my husband, who can be articulate when he chooses, has informed you of events up to now. Therefore, I will not be prolix. He telephoned to me this morning from Briscoe and said among other things it was possible that nobody was manning the field station, so I came to serve. For a time I was alone, then Miss Buddley came along wearing unsuitable garb. I sent her back to change into something more appropriate, which she has still not done."

"I told you this is the only dress I own," Viola protested.

"True, and I gave credit for good intentions, even though I deplored the result and mistrusted the motive. Even more I mistrusted the person Miss Buddley brought with her and introduced as her landlady. It was clear to me that I was supposed now to leave these two alone so that they could wreak their will on our Winifred when she returned to the station."

One of the Clavaton officers had started taking notes. He looked up from his notebook. "How did you know that, Mrs. Svenson?"

"They talked between themselves while I was making coffee, thinking I could not hear, which was absurd. They have high opinions of their own cleverness and little respect for the acumen of others; this has been their downfall. They thought Mr. Debenham would bring Winifred back as was usual when she went to Clavaton and that he would be a pushover. They were, of course, wrong. Anyone with eyes can see in his face the courage of a lion and the wisdom of a sage. Am I not right, Winifred?"

"I have always thought so, Sieglinde."

By George, Peter thought, she's blushing.

"So," Sieglinde went on, "I was deaf to their hints that I go. My husband knew I was coming to the field station. I reasoned that he would call our house when he reached Clavaton. Not finding me there, he would stop here, as he has done, and I would deliver them over to him. You doubtless regret, dear husband, that you missed the fray, but I tell you these are not opponents worthy of your prowess. Also it would have been unseemly for you to engage in wrestling with a woman of indelicate propensities and poor taste. As for this other, it was plain to me at once that he was a man in disguise. It is also plain to me, Peter, that you are wearing his suit, which becomes you ill. Thorkjeld, did you remember to bring Peter's own clothing off the tugboat?"

"Yes, wife. Have they talked?"

"They have done nothing else. However, they made no sense as both talked at once with much screaming and use of unseemly words. Perhaps these kind officers will now arrest them and take them away."

"Happy to oblige, ma'am," said the one with the sergeant's stripes on his sleeve. "What charge do you want to lay?"

"A good question. What charge, Peter?"

"M'well, let's see. The one in the rubber boots was arrested on Saturday by Chief Ottermole of Balaclava Junction under the name Fanshaw, which is how he'd introduced himself here at the station on his first appearance. At the time he was pretending to be employed by the Meadowsweet Construction Company and looking for that chap Emmerick who'd been murdered the night before, as you may recall. So he's wanted in

Balaclava Junction as an escaped prisoner. He was the one on the tugboat who called himself Tugboat Annie Brennan when President Svenson and I found him and his cohort holding Professor Binks captive. Your river police pinched him then on a kidnapping charge, but he got away again. Do you still have the other chap, by the way?"

"Oh yes. He claims this guy's name is Dewey."

"So that's three names and three charges so far. I suppose you could also get him on imposture or whatever they call it, though that seems a bit redundant. How about attempted murder? It's a fair supposition he hoped to drown us when he set us adrift. He'd have succeeded, no doubt, if President Svenson weren't such a capable seaman."

"You might further add conspiracy," added Sopwith. "It has taken me some time, I confess, to penetrate his disguise since he was wearing a beard when he approached me on a matter I—ah—would prefer not to discuss before having legal advice; but I can now identify him as the George Dewey who claimed to be a vice-president of Lackovites. The—ah—lady with him was also a party to the conspiracy."

"The—ah—lady was, if I'm not mistaken, a driving force behind the conspiracy," said Peter. "Mr. Sopwith, would you mind telling us whether, on leaving here Saturday morning after the interview in which Professor Binks instructed you to sell certain stocks and invest the proceeds in a—er—different company, you were accosted by Miss Buddley and told to circumvent your client's orders by any possible means?"

"Um—ah—I'd rather not say."

"Thank you. Did you drive Miss Buddley farther down the road from where you picked her up, tie her to a tree, and leave her there alone?"

"She forced me to!"

"I'm sure she did. Was her object in doing so to get herself regarded as a victim instead of a co-conspirator of the villains involved in murder committed the night before?"

"I—ah—couldn't say."

"Did you recognize her then as the same young woman whom you'd previously met in Boston, calling herself Toots?"

"I didn't have my glasses with me."

"You told us back at Clavaton this afternoon that after having met Miss Buddley, whom you then knew only as Toots, you were next approached by a Mr. Emory. You took him to be an associate of Mr. Dewey here, did you not?"

"I had every reason to think so."

"Are you aware that the man who called himself Emory was also passing himself off here at the station as Emory Emmerick, a site engineer for the Meadowsweet Construction Company?"

"No!"

"You didn't, from media reports, identify him as the man who was murdered Friday night?"

"How could I, if he was using a different name?"

Peter didn't pursue that question, Sopwith looked ready to start crying again. "Getting back to Miss Buddley: when you met with Miss Binks and the rest of us here Saturday morning, you brought along Mr. Tangent, whom you introduced as the accountant for the Binks Trust. Is that his true position?"

"Absolutely. He's been with the bank for many years."

"Did he assist in the fake kidnapping of Miss Buddley?"

"No, Tangent was and is in no way involved. What happened"—Sopwith didn't want to talk but apparently couldn't help it—"was that Miss Buddley came out of the woods shortly after we'd left the station in my car, and flagged us down. She claimed to have an urgent errand in Whittington and asked for a lift. Since Tangent lives in Whittington, I acquiesced and took him home first."

"Because you realized Miss Buddley wanted to get you alone for some purpose connected with your mutual enterprise?"

"Because she'd given me to understand that her objective was—ah—farther along my way."

"But you knew what she was really after," said the sergeant.

That was one too many for Sopwith. "I refuse to allow this interrogation to continue until I have taken legal advice. Debenham, you're a lawyer, can't you intervene for me against this unlawful intimidation?"

"I don't quite see where you're being intimidated, Mr. Sopwith. In any case, I couldn't act for you because I already represent Miss Binks."

"But I'm cooperating in her behalf! I've come forward with information."

"As was your duty as a citizen, Mr. Sopwith. I'm sure Miss Binks won't mind your using the office telephone to call your own lawyer."

"Of course not," said Winifred. "Please go ahead, Mr. Sopwith. The sooner the better, I should think."

"Ah—er—thank you." A most unhappy man, the trust officer slunk across to the chair that Sieglinde had by now vacated.

"And now," Winifred went on briskly, "what about these other two? Won't you tell us your real name, Mr. Fanshaw? Or should I say Miss Atakuku?"

"Shut up, Chuck," snapped Viola. "Don't tell them anything."

Peter smiled. "So you are the ringleader, Miss Buddley. I've thought so ever since that first time you had yourself abducted, and was sure of it when Professor Binks and I encountered your sister this morning, planted as receptionist at Golden Apples to prevent any dangerous messages from getting through to the Compotes. Rather an hysterical type, isn't she? I assume that's why you had Fanshaw hypnotize her."

He took out the gold piece and began swinging it back and forth on its chain, directly over their recumbent heads. "Look, Fanshaw, I've got your lucky piece. Watch it, Fanshaw. Watch it, Miss Buddley. Keep watching, Fanshaw, keep watching, Miss Buddley. Look at it swing. Back and forth, back and forth. You're getting sleepy, Fanshaw. Go to sleep, Miss Buddley. Sleep, Fanshaw. Sleep. Sleep. Sleep."

Great Scott! It was working. Both prisoners' eyes were closed, they were breathing slowly and deeply. Was this a trick? Peter kept swinging and droning. No, it was really happening. Sieglinde and the president were watching in awe, so were Winifred and Debenham. So were the two Clavaton policemen; in fact one of them was beginning to look about the way Ottermole and Dorkin had looked Saturday morning. He'd better get on with the next step.

"Fanshaw, can you hear me?"

"I hear you." The voice was drowsy, relaxed.

"What is your real name?"

"Chuck Smith."

"Are you related to the Fred Smith who works at Golden Apples?"

"No. There are Smiths everywhere. I hate being Chuck Smith. I like being Francis Fanshaw. I like being George Dewey. I like—"

"Good, we get the picture." Peter wasn't about to spend all night listening to this chameleon work through his repertoire. "Tell us about Friday night, Fanshaw. What was your role in the plot?"

"I came from Clavaton to Hoddersville on the bus. Then I took a taxi to Balaclava-Junction and walked to where Emory had left a rented car. The key was under the seat. It was late. I drove out into the country and spent the rest of the night in the car."

"And that's all you did? You took no part in what happened on the owl count?"

"None."

"But you knew it was going to happen?"

"No. When Viola hired me, she'd said something about kidnapping the heiress and holding her till she agreed to sell her Golden Apples shares, but I said nothing doing. I'm a con man, not a thug. So she said okay then, work out a swindle. So I did."

"This was on behalf of Lackovites?"

"Yes. It was a beautiful swindle, it would have been the crowning achievement of my career. But Viola went and spoiled it by getting physical. I should have known."

"Then when you came here on Saturday morning, you really didn't know Emmerick had been killed?"

"She didn't have to get physical. You could have knocked me over with a feather."

"Sorry. You say Viola hired you. Then she bossed the affair?"

"She had the connections."

"How much was she paying you?"

"It's vulgar to talk about money. She said two hundred thousand, but she may not have meant it. I don't trust her any more."

"Who was that so-called lawyer who showed up at the police station?"

"Viola's brother Herman. He used to specialize in mail fraud, but he developed an allergy to stamp glue, so now she uses him for odd jobs."

"Why did you come looking for Emmerick Saturday morning?"

"It was part of the plan. Sopwith was meeting with the heiress. I'd been working on him, I had him right in my pocket. Emmerick had this place bugged, I meant to listen in and make sure Sopwith got her to dump Golden Apples and buy more Lackovites."

"You'd have been disappointed."

"I know. Viola phoned me."

"Where?"

"On the tugboat. I went there after I got away from those half-wit cops. She said my plan was a washout. She'd have Keech kidnap the heiress and bring her to me."

"Who's Keech?"

"Her boyfriend. You met him on the boat. She likes them big and stupid."

"Was he involved in Emmerick's murder?"

"Yes. He told me on the boat, before you came. He worked the owl. It was just a bunch of white feathers on a long fishline he'd strung through the trees. He was hiding in the bushes, waiting for you all to come along. Emmerick was dressed the way the heiress usually does, in slacks and a sissyish sweater. He was supposed to lead her into the net and knock her out when the fireworks went off and everybody panicked. Viola would haul her up. They'd rigged a slide of black plastic, Keech would hold it steady while she slid down with the heiress. They were going to ride off with her on a tandem bicycle. Emory would drop down and pretend he was her with a sprained ankle or something, to give them more time for the getaway. But he got netted by mistake."

"And Viola was in the tree alone. So it was she who stabbed him."

"She had to shut him up before he squawked. Anyway, Viola always gets physical when somebody fouls up."

"I see," said Peter. "Viola, can you hear me?"

"I hear you."

"Did you stab Emmerick in the neck?"

"Yes. It was fun."

"What did you do then?"

"Let him fall to distract you. Slid down the plastic and pulled it away from the tree. Rode off with Keech on his bike."

"Did Fanshaw help you and Keech kidnap Miss Binks on Sunday?"

"No. He stayed on the boat."

"Was it you or Keech who slugged Knapweed Calthrop?"

"I did. With a stick of firewood. He was a spy."

"For whom?"

"Golden Apples. My sister Elvira told me. The Compotes were scared Binks would—hey, wait a minute! What the hell's going on here? Chuck, wake up. He's got your gold piece."

"Huh? My God!" Incredibly, Fanshaw turned to the two Clavaton policeman. "Arrest this man! He's stolen my gold piece. And my suit."

"Not according to the law, he hasn't," said the one taking notes. "I'd say he's only borrowed it. Wouldn't you, Officer Musgrave?"

"Oh, no question, Officer Yerkes. Now everybody, it's getting on toward suppertime and you folks have had a rough day, so why don't we just arrest Miss Buddley and Mr. Smith and get them out of your hair? You want to read them their rights, Officer Yerkes?"

"Sure, then you can make the collar. Let's see, she's murder one, assault with intent, kidnapping, and conspiracy. He's kidnapping, conspiracy, escape while under arrest, and interfering with police officers in the performance of their duty by means of hypnotism. Is that okay with you folks?"

"Sounds good to me," said Peter. "How about you, Winifred?"

"I'd say that should do nicely. President, what do you think?"

"Urgh."

"And I agree with Thorkjeld," said Sieglinde.

Sopwith was not asked for an opinion and did not volunteer one. Mr. Debenham raised a technical question.

"Forgive the legal quibble, but since we're within the boundaries of Lumpkinton, shouldn't we get the local police to perform the arrest?"

"Ah, those guys won't care," said Officer Musgrave. "We've got kind of a mutual pinch agreement in Balaclava County, since all prisoners have to be taken to Clavaton County courthouse for arraignment anyway. You want to give Mr. Smith back his suit, Professor Shandy, or shall we take him in his landlady outfit?"

"I'll be glad to change if you'll bring my clothes out of your car. However, I'd suggest you take Smith and Miss Buddley just as they are, ropes and all. I'd further suggest that you not let Smith get his hands on this gold piece."

"No fear, we'll impound it as evidence. Got an envelope you can spare, Professor Binks? Okay then, here goes with the charges."

It was beautifully done, as everyone agreed. Since the prisoners had their feet tied, Dr. Svenson carried Smith while the two officers wrestled the squirming and yelling Viola into the police car. Smith wasn't making any protest. Peter had a hunch he was planning to try copping a plea like Sopwith, who'd already been collected by his own lawyer and taken away to face the district attorney and be either jugged or shriven, as the case might be. The thug known as Keech had already confessed to his share in the unlawful abduction and retention of Winifred Binks, they'd learned, implicating Viola and Chuck Smith up to the eyeballs and giving an eyewitness account of Viola's near-lethal attack on Kenneth Compote, as they now knew Knapweed Calthrop to be.

"That must be what the Compotes were looking so nervous about this morning," said Winifred. She was in no hurry to get rid of her friends; therefore, much as they wanted to get home, Shandy and the Svensons had lingered with Debenham for a miniature celebration. "I suppose we can't blame them for trying to get a line on what I was likely to do about Golden Apples. Poor dear Knapweed, as I shall probably always think of him, was never cut out to be a spy. I'm so relieved that he's conscious. I'll nip over tomorrow on my bicycle and take him some bedstraw. He may be feeling rather blue about Viola. I couldn't make up my mind whether he was stuck on her or afraid of her, but then I've never had any experience in affairs of the heart."

"Then why is this good Mr. Debenham gazing upon you with the eyes of a stricken sheep?" demanded Sieglinde. "Sir, have you a wife living?"

"Oh no. I—" Over Debenham's honest face crept a warm blush. "I am a widower of many years' standing. It's true that over a period of time I have come to feel an ever-increasing regard for the courage, high principles, and never-failing good humor of my client."

"Pussyfoot! You love her."

"I—I suppose I—yes, I admit it. I worship her."

"Oh, Mr. Debenham." Winifred was blushing, too. "But why have you never told me?"

"How could I? You, whom I knew to be sole heiress to a great fortune, and I, just an old fuddy-duddy of a lawyer with only a modest competence saved from years of unceasing toil in the service of my clients. It wouldn't have done, you know. It would have been a breach of professional ethics."

"Bah to professional ethics!" cried Sieglinde. "What is so ethical about leaving our dear Winifred alone in the wilds as the prey of spies and kidnappers because of your pettifogging reluctance to be branded a fortune hunter? Be sensible, Mr. Debenham. Join with Winifred in her zeal to disburse her grandfather's wealth in the interests of many good causes. Then you both can live happily upon your modest competence and all will be well."

"Why—why, bless my soul, so it will." Chin firm, eyes resolute, Debenham advanced to address his principal client. "Miss Binks—Winifred—do you—could you—might you ever bring yourself to think of me as Alaric?"

Peter nodded to Sieglinde. Sieglinde nodded to Thorkjeld. There was nothing left for them to do here, they might as well go home.